DARK LESSONS

JULIA SYKES

Edited by Rebecca Cartee
Cover by Popkitty Design

Special thanks to LK Shaw for listening to me ramble!

PROLOGUE

Jason

I t was back again: the choking, all-consuming fear. It tightened my chest, dark tendrils winding around my lungs. They crept up my throat to cut off my air supply. I swallowed hard and closed my eyes, willing the rush of panic to abate.

You're safe. This isn't rational.

Despite my attempts to suppress the fear that gripped me, my stomach turned and sweat beaded on my brow. Gunfire *popped* through my head again and again, penetrating the protective gear that covered my ears. I sucked in a deep breath and set down my SIG as the shooting range began to blur around me. My fingers curled to fists to hide their trembling.

Control, Harper. Get your shit together.

"Hey, man. You okay?" Hopkins raised his voice so I could hear him.

I jerked my head in a nod, unable to force words through my constricted throat.

Get out. Get to somewhere private.

It was time to dull my panic. Self-medicating was the closest I could come to control over my racing thoughts and pounding heart. I would handle this just fine on my own. No one could know I was struggling with PTSD, or my short career with the FBI would be over almost as soon as it began.

I strode out of the shooting range and made my way to the men's room, quickly locking myself in a stall so I wouldn't be seen. The bathroom was empty, but that could change at any moment, and I didn't intend to be caught. If I were found out, I'd lose my job as surely as I would if anyone knew about my PTSD.

I unclenched my fist so I could fish my pain meds out of my pocket.

I popped two pills in my mouth and dry-swallowed, closing my eyes to wait for the numbness to set in.

"Harper? You okay?"

I jumped at the sound of my surname, and the open bottle tipped slightly. Several pills spilled out to bounce against the tiled floor. The little popping sounds they made on impact ripped through me more viciously than the gunfire.

Fresh fear formed a block of ice in my gut. For several agonizingly long seconds, Hopkins said nothing. Then I saw his hand beneath the stall door, plucking up one of the damning white pills. They were so small to pose a threat of such magnitude.

A long, condemning sigh sounded through the bathroom, and my stomach twisted. Hopkins didn't utter a word. His footsteps slapped against the tiles as he left. The door banged shut behind him.

The walls began to close in, and the panic returned. Desperate, I popped another pill.

In that moment, I recognized that this wasn't control—the drugs controlled *me*. I didn't know how to function without them. Shame burned through my veins, but after a few minutes of full-body trembling, everything faded. Fear became a background buzz, and a sense of hollow peace settled over me.

It wasn't courage that made me leave the false haven of the bathroom, but a lack of any emotion at all.

MY STOMACH CHURNED, AND MY HANDS SHOOK. I

wasn't queasy at the prospect of facing Franklin Dawes, my boss and the director of the Chicago FBI field office; I was going through withdrawals.

Well, maybe that wasn't entirely true. I was scared shitless at the highly likely possibility that I was about to be fired. I'd dreamed of being an agent for years, the need to protect and serve ingrained in me. If I thought about it, that was probably a result of my shitty childhood. But I preferred not to think about it. I preferred to think of myself as some kind of hero. I'd certainly been called that after my time serving as an Army Ranger.

I'd been vain, thinking I was strong and untouchable. Now, my world was crashing down around me, my controlled façade crumbling in the face of the damning evidence that I'd become an addict.

I took a deep breath and knocked on Dawes' office door.

"Come in," came his clipped voice. It wasn't unusual for him to sound so cold, but it still made ice crystalize in my veins.

As soon as I opened the door, I stopped in my tracks.

Fuck.

My father sat in the chair across from my boss' desk. His bright green eyes practically burned with disdain.

"Shut the door," he ordered, his voice even colder than Dawes'.

Swallowing hard, I did as he commanded. I knew better than to defy my father. I hated it, but years of physical and emotional abuse made deference automatic. Especially when I knew I deserved his ire. I'd fucked up worse than ever, and I wouldn't be surprised if the barely controlled rage in my father's tightly coiled body burst out and he beat the shit out of me. I wouldn't try to defend myself. Not this time. Ever since I'd matured into my full strength, he hadn't challenged me physically, but I wasn't certain if I'd ever be able to stand up to him if he did threaten me.

Impossibly, the sense of weakness that crushed my chest magnified. I cut my gaze away from his.

I wasn't invited to sit. I was going be forced to stand here and be scolded by my father and my boss before they fired me. It wasn't enough that they were going to end my career; they were going to humiliate me first.

I drew in a shuddering breath and attempted to head them off before the reprimanding could begin.

"I'll go clean out my desk," I said, struggling for a hard tone.

"Yes, you will," Dawes confirmed.

My jaw tightened, and I nodded sharply. "I understand."

"No, you don't," my father said. "You're not being fired. You're being transferred."

I looked up at him, shocked. "What?"

His eyes narrowed. "If you think I'm going to let your fuck up ruin my reputation, you are sorely mistaken. This isn't going public."

As the Deputy Director of the FBI, my father would be publicly shamed if my failure were made common knowledge. I hadn't considered this. Perhaps his vanity would be my salvation. I should have resented his ruthless use of my image for his own ends, but I was too relieved to be angry with him.

"Thank you, sir," I said, carefully deferential.

"Don't thank me yet," he warned. "I'm pulling you from the field. You're going back to Quantico. You'll teach the new recruits and undergo psychological treatment until you deal with whatever bullshit made you a pathetic addict."

Shame burned in my gut. That *bullshit* was the uncontrollable panic that seized my chest at random intervals. I'd seen some fucked up shit, and it had lodged in my brain, warping me and making me weak.

I *was* pathetic.

But I didn't want to go to Quantico. To be

assigned as an instructor to newbie agents was tanta-mount to the harshest possible demotion. I'd be professionally humiliated while my father's reputa-tion would remain untarnished.

"Please." I hated begging, but I had no other recourse. "Send me to another field office. I'll go to therapy. I can kick this. I've already stopped taking pills."

My father sneered. "It's been less than twenty-four hours, and you're sweating and shaking. You're not fit to be an active agent. You'll go to Quantico, and you will thank me for it."

I lifted my chin and stared at him in defiance. He met my stare, his eyes glittering with malice.

"You will thank me," he repeated, his voice low and dangerous.

Rage and humiliation burned in my veins, but I knew I didn't have a choice. If I wanted to have any hope of salvaging my career, I had to comply. If I could get my head straight and prove myself, I might be reassigned to another field office eventually.

"Thank you, sir," I said tightly, the words leaving a bitter tang on my tongue.

My father nodded in cruel satisfaction.

"You're dismissed," Dawes said, as cold as ever.

I turned sharply on my heel and did my best not

to flee from the man who was ruining my life. The man who had always ruined everything.

No. I was fully responsible for my clusterfuck of a situation. Steeling myself, I resolved that I *would* make it through this. I'd find my control again and prove to my father and myself that I wasn't weak.

It was time to get my shit together.

PART I
TRAINING

CHAPTER 1

Natalie

I smiled when I stepped into the seedy dive bar. It was definitely my kind of place, and this would be my last night to let loose for a while. I would start training for my dream job at Quantico tomorrow, and I wouldn't be able to party. I didn't really drink much, but it would be nice to have a night to celebrate my accomplishments.

I'd checked into a motel near Quantico for the night, and The Community Tap had beckoned from across the street. The bar might be a bit sketchy, but I wasn't at all nervous entering by myself. I'd been taking mixed martial arts classes for two years, ever since I'd started my Master's degree in Psychology. I'd known I was preparing to apply for a job with the FBI, and I wanted to be physically equipped as well as mentally sharp. I was determined to graduate the academy and join the Bureau.

As I crossed the threshold, I registered several male gazes swinging my way. I ignored them and headed for the bar. I wasn't here to hook up. I just wanted a beer and a little atmosphere. I'd intentionally selected a conservative sweater with jeans, and I'd applied minimal makeup. I definitely wasn't dressed to impress, but I knew men found me attractive. It wasn't a vain thing; I was physically fit from training, and years of male attention let me know I was pretty enough. I could find some company for the night if I wanted to, but that wasn't part of the plan. I didn't do casual fucks, anyway.

"What can I get you, sweetheart?" The bald, bulky bartender smiled at me.

I didn't care for the casual endearment, but I brushed it off. "What craft beers do you have on draft?" I asked.

He handed me a list, and I quickly made my selection. A good IPA would hit the spot.

Taking my beer with a smile and a tip, I turned to face the rest of the bar. I grinned when I saw people —mostly men—signing up for a darts tournament.

I was so down for this. I had excellent aim, and it

would be fun to compete with the heavily muscled, macho men who were putting their names on the chalkboard and paying the entry fee. Men like that often underestimated me, and I liked proving my worth. It would be a good confidence boost before facing the fierce competition at Quantico.

I crossed the room to the sign up area and confidently wrote my name on the chalkboard, handing the bouncer the five dollars required to compete. He informed me that the tournament would start in fifteen minutes, so I decided I would people watch for a little while and size up my competition.

As I settled back in at the bar, a cluster of hard-faced men in leather jackets caught me looking in their direction. The tallest, biggest one leered and winked at me. Keeping my expression impassive and disinterested, I broke from his gaze. I didn't want to imply any sort of physical invitation.

"You any good?" A deep, masculine voice rumbled through me. I jolted and turned to face the man who had approached me soundlessly. Even though the bar was fairly noisy, it wasn't often that someone was able to encroach on my personal space without my realizing it.

As soon as his stunning green eyes locked on mine, I became very aware of his nearness. My breath caught in my throat, and my body reacted with instant attraction, the pull toward the stranger more visceral and immediate than anything I'd ever experienced. He was easily the most beautiful man I'd ever seen.

No. Beautiful wasn't the right word. He was far too ruggedly masculine for that term. With a strong, clean-shaven jaw and high cheekbones, he could have been a male model. His glossy black hair was meticulously styled, and his sharp black suit managed to convey an air of elegant power. The teasing tilt to his full lips was cocky and sexy as hell.

"What?" I managed to release the air that had been trapped in my chest. I couldn't remember what he'd just said to me. His nearness scrambled my brain and heated my insides. The sensation was utterly foreign and darkly delicious.

"I saw you entered the tournament." He gestured at the chalkboard, but his sparkling emerald eyes didn't leave mine. "Are you any good?"

I straightened my shoulders, struggling to collect myself. It wasn't at all like me to fumble like this over an attractive man.

"Yeah," I asserted with most of my usual confidence.

One corner of his lips ticked up farther, and my gaze riveted on his mouth.

"I'll enjoy the competition, then," he said, his

voice lilting with amusement. "I'm Jason." He extended his hand.

I shook it firmly, finally collecting myself. "Natalie," I introduced.

"It's nice to meet you, Natalie." His voice caressed my name, and I suppressed a shiver. Lust had never hit me so hard. The air seemed to crackle between us, and the way his eyes darkened with hunger as he held my hand told me that I wasn't the only one who felt it. He squeezed gently, and my sex contracted in response.

Slightly disconcerted, I extricated myself from his grip. He smirked. It should have irritated me, but his arrogant confidence was undeniably stoking my lust.

"I'd buy you a drink, but you seem to have that covered," he continued smoothly, flicking his long fingers toward where my beer sat mostly untouched on the bar top. "The next one's on me."

I shook my head. "I don't need to get tipsy. I plan on winning this tournament."

"Competitive," he remarked. His sharp grin dazzled me. "I like that." He tipped his head in the direction of the leather-clad men, but he still didn't take his eyes off my face. "I don't know if your admirers will appreciate it if you beat them."

I shrugged. "That's their problem."

His grin widened. "Then I look forward to

watching you kick their asses." He cocked his head at me. "Although I don't intend to lose, I'll warn you now."

I returned his smile, helplessly charmed by his cockiness. "I'll try not to bruise your ego too badly, then," I teased, slightly surprised at my husky, flirtatious tone. I hadn't been planning on hooking up with anyone, but I certainly wouldn't say no to a hot night with Jason. The physical chemistry between us was electric, and we'd barely touched.

Images of his powerful, sweat-slicked body sliding against mine as he fucked me hard flitted across my mind, and my cheeks heated.

His eyes flashed, and his lips curved in satisfaction. "Are you a betting woman, Natalie?" he asked.

"I..." I fumbled again. I took a shaky breath and tried to gather my wits. "Not really."

"I like games," he told me, his voice dropping to a deeper register. The words rolled through me, vibrating down to my core. My inner muscles fluttered, and my panties grew damp with the beginnings of arousal. "Play with me." It wasn't a question; it was a command.

My tongue darted out to wet my lips. His gaze flicked to my mouth before finding my eyes again, keeping me captured in his steady stare.

"If I win, you're mine for the night."

My heart skipped a beat. The possessive declaration set my body on fire. Suddenly, I wanted very badly to lose to this man.

"And if I win?" I managed to ask, but there was no challenge in the breathy words.

He leaned in, almost as though he was going to kiss me. He stopped when he was close enough that I could feel the heat of his words teasing across my lips. "Then I'll still make you come so hard you'll scream my name and beg for mercy by the time I'm finished with you."

My mouth went dry, and I swallowed. His sexy smirk told me he had me exactly where he wanted me. His easy confidence and commanding aura were intoxicating.

"But not yet," he murmured, dipping his head closer to mine. "Time to play." His lips brushed across my mouth in the lightest teasing contact.

Abruptly, he stepped back. I swayed toward him, and his hands closed around my shoulders to steady me. My sex throbbed with need, and he'd barely touched me.

"Let's get out of here." I urged breathily, deciding I didn't want to play darts. I wanted more time with Jason; one hot, carefree night before I committed myself to my career. "I'm staying across the street. We can go back to—"

"Not yet," he refused, his rich voice colored with amusement. "We still have a wager to settle." He gave me a crooked grin and released me, drawing away completely. He stepped back and waved toward the dartboards. "Ladies first."

Shaking myself, I struggled to find my composure. My entire body felt oddly weak, and I wasn't at all certain I'd be able to aim straight. I didn't mind losing to Jason, but I didn't want to embarrass myself in front of the whole bar.

That thought helped me still my trembling fingers. Now that Jason had given me some space, I could feel the other men's eyes on me again. The huge guy in the leather jacket watched me with undisguised interest, and he sized up Jason. He was clearly ready to challenge the man who'd captivated all my senses.

I wasn't remotely interested. I spared him a single cold glance before finding the confidence to saunter over to the dartboard. Jason chuckled beside me, keeping pace. Even though he was no longer touching me, I could feel the raw sensuality rolling off him. It kissed my skin like a palpable touch, and my sex pulsed.

He picked up the darts and pressed them into my hand, allowing his fingers to linger for a few seconds longer than necessary. The strange weakness flooded my system again, and I struggled to keep my legs from sagging beneath me. All my instincts urged me to fall to my knees before him.

"Don't disappoint me now," he ordered sternly. "I want a proper challenge. I know you're good." He positioned his body behind mine, his hard chest pressing against my back. He gripped my wrist and lifted my arm to the proper height to aim at the target. "Focus," he commanded evenly.

The world fell away around me, and I honed in completely on my task. My hand steadied, and the target was clear before me. He released my wrist, and I delivered a perfect shot, the dart embedding itself in the bullseye.

"Good girl," he rumbled.

My body felt oddly light, my mind blank except for the pleasure at his praise and the goal set out before me. I threw the darts in rapid succession. Within seconds, I'd managed a perfect score.

"Impressive," he remarked. "Maybe we'll tie."

His hands closed around my shoulders again, and he guided me away from my stance in front of the target, placing me at a high table near the competition area.

"My turn," he said. His fingers curled into my flesh briefly. "Stay."

Compelled by his command, I remained where he

left me, watching him move toward the target with predatory grace. He removed my darts from the board and took his place to make his shots.

My focus was ripped from him when a large hand settled on my hip.

"Nice shots, gorgeous."

I blinked and looked up—way up—at the man who touched me. It was the guy in the leather jacket who'd been watching me since I'd come in. His thin lips were drawn back in a lustful smile, and his dark brown eyes were sharp with hunger.

"Lose the suit and hang with me," he urged. Unlike Jason's commands, the order left me cold. My skin crawled where he touched me. I took a step back, and his hand instantly shot out to grip my upper arm. "Come on, baby. I know you're friendlier than that."

I fixed him with my most glacial stare. "Take your hands off me," I demanded levelly. "Now."

He didn't release me. "Don't be like that, sweetness. I'll show you a good time."

"I'll give you three seconds to let me go," I warned.

A dark brow rose. "Or what?" he challenged.

"Or I'll break your nose," I said, a simple declaration of fact.

He threw his head back and laughed. Fuck three seconds, this asshole was going down.

He evidently didn't expect a woman half his size to strike, so he didn't even flinch when my fist flew at his face, landing squarely on his nose with a satisfying *crunch*. Blood instantly poured down over his lips.

"Fucking bitch!" he shouted, clutching at his ruined nose. He lunged for me, his fist swinging.

Before I could react, Jason appeared between us. He caught the man's fist easily, bending his arm back at unnatural angle and forcing him to his knees.

"Do you yield, or do I need to break your arm?" Jason asked, coldly controlled.

"Jason!" I exclaimed in warning. My assailant's three large friends had decided to join the fight. They barreled toward Jason, and I stepped in just in time.

My body moved without thought, my muscles remembering how to fight after hours of training. I heard the man with the bloody nose cry out again, and the dull *crack* let me know Jason had broken his arm, just as he'd promised.

But the sound was periphery. I focused on the first of the three men rushing at us. He lunged for me, and I sidestepped, landing a vicious kick to his knee as I moved. He went down with an agonized shout. I didn't take a moment to think about the damage I'd done; I needed to focus on the other two men coming at me.

But it turned out I didn't need to. When I looked past the fallen man, I watched as Jason took down the last attacker with a brutal blow to his throat. The other man was already on the ground, clutching his stomach and moaning.

"Get the fuck out of my bar." The bouncer's roar called my attention away from the fight. He slapped a baseball bat against his palm menacingly.

Jason held up his hands and took a step back from the bleeding men strewn out on the ground at our feet.

"We were just leaving." He ensnared my hand in his and pulled me along in his wake as we rushed out of the bar.

CHAPTER 2

Natalie

I let out a burst of adrenaline-fueled laughter when the cool night air kissed my heated skin. I'd never been in a real fight before. It was undeniably exhilarating.

Suddenly, Jason caught me up in a fierce embrace and crushed his lips to mine. The kiss was nothing like the teasing seduction he'd shown me so far. In the bar, he'd touched me with the barest brush of his hand, his mouth. Now, he branded me with heat, his tongue tracing the seam of my lips and demanding entrance. I gasped in a shocked breath at the sudden, electric contact, and he took advantage of my open mouth. His tongue delved in, tangling with mine.

Visceral lust quickly swept aside my surprise, and I speared my fingers through his glossy black hair, tugging him closer. He nipped at my lower lip with a growl.

The light hit of pain and the warning rumble connected with my primal brain in a way I didn't fully understand. After the brutally efficient bar fight, giddiness rushed through my system, making my blood fizz in my veins. Jason's raw dominance in the way he handled my mouth brought forth a facet of my sexuality that was somehow both stronger and softer than I'd ever known. The riptide of desire for him was nearly overwhelming, driving me into a frenzy, and yet his teeth against my lips and the firmness of his fingers on my hips kept me trembling and compliant in his hold. I wanted to rub myself against him, to find any stimulation I could when my every nerve ending was alight with need.

Despite my physical desires, my fingers unknotted from his hair, my palms skimming down his cheeks and neck to rest submissively against his sculpted chest. I felt his muscles flex beneath my fingers, and a low sound of his approval rolled against my tongue, vibrating into my chest before sinking lower down in my body. My core heated and clenched, aching for him to fill me, to fuck me. I melted against him, my entire body softening and shaping to his hard, masculine frame.

He pulled back just far enough to allow me to gasp in a much-needed breath, and his emerald eyes caught mine. "You're incredible," he murmured against my lips. "Where did you learn to fight like that?"

"Does it matter?" I panted. I didn't want to talk about my life or my reasons for being here. I might be fiercely attracted to him, but Jason was a stranger, and he didn't need to know about my plans at the FBI academy. All we would have was one scorching hot night together, and I certainly didn't want to waste any time talking.

He grinned savagely. "I guess not," he allowed. "Where are you staying?"

"This way," I urged, stepping out of his embrace so I could lead him across the street to my motel room. Although he followed me, his fingers closed around my wrist in a possessive grip that very clearly let me know I was not in control, even if I was momentarily taking the lead.

Within minutes, we were standing under the fluorescent lights outside the motel as I fished the key out of my pocket. I hadn't bothered taking my usually overstuffed purse to the bar, so I was able to make quick work of my task.

As soon as I got the door open, Jason pushed me inside, spinning my body so my back was pressed against the wall. He slammed the door closed with a kick, and his big hands began tearing at my clothes as his mouth found mine again. I gasped against his hot lips, shocked and aroused at his intensity. I'd had rough sex before and thoroughly enjoyed it. Jason's actions boded for an extremely hot night.

His fingers fisted in my sweater, and he pulled it up my torso, his calloused palms making my skin pebble as they skimmed along my abdomen. I lifted my arms so he could fully remove the garment, and he quickly ripped it off and tossed it aside.

Catching onto his frenzied desire, I returned his kiss with fervor, my tongue tangling with his as my fingers fumbled at the buttons on his crisp white dress shirt. Before I managed to get one free, he caught my wrists and pinned them against the wall above my head, holding them in one hand. His other cupped my jaw, tilting my face up so he could plunder my mouth more deeply. I shuddered and softened. Despite the lust raging through me, I couldn't seem to help submitting. It wasn't like me to surrender to a man's strength so easily, but I'd never been kissed by a man like Jason.

He pulled back, ending the kiss. I stared up at him, wide-eyed and panting.

"You're mine for the night," he declared. "I'm in charge, and I'm going to give you more pleasure than you've ever known."

"And how would you know that?" I managed in a weak attempt at a challenge.

He brushed his knuckles down my cheek, keeping my wrists pinned with his other hand. The firmness of his grip contrasted with the gentle touch on my face, making my head spin. He was a study in contradictions: hard and unyielding, but tender and careful. Although I wouldn't be able to escape him in this position, he wasn't holding me cruelly. He'd subjugated my body, but he wasn't hurting me.

"Because beneath all your fire, you're a sweet submissive, and I don't think anyone knows it. Not even you."

"What are you talking about?" I asked, genuinely confused.

"You like when I take control." He squeezed my wrists for emphasis. My sex contracted in response, and I squirmed against him. He smirked. "I could tell as soon as I touched you for the first time. You sauntered into that bar, confident you could take on any man who challenged you. And after how you handled yourself in there, I know you could. But when I Topped you, you melted."

"Topped?"

He cupped my cheek in his big hand. "I dominated you, kitten. I took control, and you loved it."

"Kitten?" I demanded, not caring for an overused endearment. "Is that what you call all your one-night stands?"

"No," he said earnestly, and the slight surprise in his eyes let me know he wasn't lying. "I've never called anyone that before."

"Then why did you?"

One corner of his lips twisted up in a cocky smile. "Because I know you're a strong, capable woman, but I'm going to make you purr."

My core contracted, and I struggled to maintain a hard mask. "What if I don't like being called kitten?"

"You do."

I tried my best to scoff. "You think you know everything."

"I know enough." Keeping his hold on my wrists, his free hand dipped between us. He deftly opened the button at the front of my jeans, and his fingers slipped beneath the elasticized band at the top of my sensible blue cotton panties. His touch danced over my clit. I rocked toward him, but he explored farther, sliding his fingers through my embarrassingly wet folds to press inside me. He filled me slowly, and I gasped at the intrusion. He watched me intently, his bright green eyes trapping me as securely as his hold on my wrists. "Good little kitten," he rumbled. My inner muscles squeezed his fingers, and a humiliating whimper slipped through my lips.

His low, arrogant chuckle made my core clench again. "You see?" he said, his warm breath fanning my neck as he leaned in close. "You love it. You want to be my good little sex kitten, don't you?"

"Jason," I said tremulously, struggling to hold on to some semblance of control.

"Sir," he corrected.

"What?"

"Address me as *Sir*. I'm in charge tonight. I know this is different for you, but if you let go and trust me, I promise I'll make you come harder than you ever have in your life."

I bit my lip, hesitating. Could I trust a man I'd only just met? This was insane.

"Say yes, kitten," he commanded, his voice dropping impossibly deeper. The sound vibrated through my bones, and I shivered in delight.

This felt so *good*. What harm could come of it? We would only have one night of wild sex.

"All right," I agreed, deciding to engage in his game.

His chin tilted back, and he seemed to grow suddenly taller as he stared down at me. "I want you to beg me," he said, still coolly controlled.

"What?" I asked again, aghast at his demand.

"Beg me to fuck you," he said, leaning in close. His lips ghosted across my neck, his teeth nipped at my throat. "Beg me to make you mine. I want to hear you say it. I need to know that you trust me before we continue."

"I... Yes. I trust you." I knew he wouldn't hurt me. If he wanted to, he would have tried it by now. He wouldn't be asking for my permission.

"Then beg," he whispered against my throat, the words sliding over my skin.

I shivered. "I... Please. I want you to fuck me."

"*Sir*," he prompted, his voice taking on a dark edge. It made my core flutter around his fingers.

"Please fuck me, Sir," I panted, aching for him to take me. I wanted him to shove down my jeans, free his cock, and fuck me hard.

His fingers curved against the secret spot at the front of my inner walls, and I moaned as pleasure lit up my system.

"Such a sweet little kitten," he praised. His warm approval heated my insides with more than simple lust. "We'll get to that part later."

He slowly withdrew his fingers from inside me, leaving me feeling desperately empty. I whined at the loss, but he hushed me with a quick brush of his lips against mine. Then he released my wrists and hooked his fingers through the top of my jeans and my panties. He pulled them down in a smooth motion, sliding down my body as he dropped to his knees before me. I stared at him, panting in need. I wanted to tangle my fingers in his thick black hair and guide his mouth toward my sex, but I remained still, trembling with the effort of resisting my carnal urges. After the way he'd dominated my mouth and my pussy, I knew he wouldn't approve of me taking charge. He was utterly in control, and I'd willingly surrendered to him.

He pressed a feather light kiss directly above my clit.

"Please," I begged, sweat beading on my brow with the effort of resisting the impulse to rock my hips toward him.

"Shhh." His breath blew across my heated lower lips in a cool stream as he gently silenced me. A small, strangled noise of pure need teased the back of my throat, but I didn't speak again. He gently gripped my ankles, one after the other, guiding me to step out of my flats and jeans, leaving me wearing nothing but my bra. Once he'd stripped me, he eased my thighs apart with a firm grip. Suddenly, his thumbs parted my pussy lips, and he studied me intently, as though my sex was the most fascinating thing he'd ever seen. I watched him with rapt attention as he toyed with my wet folds, exploring my shape and the slick readiness that coated my swollen folds.

"This is a very pretty pussy," he said, his voice rough with lust. Although he was on his knees before me, there was nothing supplicant about his position. He boldly examined my most intimate area, as though he had every right. As though he owned every forbidden inch of me.

Finally, he mercifully explored me with his mouth as well as his hands. Keeping my folds parted with his thumbs, he traced my entrance with the tip of his tongue. I cried out at the teasing contact, my entire body wound so tight with anticipation that even the light touch sent bliss crackling through my system.

I couldn't help myself; I lifted my hips toward him, and I buried my fingers in his thick hair. He nipped at my clit, grazing his teeth over the hypersensitive bud. My knees collapsed, but he caught me, his strong arms bracing beneath my ass to keep me from falling. His low, triumphant laugh made me shiver. He had me exactly where he wanted me: wet and needy and thoroughly chastised.

He got to his feet, lifting me as he righted himself. Suddenly, I was in his arms, cradled against his hard frame. I only had a moment to revel in the strength of his hold before he turned and abruptly dropped me onto the bed. The sensation of falling made adrenaline spike through my system, and a giddy giggle bubbled from my chest when I landed safely on the soft mattress. I felt drunk, even though I'd barely touched my beer in the bar. It was Jason; he was utterly intoxicating. I was completely enthralled, and I couldn't have broken free from his power over me even if I wanted to.

And I definitely didn't want to. I watched him as he shrugged out of his suit jacket. He grinned at me sharply as he loosened his tie. I only had a few seconds to puzzle over his almost cruelly arrogant expression before his body settled over mine. His weight pressed me into the mattress, pinning me down. He kissed me again, hard and demanding. I could taste myself on his tongue this time, and I moaned into his mouth at the wicked flavor.

He reached beneath me and unclasped my bra before sliding the straps down my arms. I moved compliantly, wanting to be bare for him. My peaked nipples rubbed against his shirt, and although I ached to feel his skin against mine, there was something undeniably erotic about me being naked and exposed while he was fully clothed. It enhanced the power dynamic between us. I kissed him with greater fervor, physically communicating how much I wanted him.

He gathered up my wrists and directed them over my head. On instinct, I pulled against the restraint.

Allowing someone to overpower my naked body and trap me went against all my training.

He gripped my arms firmly, stilling my efforts. His body over mine prevented me from kicking out, and all I could do was squirm beneath him. He leaned in and whispered in my ear, his hot breath tickling over my neck.

"Calm down, kitten," he said, soft and soothing. "I'm not going to hurt you."

"I don't know how I feel about this," I said on a shuddering breath.

"Don't you?" he challenged softly. He reached between us and caught one of my nipples between his thumb and forefinger, pinching hard enough to elicit a flare of pain. At the same time, he bit down on the sensitive spot on where my neck curved into my shoulder. I cried out at the flash of pain, but hot lines of pleasure shot from the abused areas, lancing all the way to my core. It throbbed, aching to be filled.

I whimpered beneath him, confused at my body's reactions but more aroused than I'd ever been in my life.

He released me from his bite, and his touch on my nipple eased. He rolled the bud between his fingers, soothing me as his tongue traced the little indentations his teeth had left in my flesh. I shuddered, and my body relaxed completely as pleasure rushed to my head.

"Good kitten," he praised, stroking his fingers through my hair as though I was his favorite pet. Mindlessly, I leaned into his touch, craving more. "You trust me, don't you?" he prompted.

"Yes," I whispered. A warm glow pulsed in my chest, filling me with a sense of security. Jason had dominated my body, but he was also taking care of me, seeing to my comfort and pleasure.

"Stay." He pressed a tender kiss against my forehead before he pushed up off me, getting to his feet. I made a small sound of protest at the loss of his heat, but my disappointment quickly dissipated when he began working the buttons on his shirt free. My tongue darted out to wet my lips at the sight of his sculpted body. I'd felt the smooth planes of his muscles through his clothes, but nothing could have prepared me for his perfection.

His green eyes darkened as he watched me lick my lips, and he increased his pace in undressing. Within seconds, he'd stripped completely. My gaze riveted on his cock, and I swallowed hard. He was big and perfectly formed *everywhere*.

He moved onto the bed, his heat rolling over my skin again.

"Do you have a condom?" I asked. I was on birth

control, but Jason was a stranger, and I didn't want to take any unnecessary risks.

"I do," he replied. "But I'm not finished tasting you yet. Keep your arms above your head."

He eased down my body and settled between my thighs. His fingers sank into my flesh, almost firm enough to bruise as he pinned my legs down. The demonstration of his power over me only got me hotter. I could feel the wetness coating my lower lips, a wanton sign of my desire for him.

He didn't tease me this time. With a low growl, he buried his tongue in my pussy, devouring me like a starving man. I moaned and thrashed beneath his onslaught, but his harsh grip on my thighs rendered me immobile. All I could do was surrender to the pleasure he was giving me.

He took me to the edge, his tongue stroking and tasting, exploring every inch of me until I felt thoroughly conquered. He owned my pussy, my ecstasy. I was so close...

"Come for me," he rumbled against my heated flesh. The command vibrated into my core, and he sucked my clit into his mouth.

"Jason!" I screamed out his name as white-hot bliss surged through my veins, burning me up with bliss. He continued to lick me through my orgasm, drawing out every last drop of my ecstasy, until I was trembling and weak.

His heat left me briefly again, but I couldn't focus enough on my surroundings to see what he was doing until he was before me again, kneeling between my thighs as he rolled on a condom. Even though I'd just had the most intense orgasm of my life, my inner muscles contracted at the prospect of having him inside me. I craved for him to fill me, to fuck me hard and finish claiming me completely.

"Please fuck me, Sir," I begged, adding on the honorific without a thought.

He grinned. "Greedy girl. I like that."

His weight settled over me, and his mouth came down on mine. At the same time as his tongue surged in, he entered me in one smooth thrust. Even though my orgasm had prepared me, there was still a slight burn as he entered me. I'd never been with anyone as big as Jason, and he stretched me almost to the point of pain. A soft whine slipped from my mouth into his.

"You can take me," he murmured against my lips. "Relax." As he spoke, he began to pet me again, his fingers running through my hair. He kissed me deeply, his tongue sliding against mine in firm strokes. His mastery of my body reassured me, and I softened beneath him. My inner walls eased, and he pulled out slightly before gently thrusting back in. He fucked me slowly, gradually stretching me as my body yielded to his. With every drag of his cockhead across my g-spot, pleasure pulsed through my system. I wrapped my legs around his hips, my heels digging into his ass as I urged him to take me more deeply. He groaned into my mouth and increased his pace, fucking me hard and fast. With each harsh thrust, I went spiraling higher on bliss, my body tightening until all my muscles shook. When I couldn't take any more, my orgasm exploded through me, and I screamed against him as pleasure wracked my system. My core contracted around him, and he groaned into my mouth as his cock began to jerk within me, his release triggered by my own. He gripped my hips and rolled us onto our sides as he collapsed in sated exhaustion, but he didn't withdraw from me. I floated in warm darkness, high on *him*.

He brushed light kisses over my cheeks, my eyelids, my lips. I felt safe, cared for. I sighed and snuggled into his chest as I basked in the warm glow that pulsed from the center of my being. I fell into sleep, Jason still buried deep inside me.

CHAPTER 3

Jason

A sense of masculine satisfaction filled me as I idly traced the curve of Natalie's hip. She was beautiful, peaceful as she slept. I'd been awake for nearly an hour, but it seemed I'd thoroughly exhausted her. She'd barely stirred when I'd withdrawn from her and prepared for bed. I'd thought about going back to my own motel room, but the temptation of her sweet, sated body was too much to resist.

I should go, I reasoned, but I didn't move away from her. For the first time in over a year, I felt at peace. The heady sense of control I got from dominating Natalie was far better than the hollow nothingness of my drugs. I hadn't allowed myself to Top anyone since I'd started using. I'd barely scratched the surface of kink with Natalie, but I'd found our night together more fulfilling than any scene I'd ever shared with another woman.

She'd been so strong and fiery in the bar, and watching her kick the shit out of the man who'd touched her without her permission had been one of the hottest things I'd ever seen. Usually, I liked my women soft, submissive.

Natalie had proven to be submissive, but she certainly wasn't outside the bedroom.

And the knowledge that she'd softened just for me got me hard again. I was sporting almost painful morning wood, but I didn't want to rouse her.

I couldn't stop petting her, though. She was precious, my redemption after long months of weak addiction. One night with her had helped me find myself again. I didn't plan on jeopardizing that by waking her up for a quickie. The self-control I found in resisting the base urge helped remind me of the man I used to be. I relaxed fully for the first time in longer than I could remember, sighing in contentment.

The small sound of pleasure finally roused Natalie. She blinked slowly, revealing her striking sapphire eyes. I gave her a lopsided grin.

"Morning, kitten."

She returned my smile and stretched, making a happy little hum as she moved. I wasn't the only one basking in the afterglow of our night together.

Suddenly, she sat bolt upright.

"Shit! What time is it?"

"Not even seven yet," I assured her.

"How close to seven? Crap!" she exclaimed and tried to slide off the bed. I caught her wrist, stopping her. She tugged against my hold. "I have to take a shower. I'm going to be late. Fuck, I can't be late." She seemed to be talking to herself as much as to me.

I reluctantly released her, allowing her to scramble away. I got to my feet as well. Her eyes dropped to my jutting cock, and she licked her lips.

"I'll shower with you," I told her.

She shook her head, tearing her gaze away from my dick. Her dark eyes were almost frantic. "No, I'll never leave if we shower together. I'm sorry, Jason, but you have to go." She picked up my clothes and began tossing them at me. I caught them in an automatic action. I'd rather throw them to the ground, scoop her up, and carry her into the shower.

But the panic in her eyes kept me immobilized.

"Okay," I allowed after a beat of silence. "I won't keep you." I began to pull on my clothes. When I was fully dressed, I pulled out my phone. "What's your number?"

"My number?" She appeared puzzled.

"Yes. I'd like to see you again."

She shook her head again, more wildly this time. "I can't. I'm sorry."

I frowned. "Why not?"

"Look. It's not you. Last night was... Well, it was amazing. But it was just one night. I have things I need to do. I'm sorry." Her eyes widened, almost pleading. I could tell she really was sorry, but that didn't stop bitter disappointment from flooding my chest.

"All right," I allowed, summoning up a cool façade. I had things I needed to do, too. For one, I needed to get to Quantico and set up my new life there. For another, I didn't need to get into a relationship while I was trying to get my life back on track. I might have gotten through the detox phase of my recovery, but my life was still a shit storm. I had no business bringing Natalie into it.

I tore my gaze from her naked body and walked past her, opening the door just enough to exit but so that no one would be able to see her. The idea of anyone looking at her perfection made anger spike through me. And that was completely irrational.

I'm only getting attached because she's the first woman I've fucked since I got sober, I reasoned.

Firmly pushing her from my mind, I jogged away from her motel and made my way back to my own room. I'd leave Natalie in my broken past. It was time to put my life back together, and getting involved with anyone would break my focus. Salvaging my career was my number one priority, and I couldn't allow anything to get in the way. Not even the most incredible woman I'd ever met.

❧

"Jason Harper. I have to admit I'm surprised to see you here," Director Georgia Parkinson said, her brown gaze pinning me in place. The whites of her eyes contrasted with her dark skin, making her stare all the more striking.

I lifted my chin and faced her head-on, tamping down the shame that threatened to rise up and consume me. "I assumed you would have been briefed on my reassignment," I said stiffly.

She speared me with a hard look. "Oh, I was briefed by your father personally. That's why I'm surprised. I was impressed with you as a recruit. I never expected we'd meet again under these circumstances."

Humiliation burned through my veins. So, my father must have told her everything. My suspicions were confirmed when she continued on.

"You will see a psychologist twice every week to work through your problems. I know you're clean now, or I wouldn't have allowed your presence here. But I will not tolerate a backslide. Whatever it is that caused your lapse in judgment, I expect you to work through it with Dr. Larson. If I get an inkling that you're using again, I will expose you, no matter what your father threatens me with. You won't work another day for the Bureau. Am I clear?"

"Yes, Director," I said as coolly as I could manage.

"However," she continued, as though I hadn't spoken. "I remember that you were one of my most promising new agents. I won't waste your talent. Once Dr. Larson clears you for re-entry into the field, I'll recommend you to a new field office. This assignment at Quantico doesn't have to be permanent if you don't want it to be."

"I... Thank you." I wasn't sure what to say. I was shocked that Parkinson was being remotely kind to me, knowing what I was.

Addict. Failure. Weak.

"Don't thank me. Show me you can do this. You father might think he can punish you for the rest of your life, but he's not God. He can't keep you here forever without raising suspicions if I recommend a transfer for you." Her lip curled in disdain, and I realized that maybe I wasn't the only person who hated my father. "But," she added sharply. "I won't do that until I know you're good to go back into the field. So work with Dr. Larson. How long you're here depends on how hard you work to get through your issues."

I stiffened. I didn't want to talk to a shrink. I could handle my problems on my own.

Yeah, and look what a great job I've done with that, a nasty little voice needled me.

"All right," I agreed, the fight draining out of me. If spilling my guts to a shrink was what I had to do to get back into the field, then I'd do it. I could handle a few months training recruits if there was hope to get away from Quantico soon. "I'll talk to Dr. Larson."

"Good." Parkinson nodded in satisfaction. "You'll be teaching hand-to-hand combat while you're here."

"I can do that." I'd excelled at hand-to-hand combat during my training, and even though I'd lost some muscle weight while I was using, I could still fight.

She nodded again. "Not a toe out of line while you're here, Harper," she warned. "Don't make me regret helping you."

"You won't," I swore. "Thank you, Director."

"You're dismissed." She waved me out of her office.

When I closed the door behind me, I heaved in a deep breath. It definitely could have gone worse. Parkinson seemed to dislike my father, which meant I had a powerful ally. All I had to do was rip open my soul and expose my darkest secrets to a stranger.

I straightened my shoulders. I'd talk to Dr. Larson. I had to. Nothing was more important than getting my career back.

Not even the scorching hot little brunette who I couldn't seem to shake from my mind. Natalie's scent seemed to cling to me, even though I knew that wasn't rational. I'd left her hours ago, showered, and changed clothes. There was no reason for me to think I could sense her in any way.

But try as I might, I couldn't shake her. Images of our hot night together flashed through my mind, tormenting me. I wished she'd given me her contact details.

No. It's for the best, I reminded myself.

Sighing, I resolved to push her from my mind and headed toward the large lecture hall where the New Agents in Training—the NATs—would be given their orientation speech. I didn't necessarily have to attend, but I was curious to assess the group I'd be training. If they were anything like my class at Quantico, there would be a few who excelled, some who scraped by, and several who weren't up to scratch.

I was a little relieved I'd been assigned to a more physical aspect of their training. I wasn't in the right headspace to test the NATs on logic puzzles, and those had never been my strong suit, anyway. I left the more difficult mental hurdles to the analysts and enjoyed being in the field. That didn't mean I was incapable of putting my mind to a difficult problem, but it certainly wasn't my favorite part of my job.

When I arrived at the lecture hall, I realized orientation had already started. I could hear the NATs swearing to uphold their duties in unison, the sound of their combined voices emanating through the closed doors. Deciding it wouldn't be a good idea to burst into the hall partway into orientation, I settled for leaning back against the wall and waiting for them to emerge. I didn't have anything to occupy my time at the moment, anyway, and sizing up the new recruits was the most useful thing I could think of. Until my first class or first therapy appointment was scheduled, I had nothing to do.

I hated lacking purpose or direction. It brought back my feelings of ineptitude, reminding me of my weakness and my failure.

I shoved back the shame that threatened to rise up and consume my thoughts.

I'm starting over, I reminded myself. I could think of this time in the next few months as Quantico two-point-oh for me. I was working my way to becoming a field agent, just as I'd done a year ago. I might not be participating in the same challenges as the NATs, but I had my own obstacles to overcome. I had to prove myself all over again, and I wouldn't fail. I'd excelled at training the first time around. I could do it again.

My conversation with the Director had given me hope that my time here would be short. All I had to do was prove to the therapist that I was clean and stable.

I certainly felt more stable than I had in months. My night with Natalie had helped remind me of the man I used to be before the drugs. Before the waking nightmares had taken hold deep in my brain, tormenting me and making me weak.

Blood and flesh and bone. Mutilated bodies strewn everywhere. Pieces of what used to be people littered through the rubble.

I closed my eyes and took a deep breath, struggling against the memory that had triggered my PTSD. I'd served in Afghanistan as a Ranger, and I'd seen fucked up shit. I'd done fucked up shit. But the bouts of uncontrollable panic hadn't started until the day I went to the bombsite.

I'd barely been with the Bureau for two months when I was called out to the site of the domestic terror attack. A thirty-foot radius of the Water Tower Place Mall had been obliterated, along with the people who had stood in the suicide bomber's path. The carnage that day had brought back every horrible thing I'd ever seen or done in the line of duty.

A few weeks later, I'd been chasing down a drug dealer, working a different case as though my brain hadn't been shattered by what I'd seen. Out of nowhere, the roar of a passing train overtook my senses, thrusting me back into a world where explosions ripped the air around me.

I'd stumbled, fallen. And broken my fucking wrist.

That's when I was prescribed the oxycodone. It didn't take long for me to start self-medicating to stave off the panic attacks.

That's all over now. I'm clean. I'm going to get my life back.

My brooding was interrupted when the doors burst open, and sound swelled from the lecture hall. I tried not to jolt at the sudden burst of noise.

I took another deep breath.

Focus. I'd come here to observe the new recruits.

From my position against the wall, I could watch them pass.

There were your typical clean-cut jock types. Some with more lithe runner's bodies, others bulked up like they lifted weights every day. The women were fit, too. If they weren't, they wouldn't be here. The rigors they'd face at Quantico were physically demanding, and trainees needed to be in peak condition to make it through.

My eyes roved over them as they streamed out the double doors, many of them practically bouncing with anticipation. They wouldn't be so energized and eager by the time they made it through their first day.

One woman caught my gaze. Held it. She stopped in her tracks, her mouth hanging open. A few recruits bumped into her, but she didn't seem to notice. Her attention was fully focused on me. Her cheeks, which had been rosy and flushed with pleasure just a few hours ago, had gone pale.

Natalie.

Oh, fuck.

CHAPTER 4

Natalie

Startlingly green eyes caught mine and held. I stopped breathing.

Jason.

He leaned casually against the wall, but there was nothing casual in the taut lines of his suit-clad body. His nostrils flared when our gazes clashed, and his jaw firmed.

Shit, shit, shit.

The curse word rang through my head over and over again in a panicked mantra, and I struggled to keep my face impassive. I'd fucked another recruit. The hottest night of my life was turning into the biggest mess of my life. It was only supposed to be one night. And although the sight of Jason walking out the motel door this morning had pained me more than I would have liked, I'd known it wasn't practical to give him my number.

But now he was here. At Quantico. Where I was supposed to be focused solely on training to become a field agent. I didn't need any impossibly gorgeous, domineering distractions.

Someone shoved me particularly hard as they passed me, and I realized I was in everyone's way. We were supposed to be moving to the dorms, where we'd be assigned our roommates and get settled in before our first challenge of the day.

I squared my shoulders and resolved to face this head-on. I'd calmly explain to Jason that this was an unfortunate coincidence, but nothing more would ever happen between us.

Forcing my feet to unstick from the floor, I made my way over to him. He straightened as I approached, and my steps turned more hesitant. I'd forgotten how imposing he was when he stood at his full height. It was more than simple physical size; he owned the space around him.

Lifting my chin, I steeled my resolve and closed the rest of the distance between us.

"Jason," I began in a clipped greeting. I tried to remain coolly collected, but the memory of screaming his name out in ecstasy only hours ago made my cheeks heat. I continued on quickly. "Listen, this is... not ideal. I guess it's not unreasonable that we both stayed near base last night before orientation. But I want to make it clear right now that I'm here for my career, and nothing else. I'm not interested in dating another recruit." I flushed hotter when I said *dating*. I hadn't meant to sound like I'd even thought about any kind of relationship beyond a one-night stand. "Or anything else," I amended.

His jaw ticked. He seemed angry with me. Was he really getting pissed that I was rejecting him?

"I'm not a recruit," he said tersely.

"What? Then what are you doing here?" My confusion pushed aside my initial panic, and I noted his suit, assessing his appearance for the first time since I'd locked eyes with him. He wasn't wearing the matching t-shirts that marked us as new recruits.

"I'm an instructor," he bit out.

My stomach dropped. "What?" I asked, more faintly this time.

His eyes flashed. "I don't know how to be any clearer. I'm an instructor, and you're—" He ground his teeth together, cutting off whatever he was going to say. "You should catch up with the others." He jerked his chin in the direction of the recruits who were headed away from the lecture hall.

"Jason, I—" I wasn't sure what I wanted to say, but he cut me off before I could get any words out.

"Go to your quarters, recruit. That's an order."

I gasped and took a step back. I'd enjoyed his sensual commands last night, but this cold order sent me reeling. Hurt and mortification burned through my chest. I couldn't even begin to sort out my emotions, but my body obeyed. I turned on my heel and half-ran after my fellow recruits, anxious to put space between me and the man who'd given me more pleasure than I'd ever known in my life.

※

BY THE TIME I MADE IT TO THE DORMS, I'D managed to stop my fingers from shaking. Outwardly, my appearance was calm, controlled. Inside, I was reeling.

Jason's here. He's at Quantico. And he's an instructor.

This was so much worse than if he'd been a recruit. That would have been mortifying enough, and the temptation of his nearness over the coming weeks would have tormented me. But knowing that he was one of the people I was going to have to impress if I wanted to graduate from the FBI academy made my stomach turn.

After the way I'd reacted to his nearness outside

the lecture hall, I knew it was going to be impossible for my body to forget how he'd subjugated it, and how much pleasure I'd found in surrendering to him. How could he ever see me as a competent agent after I'd begged him to fuck me and called him *Sir*?

Fuck.

I was going to have to call him *sir* again, but in a completely different scenario. Would I be able to keep my core from clenching every time I used the honorific?

"Simmons." I snapped to attention when someone barked out my surname. "You're with Briggs."

Shaking my head slightly to clear away my roiling thoughts, I focused on the woman who was organizing the room assignments. She gestured to a petite blonde a few recruits away from me. I smiled at the blonde—Briggs—and her pale blue eyes narrowed on me, assessing. She didn't smile in return.

Okay, so my new roommate was the competitive type. A friendly pairing would have been a small mercy, especially given my current emotional turmoil, but I was used to hypercompetitive environments from my grad school days. I was barely fazed by Briggs' small show of hostility.

The roommate assignments continued on for a few more minutes, and then we were allowed a small lapse in organized time so we could settle in. We'd be attending our first class in half an hour, and an excited buzz filled the long dormitory hallway as recruits broke off into conversations. I made my way over to Briggs to introduce myself properly. She might warm to me after her initial tough-girl act.

"I'm Natalie," I said, extending my hand for her to shake.

She briefly attempted to crush my fingers. "Elena," she said with a harsh grin.

I gave her my best cold smile, an icy curve of my lips that didn't reach my eyes. "It's nice to meet you," I said, perfectly polite, just as my mother had drilled into me. My debutante days might have felt like a waste of time, but in that moment I was grateful for the perfect bitchy poise I'd learned. Elena's grin slipped when I squeezed her hand just as hard as she gripped mine. That trick was compliments of my dad. My mother might have wanted me to be a perfect lady, but my father had taught me how to shake hands properly.

Elena's death grip eased, and I released her.

"Damn, I was hoping for a catfight," a new, masculine voice interjected. "But I guess I'll get to see you ladies go at it during combat class later."

My cold smile dropped to a glacial blank stare as I turned my gaze on the perv who'd sidled up to us. He grinned at me, white teeth flashing against his darkly tanned skin. He looked like a golden boy football star, with a perfect smile and twinkling hazel eyes. I wasn't remotely impressed by his appearance, considering his opening remarks.

"I'm Trent McMahon," he introduced himself, still grinning. I pointedly glanced down at his proffered hand and didn't extend my own.

"Elena Briggs." My roommate warmed to him instantly, and I noticed her knuckles didn't turn white when she gingerly shook his hand.

I suppressed a shrug and started to turn away. I'd already taken a dislike to both of them, so I had no issue with them being friendly.

Trent, however, wasn't content to let me disengage.

He dropped Elena's hand and grabbed my upper arm, stopping me. "Wait. I didn't catch your name, beautiful."

I fixed him with my deadliest stare. "My name is Natalie Simmons. And the last man who touched me without my permission got his nose broken. The only reason you're not crying on the floor right now is that I don't want to get kicked out on my first day at Quantico. But let me be clear: I will report you for sexual harassment if you don't take your hand off me right now."

His jaw dropped, and he jerked his hand away

from me as though I'd burned him. But his grin was firmly back in place an instant later. "Damn, Natalie," he chuckled. "I know not to fuck with you. I didn't mean anything by it. I'm from Texas. We're real friendly there, is all."

"My daddy's from Texas," Elena said quickly. "I totally get it. Don't be such a bitch, Natalie."

I crossed my arms over my chest. "I'm from North Carolina, and where I'm from, real gentlemen know to keep their hands to themselves."

He seemed completely unfazed. "Carolina girl, huh? That's a cute accent."

Cute? Was this guy for real?

Elena certainly seemed to find him charming. "I'm from Florida," she provided, although no one had asked. "Where in Texas are you from, Trent? My dad's from Austin."

Trent opened his mouth to answer, but I stalled him. "If you'll excuse me, I'll let you two get to know each other."

I had no interest in the flirtation that was taking place. Trent was clearly a man who liked a challenge, because he seemed to have focused in on me, despite my attitude toward him. Elena couldn't seem to stand for that. She was practically fawning over him in an effort to divert his attention from me.

I didn't have time for stupid games. I was here to

earn my place as a field agent, not flirt with other recruits. For all I knew, Trent might be making a power play to edge me out by exploiting my femininity in front of the others.

Or he could just be an entitled pretty boy who wanted what he couldn't have.

Regardless, he didn't have a shot with me. Having excused myself, I withdrew from the conversation and started to make my way to my first class: hand-to-hand combat.

◈

THE TRAINING ROOM FILLED WITH HUSHED conversation as our class waited for the instructor to arrive. I glanced at the clock mounted on the wall above us. He only had twenty-three seconds left to arrive before he'd be officially late. As it was, we'd all been waiting for nearly ten minutes, because no one had dared to be tardy for our first lesson.

I rolled my shoulders, loosening up my muscles. I'd trained for this for two years, and I felt confident about my ability to excel in this particular area. I might be considerably smaller than most of my male counterparts, but I'd learned to use my size to my advantage. I moved faster than my larger opponents, but I knew many of my fellow recruits would have trained for this, too. It would provide a greater challenge than I was accustomed to.

The memory of my performance in the bar fight the night before helped bolster my confidence. Those men had been huge, and I'd taken them down easily. I'd been outnumbered, and things might have turned out differently if Jason hadn't been there to assist. As it was, the adrenaline rush from the fight had only added fuel to the lustful fire that burned between the two of us, and it had led to the hottest night of my life.

As though summoned by my thoughts, the man I was fantasizing about stepped through the door. The recruits instantly fell silent. Could they feel the raw power pulsing off him as keenly as I did? Jason utterly commanded the space around him, radiating authority. No wonder he'd been selected as an instructor.

He was physically fit to teach combat, too. My mouth went dry as I watched his bulging muscles flex as he moved with fluid grace. He'd traded his sharp suit for a tight black t-shirt and track pants, and the material shaped to his perfect ass.

I remembered how firm it had been beneath my heels as I wrapped my legs around his waist and drew him deeper inside me, welcoming his cock.

I tore my gaze from him. How was I going to focus on my training when I couldn't stop thinking about how his sweat-slicked, powerful body felt pressing mine into the mattress, trapping me with his superior strength?

"Welcome to Quantico," his deep voice boomed out. It was clipped, professional, lacking the dark velvet caress of last night. The sharpness of his tone helped give me the courage to look up at him again. His stunning green eyes roved over the recruits. They skipped right over me, as though I wasn't even there.

My stomach dropped as an irrational sense of rejection flooded my gut.

Don't be stupid, I berated myself. Of course I didn't want his special attention. I wanted him to treat me like any other recruit, to pretend nothing had happened between us. That was the only way I'd be able to get through this. My career was far more important than my infatuation.

"I'm Agent Jason Harper, and I'll be training you in hand-to-hand combat," he continued on, still not looking at me. "I know most of you will have experience with some form of physical combat, but it's my job to teach you the way the Bureau does it. This isn't boxing class at your local gym. We'll start with the basics today. Pair up." He barked the final order.

Everyone scurried to do his bidding. I noticed Trent making his way toward me, and I quickly turned to the first alternative person I could find. The massive man beside me was my fastest option.

"I'm Natalie," I introduced myself with a firm handshake. "Want to partner up?"

He beamed at me, his perfect white smile contrasting with his flawless ebony skin. "Sure. I'm Nathaniel Cross," he said, "but you can call me Nate."

I glanced over to find that Elena had intercepted Trent, and I breathed a small sigh of relief. Maybe he'd leave me alone if she continued her efforts to win his attentions.

"Nate." I smiled at my new partner. "Do you have any experience with hand-to-hand combat?"

His smile turned self-deprecating. "I'm afraid my experience with boxing won't help me much, considering Harper's introduction. What about you?"

"Two years of mixed martial arts," I replied.

"Damn. Go easy on me, will you?"

I was pleased that he recognized my experience rather than assuming his brawn would do him any favors. I respected a man who recognized his own limitations and was willing to learn new skills.

"We're just learning basics today," I assured him. "I don't know how much of what I know will align with the Bureau's protocols. This is new territory for both of us."

He tipped his head in gratitude. "That's nice of

you to say, but I overheard you putting McMahon in his place. I'm pretty sure you could break my nose if you wanted to." He winked.

I laughed. "I wouldn't do that. You're not a misogynistic ass."

"You read him that fast? You should be an analyst, not a field agent." I could tell by the teasing tilt of his lips that he knew just as well as I did that Trent was a dick.

"I did just finish my M.A. in Psychology," I admitted. "I'll go wherever the Bureau chooses to place me, but I'm hoping to be in the field more often than I'm at a desk."

"You and me both," he agreed. "Where are you—?"

Before he could finish his question, Jason's voice boomed out again. "Quiet," he demanded. "You can all socialize after your lessons. If you have the energy left for conversation. This isn't college. You're not here to make friends. You're here to learn to be an efficient agent. Those of you who make it to graduation, that is. Thirty percent of you won't. Keep that in mind."

With the cruel warning, Jason began the lesson, selecting one of the bigger men from our group to demonstrate the first basic moves we would practice. Luckily, they were familiar to me.

Nate wasn't as fortunate. Although he was muscular and fit, he wasn't accustomed to moving with the fluidity and speed necessary. While the moves weren't particularly difficult, I had to consciously slow my actions to allow him to catch up.

Jason prowled around the room, pausing to critique and correct. When he neared me, I felt him more than I saw him; I was studiously focusing on Nate instead. But I couldn't deny the magnetic pull of his presence. His deep voice rumbled through me as he assessed the sparring pair beside me.

I held my breath, bracing myself for his nearness.

He passed right by without a word.

The knot in my stomach loosened, nervous anticipation giving way to indignation. How was I supposed to learn if he ignored me completely?

In my distraction, Nate managed to land a light hit. Startled, I turned my attention back on him.

"Got you." He beamed with pride.

I made an attempt to return his smile. "Good one." Trying my best to shake off my irritation with Jason, I focused on my task. If he wouldn't teach me, I'd just have to work that much harder to learn without individual help. "Let's go again," I urged Nate.

By the time we finished, sweat covered my body, and exhaustion was already seeping into my muscles.

But we weren't anywhere close to being finished for the day. We only barely had time to hit the showers and change for our next class, in which we were shown gruesome crime scene photos and instructed in the basics of casework.

At the end of the day, I tried to talk with Nate over dinner in the dining hall, but I could barely carry a conversation. I'd never been so physically and intellectually spent in my entire life, and I still had to go back to my dorm room to study. I fell asleep on my books, too exhausted to worry about Jason. It was a small mercy.

CHAPTER 5

Natalie

Despite my exhaustion, I forced myself to wake up at four-thirty the next morning and go for a swim. The exercise would help wake me up so I wouldn't be a zombie for my first class. Besides, I found swimming soothing. It was a solitary activity, and it gave me a chance to clear my head.

As soon as I awoke, thoughts of Jason invaded my mind again: lust, irritation, uncertainty. I didn't know how to handle this situation. I was mortified that I'd slept with one of my instructors, but I was also pissed at him for ignoring me. And I wasn't entirely sure if my anger was simply because I needed to learn from him. A little voice in my head told me I was also angry because I felt like a spurned lover.

Which was ridiculous, because we'd only shared one night together.

Sighing, I straightened my goggles and dove into the pool. The cool water parted, welcoming me in a smooth glide. As I began my laps, my mind slowly calmed. The pool was completely empty at this time of day, and I was grateful for that.

When I reached the end of my tenth lap, I paused. I popped up out of the water and removed my goggles, rubbing residual water from around my eyes. When my vision cleared, I stopped breathing.

Jason was staring down at me. His mostly naked frame was propped up against the wall, his powerful arms crossed over his chest. He was dressed only in tight swim trunks, and they did little to hide his growing erection.

He was aroused, but he was glaring at me as though I'd offended him deeply.

My anger surged back to life. I pushed up out of the pool, water sliding off my body. His nostrils flared as his gaze darted down to my breasts before snapping back up to my face.

I strode over to him, riding the wave of my anger. "What is your problem?" I demanded. "You're treating me like I've done something wrong. Well, I haven't. It's a shitty coincidence that we're both here, but I didn't—"

"Of course you haven't done anything wrong," he barked over me. "I'm the one who—" He shook his head sharply and tore his eyes from mine, as though he couldn't bear to look at me. "I can't do this."

"Well, you're going to have to learn to deal," I said hotly, some of my hurt burning through my anger. "I'm going to be a field agent, and you're not going to stop me."

He blinked and met my gaze again. "Why would I stop you?"

"You completely ignored me in class yesterday," I railed at him. "How am I supposed to learn if you're determined to act like I'm not even here?" I threw up my hands, too exasperated to continue the conversation. I couldn't stand to be this close to him. Despite my righteous anger, my body was reacting to him. My core throbbed, and wetness gathered between my legs. Even when he was glowering at me, he was so damn perfect it was almost painful to look directly at him. Especially knowing that I'd had him once and never would again.

I shook my head and turned away. "I'm going to shower off," I announced. "See you in class."

I stalked to the showers without waiting for a response. Just like the pool, they were deserted, and I was grateful for the privacy. I didn't want anyone to see my shaking hands as I stormed in and ripped the curtain aside on one of the stalls. I quickly stripped and turned on the water, keeping the temperature colder than usual. My body felt hot, and my clit throbbed.

"Damn you, Jason," I muttered.

The shower curtain slid back. "That wasn't very nice," he rumbled and stepped into the stall with me as though he had every right, as though I wasn't naked.

I quickly tried to cover myself with my hands. He lifted a dark brow.

"You weren't so modest before."

I gasped. "You asshole!"

"You're right," he said, his voice roughening with unmistakable lust as his eyes made a slow appraisal of my body. "I'm definitely an asshole. But you know what? I don't fucking care."

He closed the small distance between us and crushed his mouth to mine. I pressed my hands against his chest to shove him away, but he caught my wrists with a low growl. Moving faster than my shocked brain could comprehend, he pressed my back against the cool tile wall and pinned my wrists above my head. The reminder of how he'd held me like this in the motel room made me moan into his mouth.

He tore his lips from mine and pressed his hand over my mouth.

"Don't make a sound," he warned in a husky whisper. "I love when you scream my name, but I don't want anyone to hear you crying out when I make you come."

I whimpered against his hand as lust overwhelmed me at his dark promise. His hand firmed against my mouth, and his fingers tightened around my wrists, reinforcing his control over my body. I didn't even think about fighting him. All I could think about was the ache between my legs and the almost painful craving for him to replace his hand with his mouth, to feel his tongue sliding against mine in frenzied desire.

I shuddered and softened in his hold, swallowing a lustful groan as I struggled to comply with his order for silence. He released my mouth and trailed his fingers down the column of my throat.

"That's my good little kitten," he whispered before capturing my lips with his. He turned the knob on the wall beside me, and the water heated, the warm spray pinging over my sensitized skin, tormenting me with sensation as my entire body came alive for him. Just as before, I was helpless in his hold, unable to even contemplate resisting him when his firm hands and skillful tongue felt so wickedly decadent.

Keeping my wrists trapped in one hand, his other dipped between us to tweak my nipples. I was grateful for his mouth over mine when he caught my sharp gasp on his lips, smothering the soft sound. My muscles drew tight as I concentrated on staying quiet, even as he began to torture my breasts. He pinched and rolled my hard nipples, tugging them until my back arched toward him in a silent plea for mercy. Despite the pain—or perhaps because of it— my core fluttered and throbbed in response to his cruel treatment. I didn't understand why my body reacted this way to him, but in that moment, I didn't care. All I could do was focus on keeping silent while he tormented me.

When I could barely resist the urge to cry out, he shifted his touch, palming my breasts and soothing the ache he'd inflicted. My knees went weak as I began to float, growing drunk on his powerful influence. His grip on my wrists tightened, steadying me.

His touch trailed lower, his fingers sliding down my abdomen until they rested just above my clit. I rocked my hips up toward him, begging in the only way he allowed me. I suddenly craved to plead for him to fuck me, to call him *Sir* again as I begged for his perfect cock to stretch and fill me.

But his mouth on mine and his order for my silence kept me quiet, compliant in his steely hold. I surrendered fully, giving over to mindless lust as I squirmed against him, desperate for more.

Finally, he rewarded me by touching my clit, bringing his thumb down on the hard bud and rubbing in a firm, practiced circular motion. Two thick fingers thrust between my soaked folds, entering me easily. He found the sensitive spot at the front of my inner walls with unerring accuracy, and he curled his fingertips against it as he continued to rub my clit.

I shattered in his arms, unable to hold back a soft cry as my core contracted around his fingers.

"Hello?" a feminine voice called out.

Jason froze, his fingers stilling inside me. I continued to flutter around them, my body still riding the final aftershocks of my orgasm even as panic spiked through my system.

"Are you all right in there?" the woman asked.

Jason slowly pulled away, breaking our kiss and releasing my wrists. I struggled to stand on my trembling knees when his hold eased.

"I'm fine," I managed, my voice shaking. I cleared my throat. "Cut myself shaving," I lied quickly.

"Natalie? Is that you?"

Fuck. Elena was the last person I wanted to encounter right now.

"Yeah. I'm almost done in here."

"Whatever," she said, her tone turning cold now that she realized I was the one in the showers. Ever since Trent had decided to fixate on me rather than solely on her, she'd settled into bitch mode whenever we spoke.

I heard the shower beside me turn on.

"You go," Jason whispered, his voice so low it was barely audible over the sound of water spraying. "I'll try to get out without anyone seeing."

He turned off the shower and reached for two towels, wrapping one around me before slinging the other low around his hips. He still wore his swim trunks, but his bulging erection was obvious until he covered it with the towel.

I stared at him for a long moment, at a loss. I was stunned by the shocking turn of events, first his decision to join me in the shower, and now almost getting caught by Elena.

"Go," he urged, gripping my shoulders and spinning me away from him.

I slipped through the curtain, barely parting it in case anyone else was waiting. Luckily, the room seemed to be empty except for Elena, who was now humming in her own shower stall, out of sight. I quickly went to my bag and tugged on my clothes before fleeing. If Jason were caught sneaking out, I couldn't be anywhere near him. I had no idea how he'd explain his presence in the women's showers, but I couldn't worry about it now. All I could do was put as much distance between us as possible. If anyone ever found out, I'd be ruined. And so would he.

CHAPTER 6

Jason

Fuck!

I waited as long as I could to leave the showers, but I couldn't afford to give Natalie much of a head start. The other recruit currently humming to herself in the stall next to me could finish at any moment, and if I lingered long enough for her to leave, I'd risk more recruits coming in as the morning grew later. I'd chosen to swim before the crack of dawn to clear my head. But, of fucking course, Natalie was already in the pool, the smooth, confident movements of her lithe body tormenting me.

So fucking stupid, Harper, I berated myself. What

the fuck had possessed me to follow her into the women's showers?

Lust, that was what. Infatuation. Obsession.

It had taken everything in me during class to avoid looking at her. If I watched her perfect body flow gracefully through the motions, I'd have gotten a raging hard-on in front of everyone.

But then when she'd confronted me this morning, she accused me of trying to stop her from becoming an agent. I'd followed her into the showers to apologize. And because her fiery diatribe had awoken the beast in me, and I couldn't resist the urge to take her in my arms and torment her until she yielded. The soft, sweet little kitten I'd played with during our hot night together was still there, hidden under all that fire. I found the dichotomy painfully arousing; knowing that she was a strong, capable woman who melted just for me called to my Dominant nature. It was a side of myself I had lost touch with since the PTSD set in and I started using. Natalie's submission was as addictive as the drugs I'd abused.

Just as addictive and equally as dangerous. If I were caught sneaking out of the women's showers, I'd be fired for sure.

Bracing myself, I slipped out of the stall. No one else was in the room, but I wasn't in the clear yet. I scarcely drew breath as I quickly padded across the tile floor, my bare feet helping mask the sounds of my movement. When I got to the door, I eased it open a centimeter and peered out.

Two recruits were now in the pool, but they were focused on their exercise. I moved as smoothly and casually as possible, pushing the door fully open and striding the short distance to the men's locker room. A few more recruits were changing to work out, but no one even glanced in my direction. I was experienced enough in hiding my emotions that my internal tension would be undetectable in the lines of my face or my body.

There was still the issue of my erection. It wasn't as pronounced as it had been when I'd had Natalie trapped in my arms, but my panic hadn't fully quelled it, either. I found my workout bag and kept my back turned on the recruits as I hastily tugged on my clothes. I managed to get my hard-on mostly under control by the time I was fully dressed, but lust still raged through my veins. Watching Natalie come apart under my hands had been one of the hottest experiences of my life. I'd been seconds away from fucking her against the tile wall when we were interrupted.

I had to get back to my apartment and deal with this. Within fifteen minutes, I'd jogged my way across base to where I'd been assigned quarters for the duration of the training period. I hurriedly tugged off my clothes and took a hot shower on my own, fiercely wishing Natalie were with me under the warm spray. Still, the memory of her body softening under my harsh treatment was hot enough that I came in just a few strokes, lust and a shadow of shame riding me hard.

I'd made a stupid decision when I'd followed Natalie into the showers. Hell, it hadn't even been a decision at all. My body had acted of its own accord, drawn to her.

Control. I'd have to find it again somehow. I'd thought Natalie had made me feel in control of myself again when I was dominating her, but I obviously still struggled with mastering my darker urges. First, it was the cravings for drugs. Now, it was a craving for *her*.

I took a deep breath and steeled my resolve. I'd have to learn how to deal. She was right. I owed her the chance to become the best agent she could possibly be, and she wouldn't graduate without proper training. Watching her in class, correcting her, was going to be torture.

But I could manage, if I could get my head screwed on straight. Suddenly, I was grateful for my appointment with the shrink this morning. Maybe Dr. Larson would be able to help me find my self-control again. Because right now, my life was a shit show, and I would do anything necessary to get everything back, everything I'd lost the day I went to the bombsite.

I grimaced. Facing those memories wouldn't be easy. But I didn't have any other options. My choice to pursue Natalie this morning proved that.

I'd go to therapy, and I'd learn to master my dark urges.

☙❧

Dr. Patricia Larson was a benignly attractive woman in her mid-forties; her kind caramel eyes and gently waved blond hair softened the more severe lines of her pronounced cheekbones and jaw. She had an air of calm about her, and her low, honey-smooth voice was undeniably soothing.

"May I call you Jason?" she asked, peering at me intently, as though my answer was very important to her.

I shifted on the plush couch. "Okay," I agreed after a moment. The use of my first name invited a familiarity that made me uncomfortable, but if I was here to bare my soul, I didn't need to bother with formality.

"Let's start by establishing why you're here,

Jason," she said. "What do you want to get out of our sessions?"

"I'm sure you've been briefed on why I'm here," I said coldly, not caring to dance around the subject.

She nodded, remaining implacably calm. "I know you recently went through detox after becoming dependent on prescription drugs. I know you've been assigned here until you're deemed fit to return to the field. But that's not what I asked. I asked what you want to get out of our sessions. The Bureau's agenda doesn't matter to me. Your emotional health is my concern. Why are you here, Jason?"

The question was incisive, but her gentle tone kept it from cutting too sharply. I took a deep breath and committed myself to this process, determined to see it through.

"I want to find control again," I declared. "I want to get my life back."

She leaned forward. "Control?" she pressed. "What do you mean by that?"

I shrugged, evading. I didn't want to talk about my sexual proclivities and the internal conflict Natalie had sparked within me. I craved control, and usually I found it in dominating a woman. Or at least, I used to. Before my life fell apart.

"Self-control, I guess," I said when she remained silent for several long seconds, watching me expectantly. "I lost it when I started using. I can see that now."

"Painkillers can be highly addictive. I read in your file that you were injured about ten months ago, when you broke your wrist. Is that when you started using?"

"Yes," I bit out the word, the admission bitter on my tongue. "But I didn't take them just because I enjoyed the high."

"Why did you take them, then?"

I shifted again. "I suppose at first I thought they were helping me maintain control. But now I can see that I completely lost it when I became addicted." Shame burned through me, but I was determined to push through it.

"You were self-medicating," she surmised. "Why?"

I blew out a long sigh. "I think I have PTSD." It was the first time I'd ever said it out loud. It wasn't as painful as I'd thought it would be, especially not in Dr. Larson's calming presence.

"What makes you think that? Could you please describe your experiences?"

I closed my eyes for a moment and forced myself to think about the debilitating episodes. "It started the day of the Water Tower Place terror attack. I'd seen some fucked up shit as a Ranger, but I'd never had any issues from it. Not really." Sometimes nightmares tormented me, but nothing like the waking panic that consumed me sporadically after that day I witnessed the civilian carnage.

"And what kinds of issues did you start experiencing at that time?"

"I'd feel... I'd feel like I was dying. Like I couldn't breathe and my heart would explode. It would happen randomly, sometimes triggered by loud noises. Sometimes for no discernable reason at all." The confession of my darkest secret was like poison being drawn from a wound. It was painful, but at the same time, I could sense that the darkness was leaking out of me ever so slightly.

"I couldn't function in the field like that," I continued. "And once I got the pills for my wrist, I realized that the attacks weren't as intense when they came. I started taking them whenever I'd feel the panic setting in."

"So your PTSD was triggered by what happened on the day of the terror attack. Can you tell me more about that day?"

I flinched, not wanting to think about it.

"You don't have to go into detail," Dr. Larson soothed me. "We'll work on that over the coming weeks. Right now, I need to know why you blame yourself for the attack."

I blinked at her. "I don't blame myself. I just saw

what was left of the bodies, and..." I trailed off, my throat closing up to choke down the description of the horror I'd faced.

"I think you do," she pressed gently. "As you said, you'd faced violence before during your service. But this was different. Oftentimes, guilt plays a role in the onset of PTSD. Do you feel guilty, Jason?"

"Of course I feel guilty," I snapped. "I'd just joined the Bureau. It was my job, my duty to protect those people. I should have gotten there sooner. I should have seen it coming. They were civilians, innocents."

"So you do blame yourself," she declared. "It wasn't your fault, Jason."

"I know that," I said, frustrated. "It was that anarchist fucker's fault."

"Then why do you feel guilty?"

"Because I failed them," I barked out, the admission knifing through my chest. "I failed."

"So you feel like a failure because of another man's actions that were beyond your control. The Bureau had no leads to the perp at the time. There was no reason anyone would have seen the attack coming, including you. But you feel like you failed. Why do you think that is?"

My fists clenched at my sides. "I took this job because I want to protect people. I didn't protect them."

"And why do you feel the need to protect them so deeply? Empathy is natural. But this sense of duty is more than that. It's shaped your entire adult life: your decision to join the Army and the Bureau. Why did you decide to pursue this career?"

"To spite my father," I said bitterly before I could think.

"Your father is the Deputy Director. Surely he's proud that you followed in his footsteps?"

I glared at her. "If you think I've lived my life trying to impress him, you're dead wrong. He's a bastard. I joined the Army because he didn't think I had the guts."

"But this is about more than spiting him," she said. "You said you felt the need to protect people. There's nothing spiteful about that. Tell me more about your father. What was he like during your childhood?"

I cut my eyes away. "I told you. He's a bastard."

"He beat you." She said it as plain fact.

My gaze snapped back to hers. "I didn't say that."

"But he did, didn't he? That's why you crave control. It's why you feel the need to protect people, to be strong."

"I didn't come here to talk about my father," I said, my voice tight.

"You came here because you feel like you've lost

control over your life. You came here because your PTSD was triggered by a sense of personal failure and guilt. This is all linked to your relationship with your father. If we're going to make progress, we will need to discuss him."

"I just want to get back in the field," I declared. "That's all I'm here for."

"And I'm not going to clear you for that until I know your PTSD is under control. I can prescribe anti-depressants, but they'll only do so much."

"I don't want any more fucking pills."

"They're not addictive, but of course you don't have to take them if you don't want to. However, you won't get control over your life again until you work through your trauma. An important part of that process is examining why you feel guilt over the terror attack and learning to forgive yourself, to accept that it wasn't your fault. Dealing with your fear of failure and your need to protect those weaker than you is an important component in that. If you're not ready to talk about your father today, then we don't have to. But we won't be able to start treating your PTSD until you're ready to do the work."

I glared at her for a full minute. Damn her. I needed to get clearance to go back into the field. And she was telling me point-blank that it wouldn't happen until I opened up about my daddy issues. Just thinking about him made me feel weak, pathetic.

And I supposed that was something I had to deal with.

Fuck.

"You're right," I said hollowly. "He did beat me. But that hasn't happened in a long time. I'm over it." I could feel the lie on my tongue. It was so obvious now that I wasn't over it. Not even close.

When Dr. Larson simply continued to watch me expectantly, I sighed.

"All right. I'm ready to talk. I obviously still have... issues. I'll do whatever it takes to get back in the field."

I'll do whatever it takes to find my control again.

She gave me a soft, approving smile. "We'll get you there. The treatment process for PTSD takes eight to twelve weeks. If you're committed to it, I should be able to sign off for you to be reassigned to a field office in a few months."

Relief washed through me. My sentence here might be even shorter than I'd thought. Until Dr. Larson laid out a timeline, I'd worried I'd be trapped here for years, possibly forever. I could make it through a few months. One round of NATs and I'd be out of here.

That brought my thoughts back to one particular

recruit. *Natalie.* I'd have to make it through twenty weeks with her, training her but not touching her.

There were so many other ways I wanted to *train* her, none of which involved hand-to-hand combat. She was inexperienced in BDSM, but she was obviously submissive at her core. I craved to introduce her to the world of Domination and submission, before some other bastard saw her for who she truly was and took her from me.

Just the thought made me see red.

"Jason? Are you all right?"

I blinked hard and forced my attention back to Dr. Larson. "I'm just ready to get out of Quantico," I said truthfully. "I need my life back."

And I need to get as far away from Natalie as possible, before I fuck up my life even more.

CHAPTER 7

Natalie

Days had passed since my hot encounter with Jason in the showers, and the recruits had reached the end of Week One at the academy. This would be the last time I saw Jason before the weekend. It was time for his class to begin, and I was torn between both craving and dreading the sight of him. I ached for his nearness, but I knew that was wrong. I couldn't allow him to touch me again, unless it was for the purpose of training.

I knew myself well enough to recognize that I was hopelessly infatuated. It was stupid, but I couldn't help it. For the thousandth time, I cursed myself for hooking up with Jason the night before training began.

How was I to know? I reasoned. It hadn't seemed like the worst mistake of my life at the time. In fact, while I'd been shuddering in his arms, it had seemed like the best decision I'd ever made.

The whole situation was shitty.

Deal with it. I wasn't about to let a foolish obsession with one of my instructors ruin my aspirations. Not even if that instructor was the most intoxicating man I'd ever met.

I didn't realize I was shifting anxiously as I awaited his arrival until Trent entered my personal space.

"I need a partner for the day," he said, casually touching my shoulder to catch my attention. "What do you say?"

I jerked away from him, scowling. "I'm partnering with Nate. I'm not interested. Maybe Elena is."

His cocky grin remained firmly fixed in place. "But you're so charming. I'd rather partner with you." This time, he trailed his fingers along my upper arm in a decidedly skeevy come-on.

I grabbed his wrist and twisted. He cursed and turned his body away to alleviate the pressure, just as I'd planned. I jerked his arm up, and he fell to his knees.

"What have I told you about touching me without my permission?" I asked coldly. "Don't fucking do it again, or I'll break your arm." I applied more pressure, and he grunted in pain.

"Let him up, Simmons."

Oh, fuck. I instantly recognized Jason's booming voice.

I released Trent and took several hasty steps back. "I'm sorry," I apologized quickly. "I—"

"McMahon," Jason barked over me, his burning gaze fixed on Trent. "Get up."

Rubbing the residual pain out of his arm, Trent got to his feet. His hazel eyes fixed on me, glowering.

"Eyes on me, recruit," Jason snapped.

My gaze darted to him, but he was still glaring at Trent. He hadn't been addressing me.

"Here," he said to Trent, pointing at a spot on the floor a few feet away from him. "Now," he commanded when Trent didn't move fast enough.

Trent hurried to obey, snapping to attention in response to the fierce order. He watched Jason warily as he took his place.

"Try to grab my arm," Jason told him coolly.

Trent's brows drew together. "Sir?"

"Try to touch me like you touched Natalie, and see what happens."

"But I—"

"Do it now, McMahon."

Trent's eyes narrowed, and he lunged for Jason. Jason easily dodged, sliding to the side so Trent stumbled past him. He kicked Trent's legs out from underneath him in one smooth, continuous motion. As soon as Trent was down, Jason pinned him, pressing his forearm against the recruit's throat.

"If I ever hear about you touching a woman without her permission, you will answer to me personally," he growled.

"But I didn't do anything," Trent insisted. "I didn't mean anything by it."

Jason's arm pressed down on his windpipe, and he choked.

"We don't tolerate men like you in the Bureau," Jason seethed. "If I hear of anything like this happening again, you won't make it to graduation. Do you understand me? The only correct answer is 'Yes, sir.'"

"Yes, sir," Trent gasped out when Jason eased up on his throat.

Jason pushed up off him, his muscles still taut with suppressed violence. My shocked brain struggled to process what had just happened. Did Jason humiliate Trent because he'd dared to touch me? Or was it simply because Trent was a creep and Jason wouldn't tolerate that sort of behavior toward any woman?

"Pair up," Jason barked at us, breaking the tense silence. Everyone rushed to obey.

Nate was suddenly at my side. "Do you think Harper will try to kill me if I spar with you?" he asked, trying to lighten the mood with a joke.

I forced a smile and turned my attention to him. "I think that was for Trent's benefit, not mine," I said, even though I wasn't at all sure of that.

"If it helps, I don't swing that way," Nate said. "Agent Harper doesn't need to worry about me making a move on you. And neither do you. If anything, Trent's more my type. If he weren't a raging douchebag."

"You're gay?" I asked, surprised.

He rolled his massive shoulders back. "And proud. In any case, you don't need to worry about Trent coming near you again. I'll kick his ass. Although," he winked at me, "I think you have that handled on your own."

I beamed at him. "Thanks for the offer, but yeah, I'd rather do the ass-kicking myself if he tries anything again. I'd love to break his prettyboy face if he keeps pushing the issue."

"I'd cheer you on from the sidelines, then."

"Thanks," I said, genuinely grateful. Nate was proving to be a good friend. He had my back. He was exactly the kind of person I wanted in the field with me once I became an agent. "Let's do this," I declared, falling into a defensive stance. "We're going to graduate together."

"You know it, partner," he agreed, mirroring my movement.

Smiling, we fell into our practiced motions. It took all my concentration to focus on my task rather than the way Jason's booming voice rolled through my body. It became even more difficult when he made his rounds, pausing by Nate and me to observe us.

"Focus, Natalie," he commanded smoothly when Nate landed a hit.

Focus. I remembered how he'd helped me aim at the dartboard, his hard body pressed against mine as he ordered me to concentrate on my task.

A sense of calm settled over me, and I became hyperaware of every minute twitch of Nate's muscles. My movements became fluid, confident.

"Good." Jason's praise warmed my insides, but this time his voice didn't break my concentration. Pleasure flooded me at his attention. Not only did I enjoy his nearness, but I was grateful he respected my wishes to train me properly rather than ignoring me.

He moved away from Nate and me after a few more minutes, but I continued to perform perfectly.

❦

Despite my mounting exhaustion, I made my way to the gym that evening after dinner. I'd tried to study for a few hours, but I couldn't stop thinking about how Jason had taken down Trent. Had he done it because he felt protective of me? Possessive?

Or was it simply because Jason wasn't the kind of man to tolerate assholes who touched women without their permission?

Maybe both, although the prospect that he'd done it for me made my stomach flip. It should have made me feel like a damsel in distress, being saved by her macho hero. But I'd clearly had the situation handled on my own. Jason had only added to Trent's humiliation. It'd been an act of righteous anger, not rescue.

And I couldn't help finding that sexy as hell.

Focus. The little voice in my head sounded suspiciously like Jason's.

Shaking my head to clear it, I made my way over to one of the punching bags. A strange giddiness fizzed through my system, making me almost shaky. I needed to burn off my excess energy before I could study properly for the evening, so I'd work out some aggression before returning to my dorm room. Besides, I didn't at all mind avoiding Elena. She'd been even nastier than usual since the afternoon. I wasn't sure if she was angry with me for humiliating Trent or jealous because he'd initially chosen me as a partner rather than her.

I decided I didn't really care. Although I liked Nate, I wasn't here to make friends, and it didn't matter if Elena hated my guts. All that mattered was getting to graduation and earning my place as a field agent.

The gym was mostly empty; it was fairly late for anyone to be out of their dorms. Two women ran on treadmills, and one of the more massive male recruits was lifting weights. I walked past them and headed for the secluded side of the gym, preferring to work in quiet solitude.

Unfortunately, I wasn't the only person with that idea. Before I could pull on my boxing gloves, an annoyingly familiar voice called my name from behind.

"Natalie! Hey, wait up."

I turned and fixed him with my coldest stare. "What do you want, Trent?"

He held up his hands, placating. "I want to apologize. I promise I'm a proper Texas gentleman. Give me a chance to prove it to you?"

I rolled my eyes. Didn't this guy ever give up? "Listen, Trent. I have zero interest in you. I'm not here for a relationship. I'm here to become an agent, just like you. Now if you'll excuse me, I'm going to work out."

His jaw firmed, but his posture remained benign. "I'm not trying to hit on you," he said. "I'm here to work out, too. I know from first-hand experience that you're good at hand-to-hand combat." He had the grace to manage a wry smile. "I need to work on that. Help me practice?"

"You must be joking." He really wanted to spar with me after how Jason and I had humiliated him just a few hours ago?

"Not joking. You say you're here to become an agent, but so am I. Let's train together."

I took a moment to study him, attempting to ascertain his sincerity. He didn't appear to be baiting me.

"Okay, then," I allowed. "Let's spar."

I might not like Trent, but if this was his way of apologizing, I wasn't going to hold a grudge. He'd learned his lesson earlier, both by my hand and by Jason's. If he wanted to up his game, I didn't mind playing the part of instructor.

"We can practice what we learned in class today. You attack, I'll block." I wasn't at all concerned about allowing Trent to go on the offensive. I knew I could handle him, and he appeared to be trying to make peace.

I underestimated him. He began the smooth, fluid movement Jason had taught us earlier. I raised my arm to block, but he changed tactics in a flash, taking advantage of the opening I left for him. His fingers curled into a fist, and he landed a sharp punch against my ribs. I fell to my knees, shocked by the pain. I'd never taken a true hit like this. I'd only ever been in the one real fight, on the night I'd met Jason. And thanks to him, no one had laid a hand on me.

In the second I spent trying to process the pain radiating through my side, his foot lashed out, catching me hard in the stomach. I'd been so distracted by the agony in my chest that I forgot to tighten my abs. I dropped to the mat, my insides writhing as I gasped for air.

Trent crouched at my side. "You think you're hot shit," he hissed. "You think you're too good for me. This is a warning. Don't fuck with me again."

I could barely breathe, but rage slammed into me, giving me impossible strength. I rolled up onto the balls of my feet and launched myself at him. My fist caught him squarely in the jaw. His head snapped back, and he went down with a curse. I leapt up and brought my foot down on his exposed throat, applying threatening pressure.

"Stay down," I rasped, barely managing to gasp enough air to formulate the words. "Stay down until I leave the gym, or I swear I'll break your face. This is *my* warning. Come near me again, and I'll do much worse."

"Fuck you," he choked out, seething.

"You wish," I replied coldly, increasing the pressure on his throat incrementally. "Now, stay down."

I eased up and backed away. He glowered at me, but he didn't get up. Satisfied that he wouldn't come at me again, I turned and walked away as casually as I could manage. Every breath sent pain knifing through my ribs, but I refused to show weakness. Head held high, I passed the guy lifting weights and the women on treadmills. None of them seemed to have noticed the brutal exchange that had taken place behind them.

Good. I didn't want anyone reporting me for getting in a fight.

Briefly, I considered reporting Trent, but I quickly decided against it. I didn't need to go running to my instructors for help. He was arrogant and incompetent. It would be so much more satisfactory to see him get kicked out for being unfit to be an agent. Besides, I didn't want to be rescued by my superiors. I was perfectly capable of protecting myself.

THE WEEKEND PASSED, BUT BY MONDAY, MY aching body told me I might not be as capable of protecting myself as I'd thought. Ugly bruises marred my stomach and left side. They looked worse than they felt, but the few days since I'd been injured hadn't been enough time to fully heal, and I was still sore when it came time for Jason's class. My movements weren't a fluid as they should be, and Nate noticed.

"You okay?" he asked kindly.

"I just pushed myself a little too hard last week," I said, not entirely lying. "I'm really sore."

"I'll go easy on you."

"Thanks." I didn't want to shirk the lesson, but I was grateful for a reprieve.

We slowed, moving at half the speed of the rest of the sparring pairs.

"What's going on here?" Jason demanded when he came to observe us. "Your opponents aren't going to come at you in slow motion. Pick up the pace."

"Yes, sir." Nate immediately complied, moving far too fast. He landed a hit directly on my abs, and although I managed to tighten my muscles, the blow against the tender bruise hurt. I gasped and stumbled back, landing on my ass.

Nate's face softened with concern. "Sorry, Natalie. I didn't mean to hit you that hard."

"You didn't," I reassured him. "I'm just sore."

"Natalie." Jason's voice held a warning edge. "I want to see you in my office after class."

"Why?" I asked, nervousness making my stomach turn. "Did I do something wrong?"

A dark brow rose. "Are you questioning me, recruit?"

I shook my head quickly. "No. I'm sorry, sir. I'll be there."

He nodded sharply. "You're going to sit out the rest of the session. Cross," he turned his attention to Nate, "you'll work with me."

"What?" I burst out. "Why?"

His bright green eyes turned glacial. "I warned you about questioning me. We will discuss your infraction in my office."

My stomach dropped. *Infraction?* I didn't understand what I'd done wrong, but I didn't dare to ask.

"You're dismissed, Simmons," Jason said. His clipped tone and use of my surname stung, but I scurried away, thoroughly chastised.

I hurried toward the locker room to shower and change, trying not to look at my fellow recruits as I made my walk of shame. But a low chuckle and cruel feminine laugh caught my attention. I glanced over just long enough to catch Trent and Elena smirking at me before I tore my gaze away and redoubled my pace. Not even the sight of the dark bruise on Trent's jaw buoyed my spirits. *He* wasn't getting kicked out of class.

Once I was in the privacy of the shower, hot tears of shame rolled down my face, mingling with the warm water.

Jason had humiliated me in front of everyone. And now I had to face him in private. I feared to discover what infraction he thought I'd committed, and I chewed my lip as potential consequences ran through my mind. Was it severe enough to cost me my place at the academy? Did he think I wasn't strong enough to handle the rigors of Quantico?

If that were the case, I would just have to prove him wrong. I certainly couldn't tell him that Trent had gotten the upper hand in a fight, because that would just demonstrate weakness. I had to show him that I was fit enough to be here, that I would make an excellent agent. Whatever weakness he saw in me, I'd have to convince him I was capable of overcoming it. I'd do whatever it took to maintain my place here. I wouldn't allow Trent McMahon to be the reason I didn't graduate.

CHAPTER 8

Jason

Natalie had lied to me. She might have Nathaniel Cross fooled, but he didn't know her intimately like I did. The way she cut her eyes away and the slight flush in her cheeks betrayed her. There was more going on here than simply being sore from training. Natalie was tough, and she wouldn't have reacted like that for a light hit unless something was wrong.

The thought of her in pain made my gut twist. Protective instincts raged to the fore. All I wanted to do was hold her and keep her safe from any harm.

This isn't rational, a little voice told me. She was a recruit at Quantico. Pain was part of the process.

And once she started her job as a field agent, her life would be on the line on a regular basis.

The prospect made my concern heat to anger. Not at her, but at the faceless people who might hurt her.

She's not some simpering submissive you met at a club, I reminded myself. *She earned her place here.*

But I knew how sweet and soft she was at her core, and the thought of anyone damaging that vulnerable, perfect woman made my heart squeeze.

I rounded the corner to find Natalie already waiting for me outside my locked office. She certainly didn't appear at all vulnerable now. Fierce, determined. And maybe even a little angry. Her full lips were pressed to a flat line, and her delicate chin was lifted in defiance.

Her posture awoke the darker urges that I couldn't seem to suppress when faced with her fire. Drawing myself up to my full height, I prowled the rest of the short distance between us. Something flickered in her deep blue eyes, and she shifted on her feet.

Fuck. She was so damn responsive when I turned my Dominant nature on her. Why did she have to be so perfect? All I wanted to do was trap her against the wall and take her mouth with mine, kissing her hard until she trembled in my arms and whimpered for the release only I could give her.

I tore my gaze from her and unlocked my office door, careful not to allow my body to brush against hers as I entered.

"Come," I commanded her to follow me, my tone clipped from the strain of controlling my carnal urges.

She straightened her shoulders and strode into the small space I'd been assigned for the duration of my time a Quantico. It was little more than a broom closet with a desk, but I didn't really need an office, anyway. But now, I was grateful to have a private space where I could speak to Natalie without suspicions being raised.

I closed the door behind her with a sharp snap, and she jolted at the sound.

Good. I wanted to rattle her a little. She was putting on a brave front and was obviously determined to lie to me about her condition. I wouldn't allow it.

"Why did you kick me out of class?" she asked, her voice hard with anger despite her physical hints of trepidation.

"Because you lied to me," I told her coolly.

"No, I didn't," she insisted hotly. "I'm sore. I've pushed myself a little too hard. That's my problem, and I'm dealing with it. You can't just humiliate me in front of everyone because I worked out too much over the last few days. I'm training hard because I want to be the best. I'll dial it back a little bit until I adjust. I'm perfectly fit for class."

"You're not," I told her, implacable. "You're hurt. If you've pushed yourself so hard that a light hit causes you pain, you're not training responsibly. If you've torn a muscle, I'm not going to allow you to push through the pain and cause permanent damage just because you think you have something to prove."

"Of course I have something to prove!" she burst out. "I have to prove that I'm tough enough to be an FBI agent. That means dealing with a little pain sometimes, doesn't it? I'll adjust, and I'll heal up in no time. It's not a big deal."

"Let me see."

"What?"

"Lift your shirt and let me take a look."

She crossed her arms over her chest. "You're not a doctor."

"No, but I've pushed my body to the limits often enough that I know how to look for serious damage. If you really are fine, you can go back to your classes. If not, you'll sit out of tactical training until you heal."

"You can't do that to me!" she insisted. "I won't graduate if I don't keep up with everyone else."

"You will. I'll make sure you do. I'll help you catch up. I'm not trying to end your career. But I won't allow you to injure yourself more than you already have." I reached for the hem of her t-shirt. "Now, show me."

She knocked my hands away, shaking her head wildly. "No."

Was that real fear in her lovely eyes?

"I don't want you to be afraid of me," I said, my voice roughening. "If this is about what happened in the showers, I'm sorry. I shouldn't have forced myself on you." Describing it like that left ashes on my tongue, but it occurred to me that perhaps she wasn't as willing as I'd thought when I'd followed her into the shower.

"You didn't force yourself on me," she said quickly, dousing my mounting disgust. "I... I didn't say no."

I fixed her with a level stare. "But did you want to?"

She licked her lips, and my cock jerked to life. "No," she said, her voice dropping to a husky whisper. "I didn't want you to stop."

Unable to help myself, I took a step closer. "And what about now? Do you want me to stop?"

"Jason..." she trailed off. I couldn't tell if my name was a plea for me to stop or to continue.

Selfish bastard that I was, I chose to interpret it as the latter. I took another step toward her. She didn't back away. Her head tilted, offering up her lush lips for my use. Her gorgeous eyes darkened to a deep, soft navy blue.

The last time I'd kissed her, it had been harsh, unrefined. I'd claimed her mouth in a frenzy of lust, subjugating her fiery spirit with ruthless strokes of my tongue.

This was different. She was in a precarious state, on the edge of submission. I could sense her desire, but also her trepidation. Now wasn't the time to take her forcefully; it was the time for slow, deliberate seduction.

I lowered my mouth to hers, barely brushing her lips with mine. She arched up to meet me, craving more contact. My fist tangled in her hair, tugging her back so I could continue my teasing kiss. The softness of my mouth would contrast with my harsh hold on her hair, inflicting pleasure while giving her a bite of pain. She reacted beautifully, her lips parting on a low moan as she melted against me.

I wanted to lose myself in her, to deepen the kiss and claim her mouth. But I was mindful of my purpose, and my free hand grasped the hem of her shirt, sliding it up her torso. I broke the kiss so I could examine her.

Ugly black bruises marred her perfect skin, marking her left side and stomach with the aftermath of violence. A snarl slipped through my clenched teeth, and she jolted. She glanced down in the direction of my gaze and gasped, quickly grasping for the hem of her shirt so she could cover herself.

My fingers threaded into her hair at either side of her head, applying firm pressure as I tugged. She had no choice but to look up into my eyes as I questioned her.

"Who did this?" I demanded, my voice little more than a furious hiss.

"It's nothing," she said shakily.

I tugged more sharply, lighting up her scalp with awareness of my grip on her hair. "It's not nothing. Who. Did. This?" I bit out each word, the question dripping with menace. I had to know who'd dared to hurt her so I could hunt them down and break them. I'd thought she'd injured herself by working too hard, but this was something else entirely. Someone had put their hands on her, with cruel intent.

"I handled it," she insisted. "I'm fine."

I handled it. I thought of the other injured recruit I'd seen today, his jaw bruised.

"McMahon," I ground out his name. "Did he try to touch you again?"

She glowered up at me. "I have this handled, Jason. I don't need you to rescue me."

Maybe not, but I need to punish him. I kept the words locked behind clenched teeth. I'd get a confession out of her, and then I'd go after McMahon.

The harsh set of her jaw let me know she wouldn't give her confession so easily.

Too bad for her, I knew how to draw out her submission. Keeping my grip on her silken hair, I brought my lips down on hers in a demanding kiss. I didn't coax her this time; I commanded her compliance, catching her lower lip between my teeth. She opened on a gasp, and my tongue surged in. Hers tangled with mine, defiant. I growled into her mouth and slid one hand out of her hair so I could roughly cup her pussy in a possessive hold. My fingers curved into her cleft through her soft gym shorts, and my palm ground against her clit. She went utterly still in my harsh hold, panting into my mouth as she sucked in short, shallow breaths.

Tightening my grip on her pussy, I guided her forward, moving her with me as I stepped back toward the desk. In a few shaky steps, I had her positioned where I wanted her. I kept one hand in her hair and the other on her sex even as I moved so I was beside her rather than pressed against her front. Using my grip on her hair, I slowly tugged down. She began to bend at the waist, her hips kept in place by my hold on her pussy.

"Brace your hands on the desk," I ordered.

She complied immediately, pressing her palms against the polished wood as I brought her torso parallel with the floor. Her back was arched, her ass thrust upward and locked in place by my firm hold on her sex.

"Usually, I'd prefer to have you over my lap for this," I told her. "But considering your bruises, this will have to do."

"What are you talking about?" she asked, her voice small. She was feeling particularly vulnerable in this position, as she should.

"I'm going to spank you, Natalie."

"What?" She sounded more alarmed when she questioned me this time, and she tried to squirm away. But I firmed my hold on her, my fingers tightening in her hair and tugging her head back while I ground my palm against her clit.

"Calm," I ordered. "I'm not going to hurt you."

"You just said you're going to spank me!" she protested, but she didn't struggle any more.

"Yes, I'm going to discipline you." My cock turned rock hard as I said it. I'd dominated her body before, but I'd never spanked her perfect ass. I knew from her previous reactions to light erotic pain that she would handle this well. "But I won't harm you," I promised.

She started trembling. My balls ached.

"Jason, this is crazy," she said on a whimper.

"If it's so crazy, then why can I feel you getting wet through your shorts?" I asked calmly, finding the heady sense of power that came with dominating Natalie.

"Jason..." She couldn't seem to find any words other than my name, and I was no longer certain if the whine in her voice was one of protest.

I decided to test her. Keeping my hold on her pussy, I released her hair and delivered the first light slap against her ass. Through her shorts, she'd barely feel the sting, but the first taste of my discipline shocked her. She let out a startled yelp, which quickly lowered to a moan when I continued to stimulate her clit.

"What are you doing to me?" she asked in a ragged whisper.

"I'm taking care of you," I informed her. "You need to tell me who hurt you so I can take the appropriate action to make sure it doesn't happen again. I'm disciplining you for lying to me about your injury and for not telling me who's responsible. I can't help you if you keep secrets from me."

"I told you I don't need you to rescue me," she said, but the assertion was weaker this time.

I petted her ass, soothing. "I know you don't. But I'm going to, just the same."

I slipped my hands beneath the elasticized bands at the top of her shorts and panties, pushing them down her upper thighs so her ass was exposed. One cheek was already light pink from my first slap. I intended for both to be a rosy red by the time I finished.

I resumed my position at her pussy, two fingers easing through her slick folds to thrust deep inside her as my palm connected with her clit again. She let out a strangled groan as I stretched her. She was just as hot and tight as I remembered, and my cock ached to replace my fingers.

But I had more self-control than that. With Natalie's wellbeing in my hands, it took little effort to master my base desire to fuck her over my desk. I found the sense of personal power I'd only known with her since I'd gotten clean. The rush was pure pleasure, far better than any drug running through my veins.

I fell into my Dominant headspace, and my entire world narrowed to focus solely on her: every hitch in her breathing, every twitch of her inner muscles around my fingers; the sight of her back arched, her ass practically begging to be punished.

"I'm going to give you ten for lying to me about your injury," I told her, my voice dropping to the deep, controlled register I found in Topspace. "Then I'm going to ask you who hurt you. You will be honest with me."

"I can't," she panted. "Jason, please..." As she begged, she rotated her hips against my hand, craving more stimulation.

I smacked her ass, another light slap that was meant to focus her attention rather than punish.

"*Sir*," I corrected her. "My fingers are buried in your hot pussy, and I'm going to spank your ass until it's glowing red. Your body is under my control. You will address me with proper respect."

She moaned her lust, and her inner walls clenched in response to my perverse declaration. Her head dropped forward, her cheek resting on the desk as she surrendered.

I trailed my fingers down the line of her spine as I curved the ones that remained seated deep inside her, stimulating her g-spot.

"Good girl," I praised. "This is going to sting. I want you to try to be quiet for me."

I was dimly aware of the possibility that this

room wasn't soundproof, but I knew the office beside me was empty, and the other wall was shared with an actual broom closet. No one would hear the smack of my hand against her toned flesh, but they might hear if she screamed.

"Can you do that?" I prompted, smoothing my hand over her ass in a reassuring motion.

"Yes, Sir," she whispered.

"That's my sweet kitten." I smiled down at her, and her lips curved up at the corners in satisfaction. She liked when I praised her. God, she was submissive and beautiful and so fucking perfect it made my heart ache almost as painfully as my hard dick. "Don't forget to breathe," I warned just before I delivered the first true slap.

She sucked in a sharp gasp, but her inner walls contracted around me in response to the stinging pain I'd awoken in her flesh.

"You are so fucking perfect." I didn't even realize I growled the words aloud, but a pretty flush colored her delicate face, and her white teeth sank into her lower lip.

I bit back a groan at the sight. She was innocent and sweet, and so fucking hot under my dominant hands that I could barely contain my desire for her.

I started her spanking in earnest, delivering four more blows in rapid succession, alternating cheeks to spread out the burn. I wanted her to feel the heat of my discipline deep inside, so she would learn not to defy me when it mattered most. She might not need rescuing, but that didn't mean I wasn't going to protect her.

And it didn't mean I wasn't going to hurt the man who'd caused her pain.

I paused and took a deep breath. I couldn't think about McMahon right now. The rage was too raw inside me, and I needed to remain focused on Natalie.

I took a moment to pet her burning skin, to murmur reassuring words before I continued.

"Halfway done," I told her. "You're doing so well."

Her pussy fluttered around my fingers at the praise, even though her eyes were shining with a hint of tears. I knew I wasn't causing her too much pain, but this first experience in discipline and her submissive reactions would be confusing for her. Many subs found their first spanking overwhelming. I wasn't going to show any leniency—it was my responsibility as a Dom to be consistent and follow through on my promises—but I could guide her through it. I took a few more minutes to pet her, easing the sting I'd inflicted as I gently rotated my palm against her clit.

"Five more," I told her gently. "Are you ready, kitten?"

"Yes, Sir," she answered, her voice soft and meek. Both of us were completely lost to the power exchange, utterly enthralled by one another.

I delivered the final five blows in sharp, rapid succession, leaving her writhing and gasping for air in the space of a few seconds. She was vulnerable, chastised. And my hand was soaked with her arousal.

"It was McMahon, wasn't it?" I prompted, my voice low and calm. "Tell me what happened."

"He said he wanted to apologize," she responded softly, the words flowing out of her. A single tear spilled down her cheek, but the sight of it didn't concern me. This was catharsis, not grief. I continued to pet her as she confessed. "We were both in the gym, and I agreed to train with him. Everything was fine, and then he decided to get back at me for embarrassing him in front of the other recruits. I put him down. It won't happen again."

"No, it won't," I said coolly. "McMahon isn't going to last another week here. I won't clear him to continue to graduation."

She blinked, coming back to herself a little. "But you can't do that. I told you I don't need you to rescue me."

"You don't need me to, but what about the other women he might abuse from his position of power? I won't allow a man like that at the Bureau." It was my job to protect the people I served, and I'd be damned if I let an abusive scumbag like McMahon poison our ranks.

"Are you all right?" she asked softly.

I shook my head slightly and focused on her again. "I just can't abide abusive men," I said truthfully. "McMahon's out of here at the end of the week when I hand in his evaluation. No one will connect it to you."

"I... Okay. Thank you."

She was relaxed, all the tension drained out of her. Her body was still bent over my desk, my hand inside her, owning her most vulnerable area. This was exactly how I wanted her: sweet and trusting and wet.

I curved my fingers inside her, and a pleasurable shudder rolled through her body.

"You were very good for me, kitten." I continued to stimulate her g-spot as I rubbed her clit. "I'm proud of you. Come for me now."

"I can't," she whimpered. "I need you inside me. Please, Jason. Fuck me."

Her brash plea shocked me to my core and tore at my control. "I don't have a condom," I forced out, even as I withdrew my fingers from her pussy to roughly grip her hip, anchoring her in place.

"I'm on the pill," she said. "And I don't have any STDs."

"I'm clean, too," I ground out, already freeing myself from my sweatpants. "I'm going to fuck you bareback," I warned. "I'm going to come in your pretty pussy and mark you deep inside."

"Yes," she moaned, wriggling her hips in invitation. "Please."

"You're going to have to be very quiet again for me," I rumbled, stepping behind her and lining up my dick with her desire-slicked entrance. "I'll help you." I leaned over her back and wrapped my hand around her mouth. The dominant act ensured we wouldn't be overheard, but it also gave me savage pleasure to subjugate her body with such primal actions. With one hand pressed against her lips and the other curved into her hip, I easily pinned her in place as I entered her in one swift thrust. She cried out, but the sound was muffled against my palm.

"Come for me," I growled the low order, gritting my teeth to hold back my own swiftly approaching release. Natalie had felt perfect the first time we'd fucked, but being inside her without a condom separating us was pure heaven. It was nearly impossible to control myself when she began to contract around me, shattering on my command. She writhed beneath me, and I tightened my grip on her hip as I took her in a harsh, merciless rhythm. I wasn't going to last long, but she would come again before we were finished.

I released her hip and shifted my hand to her back entrance. My fingers were still slick with her desire, and when I pressed my thumb against her tight asshole, it slipped inside.

Something that sounded like my name caught against my hand, and I firmed my palm across her lips as she cried out in ecstasy. Her pussy tightened around me again, and I finally allowed myself release. My cum lashed into her, marking her.

"Mine," I snarled as I fucked her through our orgasms, pressing my thumb deeper inside her. "All mine."

With a final grunt, I thrust all the way in, locking us together through our last seconds of mutual ecstasy. I released her mouth so I could catch her beneath her hips. Her legs trembled, and I barely had the strength in my sated muscles to hold us both upright.

Holding her carefully, I eased us down onto the rough carpet, slipping out of her as we went down. I hated the loss of her heat, so I laid on my back and rested her warm body atop mine. She was breathing hard, and her lovely eyes were closed as she pressed her cheek against my chest. I wrapped my arms around her, not wanting a millimeter of space between us.

She yelped when I pressed down on her bruises.

I cursed and instantly released her. She scrambled back, her eyes clouding with confusion.

"I'm sorry, kitten. I didn't mean to hurt you. I'll be more careful."

I reached for her, and she shifted away. "Jason, I..." She shook her head as though to clear it. "I don't know what..."

Fuck.

"Come here," I ordered, trying my hardest to keep my voice gentle when panic was rising in my chest. She was staring at me with something like horror. "You're going to drop. You need aftercare."

"Drop? Aftercare?" She shook her head again and got to her feet, pulling her shorts up as she went. "I don't know what you're talking about, but I'm leaving. This was a mistake."

I pushed upright as well, hastily covering myself. I suddenly felt far too exposed and vulnerable.

"Don't go." My voice held a pleading edge, and I didn't even care. "I know you must be confused, but let me explain."

"Explain?" she demanded. "What is there to explain? You *spanked* me, and we just fucked against your desk. You're my instructor, and we just fucked in your office. Oh shit, shit!"

"You're dropping," I tried to get her to see reason. She'd never been disciplined before, and now she was pulling away before I could give her the proper after-care. She needed me to cuddle her close and tell her everything was okay. As it was, she was going to spiral into confusion and self-doubt, especially considering she didn't know anything about BDSM or the power exchange that had just taken place between us. "Calm down, and we'll talk."

"*Calm down?*" she hissed, her eyes flashing. "I don't fucking think so. I'm leaving. Don't follow me, and definitely don't ever call me to your office again. I'm serious about my career, and if you have any respect for me at all, you'll leave me alone."

My hands fisted at my sides as I forcibly prevented myself from reaching out for her. "Please don't leave like this. Just stay and talk to me. Of course I respect you."

She laughed, a high, anxious sound. "If you respected me, you wouldn't have spanked me like a child."

"It's not like that at all," I said, struggling to maintain a veneer of calm. "Natalie, I—"

"I don't want to hear it," she snapped. "I'm leaving.

I'll see you in class tomorrow. And don't you dare even think about kicking me out of the training session. I told you I didn't need saving, and I meant it. I'm going to graduate without your help. Stay out of my way."

She stormed out before I could say anything else, but not before I saw the tears shining in her eyes.

Damn it!

She was dropping hard, but I couldn't go after her. She was so on edge, she'd probably start yelling at me in public. Then we'd both get kicked out of Quantico. I didn't want that for her. And I certainly didn't want it for me, either.

Was I really so far gone that I'd lost all control? How had it come to this? I was risking my career for a good fuck.

I hated myself as soon as I thought it. Natalie was so much more than that. She was an extraordinary woman, and if I'd met her at any other time in my life, I'd tie her to my bed and never let her go.

As it was, my shitty decisions were making it clear that I wasn't fit to be her Dom. Hell, I wasn't even fit to be her instructor. Being a field agent was laughably beyond my capabilities at the moment. My own life might be in tatters, but I had no business ruining hers, too.

CHAPTER 9

Natalie

I couldn't stop crying. And that made me angry, despite the sense of bereavement that had taken hold deep in my chest. I couldn't allow myself to break down in front of Elena in our dorm room, so I let it all out in the shower, swallowing my sobs so she wouldn't hear. Even after I thought my tears were all spent, the constant sting at the corners of my eyes threatened to well up again.

The next morning, I knew fine red veins crisscrossed the whites of my eyes, but there was nothing I could do about it. It took all my effort to suppress the strong, irrational sense of grief that was crushing my heart. I felt... lost. Confused.

Jason had mentioned "dropping," but this was so much worse. I felt like I was in free fall: completely powerless to stop dropping, with no end in sight.

What would have happened if I'd stayed with him? He'd said he wanted to explain. Explain what? Why he'd treated me like something between a disobedient child and a sex object? I didn't understand what had happened at all.

I wasn't completely naïve. I knew some people enjoyed a little kink, and a slap or two against my ass during sex wasn't entirely unfamiliar to me.

But what had happened in Jason's office was different from that. He'd taken charge of my body and ensnared my mind in a way I didn't understand. I'd never been so meek with a man, but I'd craved to give Jason everything he demanded of me. He'd claimed he was taking care of me. And I'd certainly felt both cherished and chastised.

I hadn't intended to rat Trent out, but the words had flowed from me without a thought.

But I had my pride, my aspirations. And allowing an instructor to fuck me over his desk was simply too mortifying, even if that instructor was Jason.

Especially because that instructor was Jason. Because I knew I wouldn't surrender to another man as thoroughly and eagerly as I submitted to him.

Submissive. He'd called me that a few times. I

didn't think of myself that way at all. I was strong, capable. I didn't take shit from anyone.

And yet, I'd spread my legs and begged Jason to fuck me after he'd *disciplined* me.

Confusion muddled my thoughts and increased my sense of anguish. It tormented me throughout the day, and by the time I made it to Jason's class, I was thoroughly exhausted, even though I hadn't worked out yet.

"You okay?" Nate asked, his dark eyes soft with concern.

"I didn't sleep well," I said truthfully. "Sorry if I'm not really completely here today. I'll try to keep up."

"I'll go easy on you," he offered kindly.

I shook my head. "Please don't. I need to keep up with everyone else. We're going to graduate together, remember?" I offered a weak smile.

He returned it tentatively, still studying me with concern. "All right. But promise me you'll get some rest tonight. I don't like when I land a hit on you. I know you're better than me, and it feels wrong."

I put on a brave face. "Then I guess I'll just have to make sure to take you down today. Twenty bucks says you don't land a single hit."

"I'll take you up on that some other time. The condition you're in today, it would feel like stealing."

He winked, keeping the tone light despite his lingering worry.

"Quiet," Jason barked out as he entered the room. He appeared even more dangerous than usual, his powerful bearing radiating barely restrained fury.

I quickly cut my eyes away so I didn't have to look at him. Even though he was several yards away from me, I felt his presence like a palpable thing. The pressure on my chest increased, and my eyes stung.

We began the lesson, and I was careful to keep my eyes averted from Jason and my focus on Nate. I couldn't afford to have him hit me where I was injured. If Jason saw my weakness, he might kick me out of class again.

I worked even harder than usual, my body screaming in protest when I twisted in a way that pulled at my bruised muscles. I set my jaw, determined to push through. Nate's movements were hesitant, his brows drawn as he watched my silent struggle.

"Don't hold back," I demanded through clenched teeth. "I don't want Ja— Agent Harper," I corrected, "coming over here."

Nate nodded grimly and came at me in earnest. I went on the defensive, and I wasn't able to gain the upper hand for the duration of the lesson. It was all I could do to block him and hold my ground.

Even though my performance was lackluster, Jason didn't come near us. I was immensely grateful. I wasn't sure if I'd be able to prevent myself from bursting into tears if he criticized my technique today. I would crack under the slightest censure from him.

I was panting and sweating by the time the lesson ended, and I dreaded my afternoon class. I wasn't at all certain that I could focus on crime scene analysis when my mind was such a scattered mess.

"Simmons. Wait a moment."

My blood turned to ice in my veins at Jason's order. It wasn't delivered sharply, but the prospect of facing him made my heart twist. Would he criticize me? Or did he want something else from me, something decidedly darker?

I considered pretending I hadn't heard him, but I knew I couldn't defy a direct order from an instructor, not when it had been witnessed by the rest of the recruits. Trent smirked at me as he passed, and Elena snickered cruelly. They certainly both seemed to be under the impression that I was in trouble again.

I glared at Trent. He had no idea how much trouble *he* was in. Even if Jason was angry with me for storming out on him yesterday, I had no doubt that he would keep his promise and kick Trent out of the academy. Jason's eyes had tightened with fury when I'd told him how Trent had hurt me.

I just can't abide abusive men, he'd said. Jason had certainly demonstrated a fierce protective streak, and I got the feeling that permeated his entire life and wasn't concentrated solely on me. He seemed to harbor a strong sense of duty as an FBI agent, and his job protecting innocents was clearly of the utmost importance to him. It only further endeared me to him, and that wasn't a good thing; I was already dangerously infatuated.

As soon as the last recruit exited the training room, Jason approached me. I felt him before I saw him. I kept my back to him, unable to face him. Stupid tears welled up as he neared, and I hastily blinked them back. Every fiber of my being screamed at me to throw myself in his arms and allow him to hold me close, to pet me and tell me how proud he was of me. His words of praise as I'd taken his discipline had touched me more deeply that I could have imagined. It should have been patronizing, at best, and perverse, at worst. But it had filled me with heady satisfaction that enfolded my soul.

"What do you want?" I asked, my voice hitching. I swallowed hard and tried again. "I know I wasn't at my best today. I'll be better tomorrow."

"That's not why I asked you to stay," he said

quietly, his tone nearly as strained as my own. "I can tell you're hurting. Please, give me a chance to explain what happened between us yesterday."

"I remember very clearly," I said, trying to sound acidic and failing miserably.

"But you don't understand. Do you?"

I hesitated, my emotions churning. No, I didn't understand. I couldn't comprehend what was happening to me or why I couldn't seem to get a grip.

He took my silence as confirmation.

"I'm going for a run in the woods tonight. Six-thirty. There's a bench halfway around the circuit. It's a good place to take a breather. I'll be there, and I hope you will be too. I'll be there every night, until you're ready."

He waited a moment, then sighed and walked away when I didn't offer an answer. Truthfully, I wasn't certain if I'd be there. I desperately wanted to get a handle on my emotions, but the prospect of being alone with Jason was unnerving, to say the least. How could I be near him without falling prey to his magnetism again?

I forced myself to start walking to the locker room. As it was, I'd barely have enough time to shower and change before my next class. I'd make my decision about whether or not to meet Jason after.

For now, I needed to focus on my studies, or I'd never become an agent.

※

DREAD SOLIDIFIED IN MY GUT, WEIGHING ME DOWN as I jogged toward the meeting point. I feared the emotional upheaval and allure of facing Jason, but I couldn't carry on as I was. I needed the answers he promised, or I would fail out of the academy. I'd barely made it through the last three days; I'd been little more than a zombie since I'd fled his office after he'd spanked me. I would have to study hard if I was going to catch up on everything I'd missed in my distraction.

As promised, he was waiting for me, seated on the bench at the edge of the path. Trees lined either side, providing privacy. No one else was jogging out here at dusk. We'd have a chance to discuss what had happened in his office without being overheard.

His attention snapped to me as soon as he heard my approaching footfalls. I slowed to a walk, my legs leaden as I forced myself to continue moving toward him. When I reached him, I paused, tense and uncertain.

He gestured at the bench beside him. "Sit with me." It was a command, not a suggestion.

My knees folded, and I perched on the edge of the wooden seat, keeping as much distance between our bodies as possible.

He was silent, waiting for me to speak first. I felt lost, helpless. I wasn't sure where to begin, and I longed for his guidance. But he allowed me time to gather my thoughts, and I was grateful for that.

"What's happening to me?" I finally asked, my voice small. I couldn't look him in the eye, so I stared at an ant that was slowly making its way across the pavement at my feet.

"You're dropping," he said grimly.

"But what does that mean?"

He blew out a long breath. "I should have explained this to you at the outset. But things moved so fast, and I didn't think I wanted..." He paused before pressing on. "Do you know what BDSM is?" he asked abruptly.

I finally looked up at him, needing to read his expression. I wasn't sure what I'd expected him to say, but this certainly wasn't it. He regarded me intently, his bright green eyes cutting into my soul.

"I've heard of it," I said slowly. "That's like, kinky sex, right? Sadism and masochism?" I supposed my time with Jason had been more deviant than anything I'd experienced before, but it was a far cry from the whips and chains I associated with S and M.

"That's part of it," he replied, still watching me with an intensity that took my breath away. I couldn't break from his gaze if I tried. "For me, it's about the power exchange. I'm a Dominant. Or at least, I used to be." His lips twisted in disgust. "You're naturally submissive, and I couldn't help responding to that. I'm sorry I didn't take the time to explain it properly before. When I disciplined you for the first time, it was an intense experience for both of us. You felt it, didn't you? The power exchange."

I thought of how I'd rested my cheek on the desk and meekly allowed him to spank me, how my core had contracted around his fingers in pleasure even as pain heated my abused ass. Everything had fallen away, and my entire world had centered on him. All I'd wanted was to please him, to be with him.

"Yes," I said softly. "I felt it."

He nodded. "I knew your submissive nature as soon as I touched you the first time. You reacted to my dominance beautifully, and I couldn't resist you. I can't resist you." His voice lowered on the last, and he reached for me. Before he could make contact, he curled his fingers to a fist and withdrew his hand. "But I have to. This isn't fair to you. I took you to a vulnerable headspace when I spanked you, and it was my responsibility to hold you and comfort you after. But I fucked up, and I couldn't stop you from leaving.

I had no right to stop you. You're not mine. And I have no business calling myself a Dominant anymore." The fine lines around his eyes deepened with anguish.

You're not mine. Yearning tugged at my chest. I wished I could be his. But everything was too complicated. I couldn't be with him, not like this. Not when it would cost me my career.

But I couldn't bear the pain etched into every taut line of his perfect face.

"What do you mean?" I asked tentatively. "Why can't you be a Dominant? Just because we can't..." I couldn't bring myself to finish that statement, but I pressed on. "I'm sure you can find someone else. A real submissive."

His eyes flashed. "You *are* a real submissive. You're so fucking perfect it makes me want... Well, it makes me want things I don't deserve."

"But what do you mean by that?"

His gaze dropped from mine, as though he couldn't bear to look at me. "I fucked up," he said, his voice rough with emotion. "It's why I'm here, when I should be in the field. I'm being punished."

"Why?" I asked, truly puzzled. "Why would anyone punish you? You're a great agent. They wouldn't have put you in charge of training new recruits if you weren't."

He laughed, a hollow sound. "I'm being punished because my father—the Deputy Director—was too embarrassed to fire me. So he chose to demote me instead; to humiliate me."

"Why would your father do that to you?"

His eyes snapped back up to mine, burning into me. "Because I was a fucking addict," he ground out. "I was weak. I started taking pills." He ran a hand over his face. "I thought I was taking back control, but I completely lost it. I lost everything. That's why I can't be a Dominant anymore. I don't have any self-control. I don't deserve any submissive's trust. And I certainly don't deserve you."

Shock rendered me silent for a few seconds. Jason had been addicted to prescription drugs? Why? He wasn't the type to jeopardize his career and the safety of those around him to chase a cheap high.

"You're a good man," I finally said. "I know you are. And I... I don't regret being with you. You deserve to be happy, Jason. Your father might be punishing you, but you don't have to punish yourself, too."

"Don't I?" he said, his voice strained. He looked at me with longing, but fear flickered in his eyes.

I reached out and cupped his cheek in my hand, unable to help myself. "What are you afraid of?" I whispered.

"I'm afraid I'll ruin you."

I didn't have a response for that. Hadn't I been worrying over how our forbidden relationship might ruin my career? Hadn't I felt frayed and raw because of our hot encounter in his office?

I'm the one who ran away. He wanted to explain, and I didn't let him.

I could see that now. He'd tried to take care of me, but I'd been scared. Scared of the intensity of what was developing between us.

"I'm afraid, too," I admitted. "Not that you'll hurt me, but that I might be willing to risk everything to be with you. I've never wanted anything more in my life than to be an FBI agent. Until I met you. You say you can't resist me, but I can't resist you, either."

"We have to," he said roughly. "I can't be responsible for you right now. I'm not in a position to care for myself properly, let alone anyone else."

"Then I'll take care of you," I promised.

He shook his head. "It doesn't work that way. I don't work that way."

"Why not? You don't strike me as the kind of man who's too proud to accept help." I considered him for a moment when he didn't say anything. As I mulled over our conversation, I came to a heartbreaking realization. "You don't think you deserve for anyone to take care of you," I surmised quietly. He flinched, and I knew I'd hit the truth.

"Natalie," he said my name like a prayer. "I—"

Footsteps slapped against pavement, and we jolted apart. My hand dropped from his face, and I quickly shifted away from him.

My stomach dropped when I saw Trent approaching us. In the fading light, I could barely make out his expression, his eyes. He seemed to be looking in our direction, but how much had he seen?

I held my breath, but he jogged on past us without stopping.

When his footsteps faded into the distance, Jason stood.

"I should go."

"Wait," I pleaded. "Stay. I want to talk to you about this. All of it." I still didn't fully understand the BDSM thing, even if I did acknowledge the power dynamic inherent in our connection. What did it mean that I was submissive? And how could I prove to him that he was worthy of love?

Love. The word terrified me. I barely knew Jason. How could I even think in those terms? This whole thing was crazy, our situation impossible.

"I can't stay," he said, his expression drawn with anguish. "If I do, I won't be able to stop myself."

"Stop yourself? From doing what?"

"From holding you down and fucking you in the dirt like an animal." His lips pressed to a thin line.

My core tightened at his crass words, craving for him to do just that. I wanted his raw power to wash over me, for him to pin me down and fuck me hard as we both lost all control.

His eyes flared as he read my arousal in my expression. "No," he bit out.

He turned from me with a curse and sprinted away, as though if he just ran fast enough, he could escape the connection between us.

It was a useless endeavor. I wondered if he knew it as keenly as I did.

I was falling for Jason, and I wasn't at all sure I wanted to resist any longer, no matter what it cost me.

CHAPTER 10

Jason

It took everything in me to prevent myself from catching up with McMahon and beating him to a bloody pulp. He'd seen me with Natalie. And while the danger of that was enough to make me want to protect her, the memory of the bruises that marred her perfect body was still far too fresh in my mind. He'd hurt her. He was a threat.

I should put him down.

No. That would be a mistake. Our situation was more precarious than ever now. If McMahon did suspect that anything was going on between Natalie and me, those suspicions would only be confirmed if

I attacked him. I had to keep my distance, or I'd destroy Natalie's career with one punch.

And probably my own as well.

That didn't matter as much to me as it once did. All I could think of was *her*. She deserved so much better than me, and yet...

You don't think you deserve for anyone to take care of you, she'd said.

How could she look right into my soul, revealing secrets about myself that I didn't dare to contemplate?

I'll take care of you. Her promise rang through my mind, tormenting me, tempting me.

All I'd ever wanted was a submissive of my own, someone to love and care for. Someone who trusted me implicitly and gave me everything, just as I would devote myself to her completely.

I'd played with plenty of women, and I'd participated in much more perverse acts than anything I'd done with Natalie. But our power exchange, our impossible connection, was more visceral than anything I'd ever known.

I knew I couldn't have her. Not until I got my shit together and found my self-control again. Then, maybe I'd be worthy of her. Maybe I could rebuild my life and beg for her to accept me.

I didn't know how long it would take for me to

get to that point. I felt so utterly shattered, I wasn't certain I'd ever get there. What if some other Dom came along and plucked her up?

Just the thought of another man touching her, another man dominating her, made rage choke my throat. I sucked in a ragged breath and struggled to center myself.

If I was ever going to have a chance with her, I had to find my control again. And to do that, I needed to commit myself to therapy. I'd already started discussing my trauma with Dr. Larson, and I'd diligently written about it, completing the "homework" she'd assigned me. Thinking about the carnage was difficult, but I had to face it. I refused to wither and waste my years at Quantico. I'd been determined to get better so I could win my career back, but now, I had a bigger prize to work toward: Natalie.

࿐

"FOR SOME OF YOU, THIS WILL BE YOUR LAST DAY AT Quantico," I said as I surveyed my class. Two weeks in, and it had already become clear to me that a handful of the recruits weren't going to cut it. I tried not to glower at McMahon too long as I spoke. He definitely wouldn't be here in twenty-four hours. I'd made sure of it, giving him a scathing assessment.

Truthfully, he wasn't half-bad. He certainly wasn't in the bottom ten percent of the class. But character counted for a lot more than skill, and I'd be damned if I let an abusive, misogynistic bastard join the Bureau on my watch. I didn't want to put Natalie in the middle of it, so I'd embellished his assessment a little. Instead of writing up his attack on a fellow recruit, I'd written that he was incompetent and unfit.

That wasn't a lie. In my mind, anyone who would beat a woman for rejecting him was both incompetent and unfit to be considered a man, much less an agent.

"The cuts will be announced at the end of the day," I continued on, allowing my eyes to rove over the recruits rather than focusing on the one I hated.

Or the one I cared for.

Don't look at her, I willed myself. I couldn't face Natalie, not after the intensity of baring my soul to her in the woods. I'd worked hard in therapy this morning, and I was feeling particularly raw, even though Dr. Larson had praised my commitment and progress. If I allowed my gaze to linger on the woman who was rapidly becoming my darkest obsession, I wasn't at all certain I'd be able to hide my feelings.

"Pair up," I ordered. "This is your last chance to impress me."

The room filled with the low buzz of conversation as the recruits split into their usual groupings. I was so focused on not looking in Natalie's direction that she caught me by surprise when she didn't partner with Nathaniel Cross.

"Agent Harper?" Her voice was soft, tentative. I didn't care for the formality; I much preferred when she screamed my name in ecstasy.

I stiffened as it took physical effort to will the surge of lust to subside. Moving slowly, I turned toward her.

"What is it, Simmons?" I asked, more sharply than I'd intended.

Instead of shrinking away from my harsh tone, she lifted her chin in defiance. God, that expression awoke all my most deviant urges. I craved to pin her down and torment her until she mewled and melted, purring like the good little kitten I knew she could be.

"I need your help," she said, bold and clear. "I've fallen behind in the last few days, and I could use some individual attention, please."

Individual attention. There were so many ways I'd like to lavish my attentions on her, none of which involved training her in hand-to-hand combat.

"I'm sure Cross can help you," I said, turning away.

Her hand shot out to close around my wrist. "Please," she begged, sounding more strained.

I stared pointedly at where she touched me, trying to ignore the heat that flashed up my arm, emanating from where our skin made contact. Reluctantly, her grip eased, but her fingertips trailed across the inside of my wrist as she pulled away, the light touch sending lust surging through my body.

I became aware of several pairs of eyes on us, and I realized we'd been too close for a few seconds too long. I had no choice but to acknowledge her request.

"All right," I bit out as I stepped into an offensive stance.

Her dark blue gaze focused on me—not looking into my eyes, but studying my body. I didn't like the analytical way she watched me, calculating my next move rather than really looking at *me*. I was a challenge, an opponent. Not the man who'd fucked her while she'd whimpered and writhed and called me *Sir*.

She took advantage of my momentary distraction, coming at me with lightning speed. I barely dodged in time, and her skin kissed mine as she slid past. I spun, facing off against her again. Grim determination settled over me. Natalie was good, but I was better, more experienced. And the animal part of my brain told me to pin her down, to conquer and claim. Her skill and the challenge she posed only made my hunger for her that much sharper.

She came at me again. I waited. Just before she made contact, I ducked under her outstretched arm and swept my foot out, lightly knocking her ankles out from under her. She dropped, and I covered her immediately, pinning her in place with my body atop hers.

My breathing came faster than it should for such little exertion. She was looking at *me* now, her eyes wide and her lips parted as she stared up at me.

A feminine giggle called my attention away from her perfection beneath me. I glanced up to find Elena Briggs smirking in Natalie's direction. McMahon was at her side, also looking at us. His lips were twisted in cruel satisfaction as he noted Natalie's position beneath me. I tensed as rage took hold.

"It's okay," Natalie breathed, her voice barely audible. "I don't care."

"I do," I growled softly. "He's gone as of tonight."

She nodded, unsurprised. "I figured."

The knowledge that she'd had faith in me to take care of this for her shocked me. I'd anticipated her resentment, possibly even her anger. She'd made it clear that she didn't want me fighting her battles for her.

And yet, she was soft and still beneath me,

trusting that I would do what was necessary to prevent McMahon from touching her ever again.

I nearly groaned as desire flooded me, my entire body aching to claim her. She turned her face away before I could bring my lips too close to hers.

"Not here," she whispered.

She moved faster than I could comprehend in my distraction, and she managed to roll, flipping our position so she was on top. She brought her forearm down on my throat, signaling her victory.

My beast in me couldn't stand for it. I gnashed my teeth with the effort of resisting my dark urges. I wanted to curve my fingers into her hips, lift her up, and slam her down onto my cock until she shuddered and surrendered.

"I have to talk to you," she urged, keeping her voice low. "Your office?"

I jerked my head in refusal. If I got her in my office, she'd be bent over my desk again in a matter of seconds. If she wanted to talk, it needed to be somewhere neutral, but still private.

"Meet me in the parking lot at eight-thirty," I murmured. "We can talk in my car." The recruits who made it through the first two weeks would be given the weekend to spend as they wished, and it wouldn't be out of place for Natalie to be in the parking lot. Many of them would leave base to let loose for the night. "It's a black Jaguar. I'll be in the back of the lot."

She nodded, then pushed up off me. The entire hushed exchange had taken a matter of seconds, but this prolonged contact in front of the other recruits was dangerous. As it was, it took everything in me to keep my hard-on under control.

"You're doing fine, Simmons," I said more loudly as I got to my feet, more for Brigg's and McMahon's benefit than for Natalie's. "Go help Cross."

She nodded and walked back over to where Nathaniel waited for her. He was watching us with open curiosity. I didn't like the keen light in his dark eyes. I knew he wasn't interested in Natalie—if he were, I would have assigned her another partner—but that didn't mean he was blind.

Struggling to keep my expression impassive, I jerked my attention back to the rest of the recruits. I'd see Natalie again soon enough. She'd said she needed to talk to me, and I owed her that. I'd thrown a lot at her yesterday, and we'd barely covered BDSM and the Dom/sub dynamic we'd been exploring without her knowledge.

The next ten hours until I could be with her again were going to be torture.

I WATCHED HER AS SHE CROSSED THE PARKING LOT, her lithe body moving toward me with confident strides. I marveled at her strength, her acceptance. I'd told her the worst of my sins, and she hadn't flinched. Instead, she'd demanded that we meet in secret again. Although I knew we were walking a dangerous path, I couldn't help hoping that she still wanted me. She'd said she wanted to talk. I certainly owed her more answers, and I needed her near me. I was a selfish bastard, and I was being reckless with both our lives.

But I couldn't bring myself to deny her. Not when I craved her more fiercely than I'd ever craved any drugs.

She arrived at the passenger door, and I popped the lock so she could get in. She slid into the seat beside me and shut the door softly. It was dark in this corner of the lot, and few cars were parked this far back. No one should have noted her approach, and even if they did, I'd been waiting in my car for over half an hour. We wouldn't have been seen together, and it was dark enough that no one would be able to see inside the car unless they were standing right beside my Jag.

"Thank you for meeting me," she said softly. "I wasn't sure if you wanted to."

"I did," I replied. "I owe it to you to answer all of your questions."

Her lips pressed together, and she was silent for a moment, as though not fully satisfied with my response. "I do have more questions about BDSM," she finally admitted. "I would have researched it on my own, but obviously I don't have the privacy here I would need to do that. I understood what you meant when you talked about a power exchange. What I don't understand is why I react to you this way. You keep saying I'm submissive, and with you, I can't seem to help acting that way. But *submissive* isn't a word I've ever used to describe myself. Just the opposite, in fact."

I nodded my understanding. "I've seen you in action. You're a tough woman. And you must have worked hard to become as skilled as you are. Why did you choose to pursue a career with the Bureau?"

"Well, if I'm being honest, I've always known I didn't want to be some simpering southern debutante like my mother wanted me to be. I never felt comfortable in cocktail dresses, making small talk with people who were just waiting for the chance to gossip about me to someone else as soon as my back was turned. That life never felt *real*. I never fit in. Training to join the FBI academy was my rebellion."

"That's pretty admirable, as far as rebellions go."

I couldn't suppress a small smile, undeniably charmed by her answer. Truthfully, it was similar to my own reasons for joining the Bureau: to defy my father, even though it might appear that I was following in his footsteps. He'd always berated me for being weak, a disappointment. I'd been determined to prove him wrong, to spite him with my success.

My plan had been working perfectly, until the nightmares set in and I became an addict.

"Hey." She covered my clenched fist with her smaller hand, calling me back to her. "Where did you go just now?"

I struggled to wipe away my grimace and school my face to a blank mask. "I used to want to be a great agent, too. But my father was right. I'm a failure."

"Don't say that," she said with surprising heat. "You might be here because you made a mistake, but you're not a failure. I don't care what your father says. He's wrong."

I bit my tongue against further argument. Now wasn't the time for me to slip into self-loathing. Natalie had asked me about BDSM, and she needed to understand her submissive nature. Her reactions to me confused her, and I didn't want her to be upset by our connection.

"We were talking about you," I redirected the

conversation abruptly. "I think I understand why you enjoy sexual submission."

"Oh?" she prompted. "And why is that?"

"You mentioned that your mother pressured you to conform to the life she wanted for you. Based on what I know of your nature, I'm guessing you always strived for perfection, even though you were unhappy with what she wanted from you."

She frowned, and her gaze turned inward. "I did have the best posture of all the girls at cotillion. And I guess I wanted to be the best ballroom dancer, too. Perfect manners, perfect poise. I hated it, but I wanted to make my mother happy. Well, until I went to college and realized I didn't have to live under that pressure to be someone I didn't want to be. That's when I started studying Psychology and making plans to work my way toward joining the FBI academy."

"You made the decision to pursue a life that would make you happy, but you've carried that perfectionism over into your pursuit to become an agent. You've been ahead of your entire class since the day you arrived at Quantico. That's natural talent, but it's also the result of hard work. You put a lot of pressure on yourself, and not just because you want to be the best. You're not vain. You want to excel because you want to please the people around you. You want to make them proud."

She bit her lower lip, considering my words. "I guess I never thought about it that way." Her eyes roved over my face, as though searching for something. "So, what does this have to do with sexual submission? I still don't really understand."

Her hand still covered mine, and I pressed my palm against hers, lacing our fingers together without a thought.

"Submissives want to please their Dominant partner. They are often empathetic and giving. I think that describes you. I've admitted my darkest secret and imposed my most twisted desires on you, and you're still here, choosing to support me despite everything. You've given me your trust, willingly placed yourself at my mercy when I desperately needed to feel in control."

"Of course I trust you," she said softly. "But I'm more selfish than that. You've given me more pleasure than I've ever known. You say I'm giving, but I'm fairly certain you've brought me to orgasm more times than I've done the same for you."

"It's not like that. The Dom/sub relationship is reciprocal. You give me the control I crave, and you honor me with your trust. In return, I give you the release you need. You put a lot of pressure on yourself, and when you put yourself in my hands, you don't have to worry about anything. When you're mine, I take care of you. That's something I need, too. I need to be needed, necessary. You've given yourself to me, and even though I don't deserve you, I—"

"I have given myself to you," she interrupted me firmly. "But am I..." She hesitated, her eyes searching my face again. "Am I yours?" she finished quietly.

"I want you to be," I said, my voice strained with the depth of my desire. "But I have some things I need to work through first. I'm trying to get better. I want to be good enough for you. Once I get back into the field, we—"

She silenced me by closing the distance between us and pressing her lips to mine. The kiss was fierce, demanding. For once, she was the aggressor, and in my raw emotional state, I couldn't resist her. I'd never been so open with a woman, revealing my scars and exposing my soul. Her touch was almost painful. Not because she was physically stronger than I, but because my nerves were frayed and vulnerable. Despite that vulnerability, I didn't feel at all power- less. As I deepened the kiss, taking her mouth more thoroughly until she shivered and melted against me, a sense of peace settled over me. She soothed me; her devotion and unwavering belief in me made me stronger than I'd ever been. She'd entered my life in my darkest hour and illuminated my world, forcing the blackness away. When I held her like this, I felt as though I truly could be the man I'd always wanted to be: powerful, worthy, *good*.

Light flashed against my closed eyelids, and I snapped back to reality. I ripped myself away from Natalie, going on high alert as instinctive panic spiked.

Someone was standing outside my car, the light on his phone shining in our direction as he recorded us.

Rage descended on me in a red haze.

McMahon.

CHAPTER 11

Natalie

I barely had time to gasp in horror before Jason launched himself out of the driver's side door and tackled Trent to the ground. I heard Trent's head crack against the pavement and the crunch of his phone shattering as it fell with him.

"Jason!" I cried out as I quickly got out of the car and darted to where he crouched over Trent.

Jason's fist came down on his jaw. Trent's head snapped to the side, blood spraying out into the darkness as his lip split.

"Jason, stop!" I spoke as loudly as I dared, not wanting to shout in case anyone was nearby. The last thing we needed was witnesses. Well, more witnesses. Trent had already seen us together.

Jason dropped his fist before he landed another blow, but he kept Trent pinned. Despite his predicament, Trent give him a shit-eating grin, his white teeth stained red with blood.

"You might have broken my phone, but the video is already uploaded to the cloud," he said, triumphant. "I have a permanent copy. You'll be fired for this. Both of you." He turned his vindictive gaze on me. "You shouldn't have tattled on me to your boyfriend, bitch."

He choked when Jason's fingers closed around his throat.

"Don't talk to her," Jason snarled. "Don't look at her."

"Jason," I said his name as calmly as I could manage. "You have to stop. You'll only make things worse."

His muscles rippled with the effort of suppressing his violence, but he eased his grip on Trent's throat. Trent gasped for air, his face contorted in pain.

"Get me back in the program," he forced out, keeping his eyes trained on Jason rather than me. He'd clearly learned his lesson. "I know you're the one who made them kick me out. I saw the two of you in the woods yesterday. You got me kicked out because of her. All I had to do was follow her tonight to get evidence on the two of you. Your careers are over if I share the video. But I won't," he said quickly, staying focused on Jason. "If you change your assessment and get me back into the academy."

A low, feral sound rumbled from Jason's throat.

"Jason," I said his name again to call him back from his blind rage. "It's okay. You have to do it. Just let him up."

"He hurt you," Jason ground out, his voice rough and primal.

"I can handle him," I replied with confidence. I addressed Trent directly. "Jason's going to let you up now. He'll get you reinstated, and in return, you won't show anyone that video. And if anyone asks how you got hurt tonight, you'll tell them I'm the one who kicked your ass. Are we clear?"

Trent grimaced at my final stipulation, but he didn't dare insult me again when Jason's fist was so close to his face.

"Fine," he barked out. "I'll keep your secret, if you make sure I get to graduation without any more problems."

"He will," I promised for Jason. "You'll join the Bureau, but how long you last in the field is on you. They don't keep misogynistic assholes in the FBI. If you touch one woman in a way she doesn't like, I will

156

personally make sure you're fired."

He shot a quick glare in my direction before refocusing on Jason. He was obviously still intimidated by my fearsome protector.

"Let's go, Jason. You can deal with his paperwork in the morning." I spoke with as much authority as I could muster. Jason might have taken the lead in our relationship thus far, but he was nearly out of his mind with possessive fury at the moment. He needed me to stay calm for both of us.

I placed a tentative hand on his shoulder when he didn't respond. He blinked and looked up at me, his fierce expression easing somewhat.

"Take me away from here," I said, softening my tone to something pleading rather than demanding.

His jaw firmed, and he pushed off of Trent without another glance. His focus was honed solely on me. He wrapped his arm around my waist and curved his body around mine as though to shield me from harm. After he ushered me to the car and secured me in the passenger seat, he quickly circled to the driver's side and slammed the door behind him. He shoved the keys into the ignition and pealed out of the parking lot, leaving Trent huddled and bloody on the pavement.

"Talk to me," I requested. "Tell me you're okay."

His knuckles turned white as he tightened his

grip on the steering wheel. "I can't do it," he seethed, not looking over at me. "I can't let him in the field. Not knowing what he is."

"He's an ass, but I don't think he's a threat. Not anymore, at least."

"He's an abusive bastard," Jason railed, still on the edge of control.

"He won't try to hurt me again," I tried to placate him. "You won't let him. And neither will I."

He sucked in a deep breath in a visible effort to calm himself. "Of course I won't let him touch you again. If he even looks at you the wrong way—" His teeth snapped together before he could go down that dark path. "I just can't stand abusive men."

"You said something like that before," I said, pressing gently. This must be linked to his need for control. He'd read me so easily, understanding why I reveled in submitting to him. I suspected I was beginning to understand why he needed to dominate me. And why he felt like he didn't deserve love. He'd spoken of his father with bitterness. "What happened to you? Was it your father?"

He stiffened, and he didn't respond.

He didn't have to. I could read his answer in every taut line of his body.

"I'm sorry," I murmured. "Whatever he did to you, you didn't deserve it."

"But he was right," he said, anguished. "I am weak, a failure. He was always right about me."

"He was not," I said firmly. "If this is about the drugs—"

"Of course it's about the drugs," he snapped. "I started using because I couldn't function. My brain decided to break one day, because I couldn't handle the shit I've seen. I became an agent to spite my father for every bad thing he'd ever said about me, but he was right. I'm too weak to deal with it."

"What do you mean? What did you see?"

"You don't want to know," he muttered.

"You can talk to me," I urged. "Please. Let me in. Let me help take care of you. You said this Dom/sub relationship is reciprocal. You take care of me, and I take care of you, too."

"You're not my sub."

"Bullshit," I declared. "You said I'm yours. When you fucked me in your office, you said it. And I'm not going to let you take it back just because you've decided to hate yourself. I won't fucking allow it. If I'm yours, then you're mine, and I'm telling you I'm not going to let you hate yourself. Not anymore. Whatever you've been through, I'll be here for you to help you heal. You said you're trying to get better. I believe you can. And you can lean on me while you do. I want this. I want *you*."

"You don't know what you're saying," he said on a pained whisper. "The kind of relationship you're talking about requires trust. I can't trust myself right now."

"Well, I trust you. I wouldn't be risking everything for you if I didn't."

"I'm sorry. I never wanted this to happen. I've put your career in jeopardy."

"I made my own choices," I declared. "And I choose you. You're mine."

A ragged laugh left his chest. "That's my line."

"I'm serious, Jason. I want to see where this goes. Our timing is terrible, but I believe we can make it work. Take a chance on us."

He stopped the car and turned to face me, his green eyes dark in the dim streetlight that filtered into the car. "I don't think I have a choice," he said wryly. "Look where we are."

I peered out the window at the half-lit *vacancy* sign. It was the same motel where we'd shared our first night together.

My heart lifted. "You mean it? You want to be together?"

He traced the line of my jaw with reverence. "Of course I want to be with you. How could I not? You're strong and beautiful, and willful enough to drag me out of my indulgent self-pity. And yet," his fingers curved around my throat, "so soft and submissive when I need you to be. You're perfect, Natalie. Far too good for me."

One corner of my lips ticked up. "There's that indulgent self-pity again," I pointed out.

His low chuckle rumbled over me, and he brushed a kiss across my lips.

"Wait here," he ordered, finding calm in his dominant headspace. "I'll get us a room."

I could have protested that I was perfectly capable of walking to the front desk and getting a room for us. But I recognized that this was his way of caring for me, and I settled in to wait while he went to retrieve a set of keys from the night clerk.

I need to be needed. His words rang through my mind.

I did need him. More than my career, more than anything. I was putting it all on the line for him, risking all my carefully laid plans.

And I didn't care. I'd only known Jason a short time, but I was already falling hard. We'd find a way to make this work. Trent might know our secret, but I was confident that he would trade his silence in exchange for a place at Quantico. If Jason and I could hide our relationship for the next eighteen weeks, we'd be free to be together publically.

I was smiling to myself when Jason returned. He

caught my levity and grinned at me as he opened my door and took my hand in his. His grip shifted so his fingers wrapped around my wrist in a possessive hold, just as he'd done on the night we'd first met.

Giddy excitement raced through my veins, and I happily followed him into the room he'd reserved for us. As soon as the door closed behind him, he was on me, his teeth nipping at my lips, his fingers tangling in my hair. He devoured me, as though he'd been starving for me his entire life.

I returned the kiss with equal fervor, tearing at his clothes as we bumped against furniture, moving in blind lust. He was my whole world, and I craved to get as close to him as possible. I needed his skin against mine, his cock buried deep inside me.

He seemed to feel the same, and he worked my clothes off as well. Within minutes, we were both naked. I reached between us, but my fingers barely brushed his hard cock before he grabbed my hand.

"No," he said sternly. I was beginning to recognize the deep, confident tone when his Dominant nature took over. It drew out my submission in the space of a heartbeat, and I instantly stilled in his hold, waiting for his instruction.

He'd been right: I wanted to please him. I wanted to give him everything, to give up control and place myself in his care. I'd never felt more at peace than I did in his firm hold.

"I'm going to push you tonight," he told me evenly. "I want to test your pain tolerance."

My confidence wavered. "Pain tolerance?"

He cupped my face in his hand, tracing the line of my cheekbone with his thumb. "I'd never harm you, Natalie. But I think you like a little pain. Do you remember how you felt when I spanked you in my office?"

My cheeks heated at the memory. It had hurt when he'd struck me, but I'd ached with arousal, and I'd lost myself in him as I ceded to his power over me. It had been the greatest high I'd ever known.

"Yes," I whispered. "I remember."

"You liked it," he said, already knowing the truth. "And I was honored by your trust. I am honored by it."

His thumb grazed over my sensitive lower lip, and I licked it without thinking, drawing him into my mouth with my tongue in wanton invitation. His eyes darkened as his pupils dilated with desire.

"There's my sweet kitten," he rumbled, working his thumb slowly in and out of my mouth in lewd imitation of how I wanted to suck his cock. "If you're good, we'll get to that later."

He withdrew his thumb from my lips with a small popping noise.

"But first, you need a safe word," he said.

"Safe word?"

"It's part of the trust we share. I'm going to test you tonight, but if I push too far, all you have to do is say the word, and I'll stop."

"Okay," I agreed. Although this talk of testing my pain tolerance made me nervous, I did trust Jason. "What's my safe word?"

He pressed an approving kiss against my forehead. "Say *yellow* if you need me to ease up or take a break. Say *red* if you've reached your limit. Everything will stop."

I frowned. "What if I don't want everything to stop?"

He tucked a stray lock of hair behind my ear. "The pain will stop," he clarified. "I'll hold you and take care of you, no matter what."

"All right," I said, squaring my shoulders. "I'm ready."

He chuckled. "Such a brave kitten." I pouted, and he traced the line of my lips. "And so cute."

"You're being patronizing," I huffed.

"And you're being adorable. My angry little kitten." He leaned in so his warm breath teased over the shell of my ear. "Don't worry. I remember how to make you purr." His teeth sank into the sensitive spot where my neck curved into my shoulder, and his fist twined in my hair at my nape, anchoring me in place for his possessive bite. I gasped and tensed as pain flared. He growled against me, and his fingers tightened in my hair in warning. His tongue teased across the abused flesh that was caught between his teeth. I sagged in his hold. It wasn't simple pleasure that made my knees weak; it was *him*. He overwhelmed me with his raw power, knowing just how to handle my body to earn my submission.

I surrendered easily, eagerly. His arm around my lower back supported me as I shuddered in his harsh hold. He finally released me from his bite, pressing tender kisses against the spot where he'd marked me.

I didn't resist as he guided me onto the bed, positioning me on my knees in the center of the mattress. His big hand pressed between my shoulders, urging me down until my cheek touched the sheets, leaving my back arched and my ass raised high like an offering.

"Stay," he ordered, lightly squeezing the back of my neck to reinforce his control before he stepped away.

I remained where he'd left me, completely still and compliant. My mind emptied as his will took over my own. I didn't have to worry, didn't have to think. All I had to do was put myself in his domineering hands, and he would see to my every need.

A soft sound whispered through the room, and I turned my face slightly so I could see what he was doing.

My mouth went dry when I saw him finish pulling his belt from his slacks where they lay abandoned on the floor. He curved the length of black leather, doubling it over before slapping it against his hand. The resultant *crack* made the fine hairs on the back of my neck stand on end.

"Easy," he soothed me, touching the cool leather against my spine, starting at my nape and slowly drawing it down to my ass. "You have your safe words," he reminded me. "I want you to use them if you need to. If everything's okay, tell me you're *green*. Do you understand?"

"Yes," I said, my voice small.

His palm smacked my ass in a light rebuke. "Address me properly."

"Yes, Sir," I said, more clearly.

He stroked me in reward. God, it felt so good when he trailed his calloused fingers over my heated skin, petting me as though I truly was his kitten. I certainly felt small when he towered over me like this, and although his belt loomed, I felt cherished, too. I decided I didn't at all mind being Jason's favorite pet.

I barely had time to register the sound of leather cutting through the air before the first hit landed. The impact shocked me first, and then my body lurched forward as the sting bloomed across my skin. My fingers curled into the sheets, and I sucked in a sharp breath.

Jason's firm hands settled around my hips, guiding me back into position.

"Are you okay, kitten?" he asked kindly, his fingers soothing the burning stripe on my ass. My nerve endings lit up with pleasure as the soothing touch contrasted with the sting. The burn turned to a delicious heat that sank through my skin, permeating my flesh until it reached my sex. My pussy lips began to swell, and wetness gathered at my core.

I blew out a shuddering sigh. "Green," I responded.

"Good girl. I need you to stay still. I don't want a hit landing somewhere unintentional. Can you do that for me?" His deep voice slid over my skin in a silken caress, his tenderness calming me further.

"Yes, Sir."

"You're being very brave for me. I'm proud of you."

I glowed at the praise. No one ever told me they

were proud of me, no matter how hard I worked. My mother was withholding, to put it mildly, and my father had always been rather disinterested.

But Jason cared. I felt a connection with him that was completely foreign to me, yet utterly enthralling. Warmth flooded my chest, and I arched my back, welcoming him to continue the torment that brought me such pleasure.

"Such a sweet kitten," he said, and I glowed as he lavished praise on me. "That first lash was to test you. I'll warm you up before the next one. I want you to relax into the pain. Do you understand what I mean?"

"I'm not sure," I said truthfully.

"You will," he promised. "You were made for this."

His confidence in me bolstered my own, and I relaxed against the mattress, waiting for the next blow. It didn't shock me like the first one. It was little more than a slight slap, eliciting heat but not the fierce sting he'd inflicted before. He delivered a twin hit on my other cheek before taking up a steady rhythm, spreading the heat evenly across my ass. My pussy began to ache, and my clit throbbed in time with each blow. A low moan left my chest as I surrendered to the blissful torment. I craved for him to fuck me, to fill me. But I desired to please him even more, and now he wanted to whip me and reveal the darkest facets of my sexuality. His pleasure washed over me, magnifying my own. It was more than physical ecstasy. This was a soul-deep satisfaction that made my heart swell until I felt it might burst with joy.

Warm tears trailed down my cheeks, but I was barely aware of them. All I could do was bask in his power over me. I was drunk on it, and I floated in intoxicating bliss, even as he increased the snap of the belt against my skin. It didn't sting anymore. Each hit thudded into me, applying a steady ache deep in my flesh. I sighed and settled into it, embracing the sensation rather than gritting my teeth and fighting through the pain.

The belt whipped against my sensitive thighs, one after the other. I shrieked as the pain flashed through me, more intense than anything that had come before it. Before I could contemplate using a safe word, he began to stroke my heated, hypersensitive skin. I heard the belt drop to the floor.

"It's over, kitten." His voice floated to me though my lust-drunk haze, his calm reassurance threading through my mind. "You did very well. I'm so proud of you."

I groaned as pleasure washed over me at his words. My entire being was flooded with physical and emotional ecstasy. I felt at peace, and yet, something was still missing. I needed him inside me, connecting us in the closest way possible.

"Please fuck me, Sir," I begged, my voice soft and husky.

"With pleasure," he rumbled.

The mattress dipped as he settled himself on his knees behind me. His hard cock lined up with my slick entrance, and he eased in slowly, allowing me to revel in the sensation of him stretching me wide as my body eagerly ceded to him.

"Fuck, you are so perfect," he said raggedly before withdrawing at the same torturously slow pace.

I whimpered at the torment. I wanted him to take me hard, to brand me with his ferocious heat. But his fingers curved into my hips, holding me where he wanted me as he dictated the rhythm.

By the time he finally increased his pace, I was whining and writhing beneath him, desperate for more. I moaned in relief when he abruptly slammed into me, his cockhead rubbing against my g-spot. His hips hit my abused ass, the little flare of pain reminding me of his complete domination of my entire being.

The knowledge that I belonged to him pushed me over the edge, and my inner walls began to flutter around him.

"That's it," he ground out. "Come for me."

I exploded with a harsh cry, my ecstasy ripping through me. Bliss sang through my veins, emanating out from my core to my fingers and toes.

His fist tangled in my hair, and he tugged, forcing my back to arch so he could take me more deeply. His free hand reached beneath me to pinch my clit.

"More," he demanded.

A ragged scream tore its way up my throat as stars popped across my vision. I convulsed around him, and his cock pulsed inside me. He roared out his pleasure as his heat lashed deep inside me, branding me like I craved.

"You're mine," he snarled as he pumped out the last of his orgasm. "Tell me."

"Yes," I gasped out. "Yours."

He gripped my waist and rolled, remaining seated inside me as he settled us on our sides. Exhaustion washed over me, and I drifted into blissful sleep as he stroked my hair and murmured words of praise.

❧

JASON'S LOW MOAN WOKE ME. HE WASN'T HOLDING me anymore, and I felt bereft without his touch. At first, I thought it was a sound of pleasure, but then an unmistakably pained groan slipped through his clenched teeth. His eyes were closed, but a sheen of sweat covered his body, and his muscles were tense.

"Jason?" I asked tentatively. His only response was to shudder. "Jason," I said more insistently, shaking him awake.

His eyes snapped open, and he moved faster than my tired brain could comprehend. He rolled on top of me, pinning me with a snarl. His forearm rested against my throat, applying too much pressure. I grasped at him, trying to push him away. But now that he had the upper hand, he was too strong for me to overpower.

"Jason," I choked out his name. It was barely intelligible as I forced it through my constricted throat. When he didn't ease up, I struggled against my instinct to fight. I released his arm and cupped his cheeks in my hands. "Wake up," I begged. His eyes might be open, but he was still trapped in his nightmare. "I need you."

Slowly, the harsh lines of his face eased, melting from rage to horror. He rolled off me in a flash, scooting away from me as though I'd burned him.

"Fuck. Oh, fuck." He scrubbed a hand over his face. "I'm so sorry. Are you—" His teeth snapped closed before he could finish asking if I was okay.

"I'm fine," I responded, suppressing the urge to rub my throat. "I'm okay. But you're not." I reached for him, and he flinched away. I withdrew slowly, sensing that he needed space. "What happened?" I pressed softly.

He tore his eyes from mine, his cheeks coloring with shame. "I told you I'm broken," he said bitterly. "I never should have let you near me. I can't trust myself right now."

"You said you've seen some bad things," I prompted gently. "Do you have PTSD? Is that why you were taking pills?"

His gaze snapped back to mine, his eyes burning. "I thought I could control it. But I can't control anything. Not my thoughts. Not myself. I attacked you. Fuck!"

"I'm fine," I reiterated. "And I understand. I studied Psychology, remember? It's not uncommon for people in law enforcement to turn to drugs to deal with what they've seen. You said you're trying to get better. You're not using anymore. Are you in therapy?"

"Yes," he bit out. "It's mandatory. I won't be allowed back into the field until the doctor clears me for duty. I'd thought I was making progress, but clearly, I'm not. I hurt you."

"You didn't," I said firmly. When I reached for him this time, I didn't stop when he tried to pull away. I boldly took his hand in mine, pressing my palm against his and threading our fingers together. "I told you that you can lean on me," I reminded him. "Let me in. Let me help you."

He shook his head. "I can't be near you right now. Maybe when I finish treatment, we can try again. It's better that way. Then you won't have to risk everything you've worked for."

"It is not better that way," I insisted. "You don't have to be alone with this. I won't let you."

He let out a hoarse laugh. "Why did I have to fall for such a bossy woman?"

My breath caught at his inadvertent admission. "I'm falling for you, too," I said quietly. "I don't want to be apart from you, not when you're going through hell. Not when I know I can help you. Will you tell me what happened? What did you see?"

He pressed his lips to a firm line.

I squeezed his hand. "Let me in," I urged again. "Please."

"Do you remember the Water Tower Place terror attack?" he asked, his voice dropping to a hollow monotone. "I was there. It was... horrible." A small shudder ran though him, and I gripped his hand more tightly to anchor him to me. "Before I joined the Bureau, I was an Army Ranger. I saw fucked up things then, too. But they didn't debilitate me. I'd served and protected. I'd done good things. But this...

It was carnage. And every horrific thing I'd ever seen spilled out of some place where it had been locked in my head."

"You blame yourself," I surmised quietly. When he was a Ranger, he'd been able to cope with the traumatic things he'd seen because he thought he was fighting for the greater good. But something about facing the aftermath of the terror attack had been different for him. Guilt had set in. I could see it in the anguished lines around his eyes and mouth, and my background in Psychology made me familiar with traits common in those who suffered from PTSD.

"You sound like Dr. Larson," he said.

"Then Dr. Larson must know what she's talking about. Why do you feel responsible for the terror attack?"

"Because I failed them," he said heavily. "I joined the Bureau to protect them, but they were innocent civilians. I should have prevented it. If I were better at my job, if I weren't a failure—"

"You're not a failure," I cut him off. "That's your father's voice in your head. You couldn't have seen that attack coming. No one did."

He blew out a long sigh. "Dr. Larson said the same thing."

I nodded my approval. "She sounds like a good fit for you, then. I'm not going to be your therapist," I reassured him, "but I do want to be here for you. You can talk to me. You're safe with me."

"But you're not safe with me," he said, his voice strained.

I ran my fingers through his hair, soothing him as he did for me. "You say you need me to trust you, and I do. Now I need you to trust me. I can help you. I want to. Please let me. Don't push me away."

"I don't think I can push you away," he said hoarsely. "I'm a selfish bastard for it, but I want you."

"I want you, too," I breathed. "We'll be more careful. We can meet here to be together while we're at Quantico. Once I graduate, we won't have to hide anymore."

"I'm going to get better," he swore. "I'm going to be better for you. When I'm cleared to go back into the field, I'll request a transfer to wherever they assign you."

My heart swelled. "You mean that? I know we haven't known each other long, but I feel—"

He silenced me with a fierce kiss, taking my mouth deeply and thoroughly, until my head spun. He pulled back slightly, just far enough that we shared every breath.

"I feel it, too," he said. "I'm not letting you go."

I smiled. "I wasn't going to let you."

He grinned. "My bossy little kitten. I think you need a reminder of who's in charge."

He flipped me onto my back and drove into me. My body welcomed him, prepared for him under any circumstances. He made love to me, long and hard. We weren't ready to say it aloud yet. It was far too soon for that. But I felt it just the same. When I shattered in his arms, I allowed his name to issue from my lips, imbuing it with the words I couldn't say.

I love you.

CHAPTER 12

Jason

Seventeen Weeks Later

"**W**hat's this?" Natalie asked as she trailed her fingers over the red satin corset.

"A corset," I responded, smiling.

She rolled her eyes at me. "I know that. I meant, why did you bring it? It'll be harder to fuck me if I'm wearing that. Wouldn't you prefer me like this?" She gestured down at her naked body.

I'd stripped her as soon as we'd made it to the safety of the motel room that had become our secret meeting place. I remained in my suit, denying her when she tried to undress me. She'd made her cute little pout, but by now, she was accustomed to the power dynamic between us.

I closed the distance between us and ran a reverent hand down her side, exploring the curve of her hip. Every time felt like the first time. I couldn't get enough of her, even though I'd had her beneath me dozens of times. I'd never tire of exploring her body.

"You're perfect like this," I told her. "But I don't think you're ready for me to show off your naked body to a room full of strangers."

She gasped, but the way her pupils dilated told me she was intrigued by the perverse prospect. I filed that away for later.

"What are you talking about?" she asked, perhaps more breathily than she'd intended.

"I'm taking you to a BDSM club."

She blinked. "There are clubs? Why would we go to one?"

"Consider it a graduation celebration." Natalie finished training at the end of next week, and her graduation was already guaranteed. Soon, we wouldn't have to hide our relationship. "A coming out party."

"And I have to wear a corset?" She eyed the ensemble I'd selected for her, including the tiny black lace skirt. "No way will that cover my ass."

I grinned. "That's the idea."

She touched the final item I'd laid out for her. "And what's this? Don't tell me they're..." She swallowed, recognizing very clearly what was attached to the black headband.

"Those are your ears, kitten."

She looked at me levelly. "I'm not actually a cat."

"No. You're my little sex kitten. And I want everyone to know it." I reached into my pocket to retrieve her final surprise. "That's why I got you this."

She stared at the thin strip of black leather. "Is that a *collar*? Really Jason, this is silly."

I cupped her pussy, teasing two fingers between her wet folds. "Is it?" I challenged. "If it's so silly, why are you creaming all over my hand?"

She flushed a gorgeous shade of pink and cut her eyes away. I touched the collar beneath her chin, allowing her to feel the supple leather as I redirected her gaze to mine.

"The collar isn't about making you my pet. Although I think you like that idea," I said with confidence as her slick juices slid over my fingers. "The collar marks you as mine." I stared into her lovely sapphire eyes, peering straight into her soul. "I love you, Natalie," I finally said the words for the first time, and a sense of completion settled over me. I'd craved to tell her how I felt for months, but now I could finally say it. "Dr. Larson cleared me to go back into the field," I told her. "As soon as you're given your assignment, I'll put in my transfer request."

She threw her arms around me and buried her face in the crook of my neck. "I love you too," she said, her voice hitching with emotion. "God, I've loved you for so long." She pulled back so she could study my face. "I knew you could do it," she said fervently. "I knew you could get better. And if you ever have an episode, I'll be here to support you."

"I know you will." I'd been humbled by her unwavering support during the course of my treatment. And the trust she placed in me, the sense of personal power I found in her willing submission, bolstered me in a way I'd never have thought possible. "I couldn't have done it without you," I said, my own voice cracking.

"I'm so proud of you." It wasn't the first time she'd said it, but every time she did, I couldn't help but marvel at her praise. My father had never offered a kind word, and my mother had left him when I was too young to even remember her.

Natalie gave me everything I'd so desperately needed to be complete: control, confidence, love. Even before the drugs, I'd lived my life to spite my father. It had been a hollow, ugly way to live. Now, I lived for *her*.

"I love you so much." I couldn't help saying it again. The words had been locked in my chest for so long, and it was the sweetest relief to release them at last.

She beamed at me. "I love you, Jason."

"Will you accept my collar?" I asked, desperate to put it around her delicate throat, to mark her as mine forever.

"If it means I'm yours, then of course I will."

"Lift your hair for me." I'd intended for the command to be gentle, but it came out rough with the depth of my emotion.

She complied immediately, exposing her neck to me. With reverent hands, I encircled her throat with the thin strip of leather. She stared into my eyes as I buckled it closed at her nape, her breath catching as I secured it in place. I traced the line of the collar with my fingertips before hooking my finger through the silver ring set into the front of the leather. I tugged her toward me, and she gasped as I imposed my control over her. I caught the soft sound on my lips, tasting it on my tongue. I took long minutes to savor her, exploring the feel of my collar around her throat, reveling in the fact that she was mine.

"I'm your Master now," I told her when I finally came up for air.

Her brow furrowed. "My Master?"

"Yes. I'm your Master, and you're my sub."

"Can't you be... I don't know, my boyfriend?"

I chuckled. "Do you want me to just be your boyfriend?"

She took a moment to consider. "No," she finally decided. "I guess that's not enough. And you're definitely not a *boy*," she purred the last, grinding her hips against my hard cock.

"I'm glad you think so. I want you to be so much more than my girlfriend, kitten. We're in a D/s relationship now. You belong to me."

"And you belong to me," she said fiercely.

"Always," I promised.

I kissed her again, lingering for a few minutes longer. Finally, I pulled away. "Time to get dressed," I prompted. "I reserved a room for us, and I don't want them to give it to someone else if we're late."

"All right," she agreed, reaching for the outfit I'd laid out. She quickly shimmied into the barely-there skirt and strappy black high heels I'd provided. I helped her into the corset, taking my time to cinch it tightly around her, making sure she felt bound by me even though she wasn't restrained. The way her skin pebbled in response let me know she felt my power slipping over her. She was so goddamn beautiful in her submission.

When I finished lacing the corset, I grasped her

shoulders and turned her so she was facing me. I picked up the headband and slipped it on so it was nestled in her dark hair. Somehow, she managed to look absolutely adorable and insanely sexy at the same time: my perfect little sex kitten.

I gripped her waist and guided her over to the mirror so she could see herself. Fuck, she looked like a wet dream in her sensual outfit, with my collar around her throat. She touched her fingers to it, examining it.

"What do you think?" I murmured against her hair.

"I love it," she whispered. She met my eyes in the mirror. "I love you."

"I love you too, sweet kitten." I'd never tire of saying it. "I have something else for you before we leave."

I shifted her so she faced the wall, and I directed her arms to either side of her head, pressing her palms flat against the wood paneling.

"Stay," I ordered before leaving her briefly to retrieve the toy from my overnight bag.

She craned her head back to watch me, and she licked her lips at the sight of the anal plug. My grin was a touch savage as I lubed it up and returned to her. I peeled her skirt up, exposing her gorgeous ass.

"Present yourself to me," I commanded.

Keeping her hands on the wall, she took a step back, arching toward me and spreading her legs so she was open for me.

"Good girl." I pressed the tip of the plug against her asshole, and it eased inside her. When it was halfway in, she began to pant and squirm. I swatted her ass in reprimand. "Be still."

"But it's so big," she protested.

"It's not as big as me, and I'll be fucking this tight little hole tonight. I've been training you for this. I'm going to claim you in every way possible. Your body is mine. Mine to play with; mine to torment; mine to command. And tonight, you're going to give me your virgin ass." She whimpered as I began to slowly pump the plug in and out of her, stretching her a little more with each gentle thrust. "You want that, don't you? I know you love when I plug your ass and fill you up. You've wished it were my cock, haven't you?"

"Yes," she whined. "Yes, I want that. I want you inside me."

I nipped at her shoulder. "Yes, *Master*," I corrected her.

"Master," she moaned out my new title. My cock strained against my slacks, aching to get inside her and claim her fully.

"Later," I ground out, for my benefit as much as hers. "You're going to wear this for me until you can't find the words to beg for release. I want you desperate, helpless. Then I'll give you what you want."

The widest part of the plug slid past her tight ring of muscles, and she closed around it. I tugged on the base, but the large toy remained firmly seated inside her. She mewled, sounding like a needy little kitten. I'd chosen her name well.

I smoothed her skirt down, covering her as much as the tight scrap of fabric would allow. I slipped my jacket over her shoulders, hiding her scandalous outfit. I didn't want anyone seeing her like this until we arrived at the club.

She walked beside me on unsteady legs, her face tight with concentration as she stepped carefully. I knew she'd feel the plug shifting inside her as she moved, and it only made me crave her more. She was being so good for me, so compliant and perfectly submissive to my will. I could hardly wait to claim her ass for the first time, but I wouldn't have that pleasure for quite some time.

It took half an hour to drive to the warehouse district where the club was hidden, and even once we arrived, I had to wait a while longer before I could have her. My plans for her dictated that we both wait, and the control I exercised over myself as well as her made me feel more powerful than ever.

When we entered the club, she stared around

with open fascination. I allowed her to observe our surroundings as I slid my jacket off her shoulders and handed it over at the coat check. Several interested gazes swung her way when I revealed her corseted figure. A strange mixture of possessive fury and intense pride washed over me.

I hooked my finger through the ring at the front of her collar and pulled her into me for a scorching kiss, making sure everyone knew she belonged to me. She opened for me, surrendering on a sigh. I indulged in her pliant mouth for several long seconds before giving her space to breathe. Then I wrapped my arm around her waist and tucked her close to my side as I moved us deeper into the club.

I didn't pause in the bar or the casual seating area. I was too intent on getting her to the private room I'd reserved to show her around properly. Although she jolted when a high, ecstatic scream emanated from the public dungeon, I didn't allow her time to stare at the display.

"We can explore later," I promised. "There's so much I want to show you. But I don't want to lose our room."

I continued to lead her around the busy dance floor, toward the corridor that led to the private rooms. We passed a woman who gyrated her completely naked body against a leather-clad man.

"I don't have to get naked in front of everyone, do I?" she asked, hesitant.

"No," I reassured her. "We're going somewhere private."

"But then why did we need to come here?"

I shot her a wicked grin. "Because the motel doesn't provide us with bondage furniture." I turned more serious. "This is the world I live in, Natalie. I want you to be part of it. But if you're not comfortable here, just say the word and we'll never come to a club again."

She glanced around at the kinky opulence that surrounded us. "I... No. I don't want to leave. But I don't think I'm ready for any public displays."

"As much as I'd love to show you off, I think I'd have to gouge the eyes out of any man who dared to look at you the wrong way," I admitted. "Come. Let's go to our room."

I kept my arm braced around her waist as I guided her down the corridor, supporting her as she teetered on her high heels. She was becoming more affected by the plug inside her now that we were in the club. It had been tormenting her ever since I'd put it in, but now she was becoming aroused by our devious surroundings. Sounds of pleasure and pain layered with the deep, throbbing beat of sensual music. I could feel it vibrate in my bones, and I was sure it was making her pretty pussy wet.

We arrived at the room I'd requested, and I was grateful to find the door ajar. No one had taken the space yet.

I led her over the threshold and locked the door behind us, ensuring our privacy. While she stared at the equipment—a St. Andrew's cross, spanking bench, and huge iron four-poster bed built for bondage—I began to loosen the laces on her corset. The hooks at the front eased, and the garment dropped to the floor. I slid her skirt down her legs, leaving her completely bare except for her fuck-me heels, collar, and cute little kitten ears. And the red base of the plug that was nestled between her ass cheeks.

I grasped her hands in mine and led her over to the spanking bench, guiding her to bend over the padded top. She didn't offer any resistance as I buckled her wrists and ankles in place. She was perfectly sweet and trusting in her submission to me.

She was the most beautiful fucking thing I'd ever seen.

I took several minutes to study her in rapt silence, watching the wetness glisten between her thighs as she began to wriggle her hips in anticipation. I allowed her to press her clit against the edge of the spanking bench, and she began to pant as carnal craving overtook her.

"Please," she begged. "Please fuck me, Master."

"Soon, kitten," I promised. "But I'm not going to fuck that pretty pussy. Do you want me to claim your virgin ass?"

"Yes, please. I want it. I want you."

"I don't think you're ready just yet," I said, drawing out the moment, tormenting her with sensual anticipation. "I want that perfect ass nice and red. I want to mark you so you know you're owned. You'll feel it every time I thrust into you. Do you want that? To be owned by me?"

"Yes," she moaned. "Yes, I'm yours. Please."

I touched the collar at her nape, satisfaction settling deep in my chest. "That's right, kitten. You are mine. Always."

I stroked her hair a few times, petting her until she calmed and relaxed against the bench, no longer trying to seek pleasure without my permission. When she surrendered fully, I left her briefly to retrieve the item I'd requested to be left in the room for my use: a new black leather paddle.

Natalie had felt the sting of my hand and my belt, but this was my first opportunity to introduce her to kinkier forms of impact play. We'd discovered that she enjoyed a bite of pain to send her into subspace, and I fully intended to take her to that place of complete abandon before I fucked her tight little ass for the first time.

I lifted the paddle from where it hung on a peg on the wall and returned to Natalie. She studied it with keen interest. I slapped it against my palm a few times, allowing her to savor the sharp *snap* of leather hitting flesh. Her tongue snaked out to lick her lips, and my mouth twisted in a knowing smirk. My kitten wanted me to paddle her pretty ass.

I was more than happy to oblige.

I stepped beside her, positioning myself at her hip. I touched the cool leather to her skin, tracing the line of her spine from her nape to her ass. She shivered and whined, thrusting her ass out in wanton invitation of the first strike.

"Greedy kitten," I chuckled.

She let out a sharp cry at the first hit, but it was more a sound of surprise than pain. I gave her a second hit on the opposite cheek, and she gasped. She jerked against her restraints, as though she could alleviate the sting if she wiggled enough. I allowed her to struggle for a few seconds, enjoying watching her beautiful body writhe helplessly against the bench. After a while, she took several deep breaths and stilled.

"Good girl," I praised before raining down sharp,

rapid blows. I spread the sting around her flesh, heating her skin until her ass glowed bright red. She moaned and whined, but she didn't cry out again until I slapped her sensitive upper thighs. She threw back her head with a shriek, and I stopped tormenting her. I dropped the paddle and ran my fingernails over her enflamed skin. A low groan left her chest, and her head dropped forward as her muscles relaxed. I continued to pet her until her breathing turned deep and even, her eyes sliding out of focus.

She was ready for me.

I gently gripped the base of the red plug and slowly worked it out of her ass. She whimpered when it slid free, a wordless protest at being left empty. Her pussy glistened with arousal, her labia puffy and pink with desire. I was careful not to touch her there. I didn't want to make her come until I was pushing inside her.

I set the plug aside and retrieved some lube from a pump by the bench. After ensuring my cock was slick enough to ease into her without causing her too much discomfort, I lined my dick up with her puckered entrance.

She'd be relaxed in her current headspace, and the plug had prepared her for me. Still, she'd never taken my cock in her ass before, and there was some resistance when I pressed against her. She whined and wriggled, her mind in a primal place of pure need and carnal instinct.

My fingers curved into her hip, steadying her. At the same time, I reached beneath her with my free hand and stroked her clit. A sharp cry left her lips, and my cockhead eased past her tight ring of muscles. She contracted around me, her body torn between pushing me out and welcoming me in. I groaned through gritted teeth, staving off my own impending orgasm. She was so tight it made stars dance around the edges of my vision, and the intensity of claiming her in this way for the first time sent me into my own animal headspace.

I continued to play with her clit, but the movements of my fingers were less refined than usual. It was all I could do to keep myself from gripping her hips in both hands and driving all the way into her tight heat.

I sucked in deep, desperate breaths as I slowly worked my way in, her body ceding to mine, even as she squeezed my cock.

"Don't come," I warned. "Not yet. Not until I give permission."

She whimpered, but she didn't orgasm, even though I knew her body was right on the edge.

"Good kitten," I praised as sweat beaded on my

brow. If she came, it would trigger my own release, and I wasn't anywhere near ready for this exquisite torture to end.

Finally, my balls pressed against her hot pussy, and I entered her fully. I held myself there for several seconds, breathing hard and savoring the feel of her inner muscles fluttering around me. Then I withdrew slowly, a long drag until only my cockhead remained inside her. A purely animal sound left her lips, a ragged, helpless cry.

I couldn't hold back any longer. I began to pump in and out of her, going a little deeper with each thrust. She continued to make impossibly sexy, primal sounds as I took her harder, faster. Finally, I slammed all the way into her. She pushed back to meet my thrust, welcoming my harsh claiming. I increased my pace to something raw and almost punishing.

"Come for me," I commanded. The words were barely intelligible, but she understood.

She threw her head back on a scream, and her muscles clamped down on my cock as her body spasmed in pleasure. I roared out in tormented ecstasy as my cum began to lash into her, marking her deep inside. I thrust in one last time, keeping us connected through the final wracking tremors of our mutual bliss.

My body was weak and shaking in the aftermath,

but I wasn't willing to leave her yet. I stayed inside her as I leaned over her, pressing a kiss against the collar at her nape. She purred and twisted her head to the side, offering her neck to me. I licked and nibbled and kissed the sensitive spot beneath her ear. She shivered and sighed, floating in her blissful headspace.

"I love you, sweet kitten," I murmured against her soft skin.

"I love you, my Master," she said in a lust-drunk slur.

She was innocently adorable and achingly erotic. Her perfection drove me to the edge of sanity. I'd do anything for her, go anywhere she led. In a few days, I'd follow her to wherever the Bureau assigned her, and we'd make a life together. We wouldn't have to hide our love anymore.

I could hardly wait to have her in my bed and in my heart forever.

CHAPTER 13

Jason

"**I** don't like it," I struggled to remain calm as I challenged Director Parkinson. "I don't want Natalie Simmons in the field with Trent McMahon. Not even for a test run."

The Director's brows rose. "Are you questioning my judgment? Let me remind you that it's within my power to keep you here at Quantico. Dr. Larson might have cleared you to go back in the field, but ultimately, it's up to me."

My fists clenched, and I forced my fingers to unfurl. "With all due respect, I don't trust McMahon. I know this is a test mission, but the team could still get into trouble if they don't support each other properly."

"And that's exactly why I'm pairing them together," she replied pointedly. "I'm well aware that Simmons and McMahon don't like each other. There have been rumors among the recruits since the first week. The way I hear it, she nearly broke his jaw twice."

"He deserved it," I said, before I could stop myself. I was coming dangerously close to revealing Trent's abusive nature. And if I did, he'd go public with the video he had of Natalie and me in my car. I couldn't allow that to happen. Not when we were so close to being together, away from Quantico.

"Yes, I wouldn't be surprised if he did," Parkinson responded coolly. "I'm also aware of McMahon's relationship with Elena Briggs. She'll be on the same team, as will Simmons' friend, Nathaniel Cross. The point of this exercise is to prove to me that they can work together, regardless of their personal feelings. Once they're assigned to a field office, they might not like everyone they work with. That can't interfere with their ability to do their jobs. If the four recruits can make it through this op without turning on each other, they'll all graduate. If not, I'll have to reconsider my assessments. That's my final judgment on this situation, Harper. You're dismissed."

I gnashed my teeth together, but I turned stiffly and strode out of her office. I couldn't argue with her, or I'd risk Natalie's career, and my chances of getting to be with her outside Quantico. If Parkinson decided to keep me here rather than putting me back in the field, I'd be separated from my sweet kitten. I didn't know if I could maintain my sanity without her. I'd become shockingly dependent on her in the span of a few months, but I didn't even care. I refused to be parted from her, and I'd do everything in my power to ensure we were together, even if that meant allowing her out on an op with McMahon.

Parkinson might have forbidden me from putting a stop to it, but that didn't mean I couldn't have a hand in the proceedings. As an instructor, I had every right to monitor their movements, and I'd make sure I was on one of the comm units as they were tested. I'd be with Natalie every step of the way, even if I couldn't be there with her physically.

I hated the distance between us. I hadn't even been able to say a proper goodbye before she was shipped off earlier this morning. The entire class had been sent away on various missions, separated into smaller groups, as they would be in a real scenario once they were part of a field office. This was their final test. And while the ops were fairly routine and would each be overseen by a senior agent, I still worried for Natalie, knowing that she'd have McMahon at her back.

I made my way to the room where the tech geeks would be gathered around their computers, monitoring the recruits' progress. When I entered, a few of my fellow instructors nodded at me in acknowledgement. I hadn't bothered to make friends while at Quantico, but we all respected one another. They wouldn't be nearly so respectful if they were aware of the addiction that had brought me here, but Parkinson had kept my secret.

The room was filled with large monitors that displayed the feed from the body cams worn by each recruit. I spotted Natalie on one of the screens, caught from three different angles: McMahon, Cross, and Briggs were all within view of her. She led their small group, one step behind the agent in charge.

I strode over to the monitor and towered over the analyst who was watching them. Feeling my presence, he looked up at me. I held out my hand.

"Give me your comm unit." I imbued my tone with the ring of command.

The man didn't hesitate to take off his headset and hand it over to me. When I stared at him for a few seconds longer, he hurriedly vacated his chair, and I took his place.

"Give me an update," I said into the receiver attached to the headset.

"Ja— Agent Harper?" Natalie questioned.

"I'm here," I reassured her. "I want a status report."

"We're moving in now," McMahon said in an angry undertone. "We don't have time to chat."

"I gave you an order, McMahon," I said, a steely warning.

"We came to case this building because there have been rumors that the Latin Kings have dealers set up here," Cross supplied quickly. "We're moving up one floor at a time. Almost on floor three now."

I could see from their body cams that they were in a brick-lined stairwell in what appeared to be a dilapidated apartment block. My chest tightened with worry. I didn't like the thought of Natalie confronting dealers affiliated with the Kings. I took a breath and tried to calm myself. This was what she had trained for, and she was going to be a damn good agent. I had to trust in her abilities.

This is routine, I reminded myself. *They're just asking the residents some questions.*

I'd barely finished my internal reassurance when the pop of gunfire exploded through the comm unit. The senior agent leading the group went down, leaving the recruits exposed. Natalie went for her gun. Her hand was on it when gunfire sprayed into the stairwell, echoing in a horrific, staccato rhythm. Her body jerked, and she fell back against Cross.

"Natalie!" My shout mingled with the panicked curses of the recruits that rang in my ears.

I watched as Cross dragged her back into cover. Briggs and McMahon had their weapons drawn and were returning fire, but they were shooting blind. The turn in the stairs only allowed them to pepper the air with bullets rather than aiming true. There was no way they could see their assailants without stepping out and exposing themselves.

I was peripherally aware of this, and I only took note of it so I could assess Natalie's chances of getting out.

"Get a team there now!" I barked out at anyone who would listen, keeping my eyes trained on the monitor.

"Cross, what's going on?" I demanded as gunfire continued to deafen me.

"Natalie!" he shouted. "Oh fuck, oh fuck."

Horrible, wet, choking noises bored into my brain, but I couldn't accept that they were coming from her. Cross cradled her in his arms, shielding her body with his own. A gory stain spread across her crisp white shirt.

"Shit, shit!" Cross pressed his hand against the wound, and a strangled cry left her lips.

"Trent!" Briggs screamed in the chaos. "Get up, get up! Nathaniel, help him!"

"I'm not leaving you," Cross promised Natalie.

Blood trickled from the corner of her perfect lips. She reached up and gripped Cross' shirt. "Run," she gasped out. "You have to run."

"Get her out of there, Cross," I snarled through my panic.

"No," Natalie groaned. "I'm sorry, Jason. I'm so sorry."

"Don't you say you're sorry," I shouted. "Say you're coming back to me. Cross, move!"

He grunted, and I watched as his body jerked. "I'm hit."

"Nathaniel!" Briggs screamed. "I need cover!"

"Don't you dare leave her, Cross," I ground out.

"I won't," he promised.

"You have to go," Natalie insisted raggedly. She coughed, and blood sprayed from her lips, leaving dark droplets on Cross' body cam. "Jason, I need you to promise me. Promise me you'll be okay."

"Stop it." I tried to command her, but it came out as a ragged plea. "I'm not promising you anything until you come back to me."

"You're so strong," she said, her eyes sliding out of

focus. "Don't let your father..." Her chest convulsed. Cross pressed down harder on her wound. Crimson streams spilled over his fingers, but she didn't seem to feel the pain. "Promise me. Jason..." A horrible rattle sounded in the back of her throat. Her eyelids drooped, and she stared up at nothing.

"Natalie!" I yelled out, willing her to wake up. "Don't you leave me. Don't you dare. I love you. Do you hear me? I fucking love you."

The monitor went black. "Someone get them back online!" I shouted, searching the room for help. A few analysts were scrambling at their computers, trying to recover the feed. The rest of the instructors were staring at me, some with pity, others with open disgust.

I could still hear Cross.

"She's gone," he said, his voice weak. "Fuck. Her heartbeat. I can't feel it. I can't—"

The gunfire stopped. White noise filled my ears.

"Natalie! Natalie!" Wet heat streamed down my cheeks.

She's gone.

A terrible, anguished roar echoed throughout the room. I didn't recognize that the sound was ripped from my own chest.

PART II
BREAKING

CHAPTER 14

Jason

"They're dead, Harper. Cross, Briggs, McMahon, and Simmons. As well as Agent Thurman, who was the senior agent assigned to their group. They're all gone."

"That's not true!" I railed, my raw voice booming through Parkinson's office. "The body cams cut out. We don't know—"

"They're dead," she said again, more sharply. There was no pity in her expression. She regarded me with contempt, her thin lips twisted in disgust. "The families have been notified. There will be funeral arrangements if you—"

"There won't be a fucking funeral," I snarled. "She's not dead. She can't be."

"You watched the footage yourself before the cameras malfunctioned," she said coldly. "Simmons died. You watched while she died. Cross confirmed it before he was killed, too."

Jason... I could still hear her voice in my head, and the horrible rattle in her throat that I refused to acknowledge. Her eyes had gone blank, her expression slack.

"We didn't get footage of the shooters," Parkinson continued, "but we believe the Latin Kings are behind it. The team was investigating their activities when they went in."

"They never should have been sent in the first place," I shouted. "They weren't prepared for a shootout. You told them it would be routine questions. Maybe call in the local PD for an arrest. That was all you said it would be. You were wrong!"

"Yes," she said bitterly. "I was wrong. We went in on the information we had to work with. But even if they had been established field agents, they would have faced the same scenario. It's regrettable that—"

"Regrettable?" I flung at her. "You got five people killed, and you're saying it's *regrettable?*"

Her eyes narrowed. "I won't be judged by you.

This is a dangerous job. They chose it. They took an oath and made a sacrifice that—"

"A *sacrifice*?" I cut her off again, raging at her. "What did they sacrifice for? What did we achieve from this? Nothing! She died for nothing." My voice gave out on the last as I admitted the truth aloud.

Her eyes... They'd lost their sparkle, their life. I'd seen death before. I knew what it looked like.

"We're launching further investigation into the Latin Kings' activities in that neighborhood," Parkinson said calmly, as though I wasn't breaking down, as though she wasn't watching a man's soul ripping apart right in front of her.

"I want to be there," I seethed, the burning need for vengeance clouding over my burgeoning grief. I couldn't face the agony, so I'd embrace the fury. "Put me back in the field."

Her lips pressed to a thin line. "You are going back in the field. I don't have a choice in that matter. But I'm sending you to Chicago. You won't be working in the D.C. area. You're not coming near this case."

"What?" I burst out. "You can't do that. You can't do that to me!"

"I can and I will," she said grimly. "You initiated a relationship with a recruit. I won't have a predator here at Quantico. I gave you a second chance when you came here as an addict, and you've only proven to me that you're not fit to be an agent. But your father won't let me fire you. So I'm sending you back to Chicago."

A predator? "I love her," I seethed, unable to say it in the past tense.

"Then I'm sorry for your loss," she replied, still ice cold. "But I won't have you here any longer. You leave for Chicago tomorrow. Pack your things and get off my base."

I slammed my fists against her desk as rage ripped through me.

"Now, Harper," she barked. "Or I'll have you forcibly removed. Then your father won't be able to cover up your mess, and you'll be out of the Bureau for good."

I snarled, but I turned and stalked out of her office. I had to get out. If I stayed for one second longer, I wasn't at all certain I'd be able to stop myself from attacking Parkinson. She'd gotten Natalie...

Killed.

She's dead. She's dead.

I ran outside and vomited into the bushes, my body rebelling against the truth.

I couldn't do this. I couldn't live without her.

Low, derisive whispers threaded through my mind, and I realized I was attracting an audience. I couldn't face them. The next person who met my eye would get their neck snapped. Impotent rage clawed at my insides, demanding to be unleashed on someone, anyone.

But I wouldn't even have a shot at vengeance. Parkinson had seen to that.

I straightened and started sprinting, putting as much distance between myself and the Director as possible. The air was cold on my face as I sped through it, cooling the hot tears that streaked down my cheeks.

I can't live without her. I can't.

In my mind, my future crumbled away. All I'd wanted was to be with her. I'd have given up everything to have her. We'd been so close to the life we wanted. We were going to leave Quantico and be happy together. I hadn't cared where we went, as long as I was with her.

There was a way for me to be with her again.

"Hold on, kitten," I murmured. "I'm coming."

I made it to my apartment and flung open the door, barely slowing my pace as I ripped my way through my belongings until I found what I was looking for.

There. At the bottom of my duffle bag. My last bottle of pills.

I'd brought them with me to prove to myself that

I was stronger than their allure. Natalie had helped me find that strength. She'd believed in me when no one else had. Not even me.

I unscrewed the cap and tossed the pills into my mouth. Some of them spilled out, but most of them clogged in my throat. I ran to the sink and sucked in water, forcing the pills down.

Then I sank to the floor, drawing my knees up to my chest and dropping my head in my hands as I waited.

Jason... Her final word—my name on her bloody lips—tormented me.

"I'm coming, kitten," I promised.

Promise me you'll be okay.

I shook my head in a sharp jerk. I couldn't be okay. Not until I was with her again.

Promise me.

She'd been in pain, but she'd forced out the words in her final moments. She'd cared more about making sure I was okay than she did about getting out of that hellhole.

My stomach twisted, and I wasn't sure if it was from the pills or the agony of losing her.

I closed my eyes. *Just a few more minutes. I'll be with her in a few minutes.*

Behind my closed lids, I saw her face. Not slack in death, but shining, alight with joy and love. God, she was so sweet and gentle. But tough as nails when I needed her to be. She'd come into my dark life and dragged me out into the light by sheer force of will.

Promise me. This time, I saw her face as she said it. Not bloody and pale, but whole and fierce. *Promise me you'll be okay.*

She'd never forgive me if I followed her into death.

I lurched toward the toilet and shoved two fingers down my throat. I gagged, and the pills I'd taken came back up. My stomach heaved until all the poison had left my system. When there was nothing left, I sank down onto the cool tiles, my body shaking with desperate sobs.

You're so strong. I heard her ragged words in my mind, and a bitter, maddened laugh choked up my throat.

I was weak. I always had been. She'd been my strength, my salvation, and now she was gone. I'd never be strong again.

I was utterly ruined.

CHAPTER 15

Natalie

"J ason?" I tried to say his name, but I barely managed a strangled croak. My mouth and throat were painfully dry, and my entire body ached. I tried to open my eyes, but they were too heavy. Half-formed thoughts swam through my muddled mind, none of them able to fully coalesce.

"You're okay, Natalie," a strange, male voice said. "Go back to sleep."

A wave of warmth washed through my system, and the discomfort ended.

MY CHEST THROBBED WITH A DULL BUT PERSISTENT ache, and my head spun. I stirred, and agony knifed through me. I stilled with a whimper.

Something was very wrong. And I was...

Where was I? I couldn't see, couldn't think.

Jason.

I needed...

"She's waking up again," the strange man said. "Put her back under."

Warmth enfolded me, and the world dissolved back into nothingness.

❧

AWARENESS RETURNED SLOWLY. MY THOUGHTS were in tatters; tangled threads I couldn't make sense of. Emotion was clearer.

Fear.

My heart fluttered with it, beating against the inside of my chest so hard that it caused me physical pain. My breaths came in short, sharp gasps. My aching lungs protested, but I couldn't stop gasping.

"Calm down, Natalie." The strange man's voice. An unfamiliar hand on my shoulder. I couldn't tell if it was meant to comfort me or pin me in place.

Panic spiked, and my eyes snapped open. I immediately squeezed them shut again when harsh, sterile light seared my retinas.

"You're okay," the voice said. It was low, deep and soothing. "You're safe."

Safe.

Horrible memories played behind my closed lids: the stairwell exploding with violence; Agent Thurman falling; agony ripping through my chest when the bullet hit.

Come back to me. Jason's furiously spoken words rang through my mind, my first clear thought since I'd awoken.

My eyes flew open again, searching for him.

"Jason." I wasn't capable of saying his name. My throat was too dry, my vocal cords hoarse from disuse.

A cup of water appeared before me.

"Here," the voice prompted, soft and kind. "Drink. You'll feel better."

My lips closed around the straw, and I sucked down several gulps. As I drank, I blinked and looked around. I appeared to be lying on a hospital bed.

I'm alive.

Somehow, I'd survived the bullet that had torn through my lungs.

But the fear remained. Something was wrong.

Something about the hospital. I couldn't focus on it, though. I could only think about one thing.

"Where's Jason?" I asked, my gaze focusing on the man who'd offered me the water.

Kind, toffee brown eyes regarded me with reassuring warmth. "I'm Dr. Alexander Stevens. You can call me Alex," he introduced himself. "We thought we were going to lose you for a while there. But you're a fighter." His white, even teeth showed when he smiled. The handsome young doctor's calm demeanor should have been disarming, but alarm bells went off in the corners of my mind.

What was wrong with the hospital?

"Where's Jason?" I asked again.

Alex tucked a lock of his shoulder-length, honey brown hair behind his ear and flipped open a manila folder. He quickly rifled through the papers inside, checking through what I assumed was information regarding my condition.

"You mean Agent Jason Harper?" he asked, still looking at my chart.

I shouldn't have used Jason's first name. He was still my instructor, and "Jason" implied an inappropriate familiarity.

But I'd almost died. I'd thought I'd never see him again. Worrying about keeping our jobs at the Bureau seemed laughable in light of the situation.

"Yes," I made myself say calmly. "Agent Harper. Where is he?"

Alex's golden eyes found mine again. This time, they studied me far too incisively.

"Why would Agent Harper be here?" he asked.

I swallowed down the urge to scream for Jason. Maybe this was for the best. If he wasn't here, then our relationship hadn't been jeopardized. Maybe he was staying away to save my career.

What's wrong with the hospital?

"Where's my family?" I asked abruptly. Jason was the first person I wanted to see, but if I'd been at death's door, why were my parents not here? They might not be the most doting people, but they loved me.

I glanced around the small, bright white room. No cards. No flowers.

Just Alex.

I don't hear anyone else, I finally realized. I should be able to hear coughs, sniffles, paperwork being shuffled, phone conversations. But no muted sounds penetrated the closed metal door to my room. The walls were painted stark white, and the floor was... concrete? Why was the door metal? The whole place looked industrial, with exposed pipes overhead.

"Where am I?" I asked when Alex didn't answer me about my family.

His hand was still on my shoulder. It firmed, pressing me down into the mattress. Instinct to fight kicked in, but I recognized that my body was too weak to fend him off.

Breathe. Assess the scenario.

"You're at a special ops facility," Alex told me. "We've recruited you because we think you'd make an excellent agent."

"What?" I asked, dumbstruck. "But where's my family?"

Where's Jason?

I didn't dare to ask about him again. A pit was forming in my stomach. Somehow, I knew not to draw more attention to my relationship with Jason.

Alex's kind smile stayed fixed in place, but his eyes continued to examine me, as though they could probe into my mind and learn all of my secrets.

"As I said, you've been recruited," he continued. "Your family would be proud of you."

"Would be? What do you mean? I don't understand what's happening."

His smile turned indulgent. "Of course you don't. Not yet."

My unease magnified. "I'd like to talk to my parents, please."

"I'm afraid you can't at the moment. You have a decision to make, Natalie. You see, you died a few weeks ago. The world thinks you're gone. We saved you. You can have a new life in our division. You'll do great things. But you have to leave your old life behind."

"He thinks I'm dead?" My voice was barely more than a whisper.

Jason. I have to get to Jason. What would he be going through right now? What would *I* do if I thought he were dead?

I'd go insane.

"Everyone thinks you're dead," Alex confirmed, speaking calmly, as though what he was telling me wasn't horrific. "And our division would like to keep it that way. You can do so much more for us if you don't exist. I'm giving you a choice, Natalie. Do you choose to work with us?"

I stared into his eyes. They were such a warm, golden color, but they sent a chill straight through my soul. Primal urges told me to fight him, to flee. But my exhausted, aching body wasn't in any shape for that.

"How long have I been here?" I asked instead of answering him right away, buying time and making a play for information.

"Nearly a month," he said. "You'll be feeling weak now, but you'll make a full recovery. You'll be an extremely valuable asset."

"And everyone thinks I'm dead?" I knew the truth even before I asked. The only thing that would have kept Jason from me was death. Otherwise, he would have been by my side every second until I awoke.

"That's right. I know this is a lot to take in. I'll give you some time to think it over. Now, you could use a real meal. I'll be back in a few minutes."

"Okay," I agreed, trying to keep my mounting panic from showing on my face. "Thank you."

He gave me one last bland smile before leaving the room. When he opened the door, I tried to look past him, but it swung shut with a metallic clang before I could see more than further white walls and concrete.

My mind spun. I took a deep breath, and the relatively light pain in my chest let me know I'd healed far more than I could have if I'd only just woken up from getting shot.

Nearly a month. Jason's thought I was dead all that time.

I couldn't leave him like that. He was strong, but he needed me to make him accept his strength. What had happened to him in the time I'd been unconscious? Were his nightmares back? Was he using again?

If he is, we'll deal with it together, I resolved. We could face anything together.

But first, I had to get out of this strange place. CIA or not, the US government had no right to hold me here without telling my loved ones that I was alive.

But something told me Alex wouldn't take it well if I refused his offer to join their special ops division. My instincts told me that he was dangerous, despite his mild-mannered appearance.

A faint, distant scream penetrated the metal door. It was high, feminine. No noise had slipped past that door since I'd awoken, and all my senses went on high alert in response to the sound of distress.

Without thinking my actions through, I swung my feet from under the covers and settled them on the floor. The concrete was cool beneath my bare soles, and air whispered through the opening at the back of my hospital gown. When I tried to stand, my legs nearly collapsed under me. My muscles had weakened during my unconsciousness.

I gritted my teeth and forced my knees to stop shaking. I began to take jerky, hesitant steps toward the door. When I managed to reach it, I eased it open a crack and peered out. The hallway was thrown into painful relief by exposed fluorescent lighting, which reflected off the white-painted blocks on either side. The gray concrete floor continued throughout.

Where am I?

My instincts had been right: this certainly wasn't a hospital.

The scream sounded again, much louder now that the door was open. Acting automatically, I pushed my way into the corridor and started stumbling toward the sound. The woman was agonized. I had to get to her, had to help.

I planted my right palm against the rough wall, seeking support as I hobbled toward the sound of pain at a lurching pace. I followed the screams to another metal door a handful of yards down from my room. I shoved it open, desperate to get to the woman.

My stomach dropped, and time froze.

She was strapped down to what looked like a gynecologist's table, her ankles bound in the stirrups where her legs were spread wide. Something silvery and metallic had been inserted into her vagina, and wires were attached at various points on her naked body.

She convulsed on a shriek, and she twisted against the restraints around her wrists. Her pale blue eyes focused on me, and they widened with terror.

"Run!" Elena screamed at me.

Forcing the horror aside, I stumbled toward her. I nearly fell onto her, but I caught myself on the edge of the table and began working at the leather cuff around her wrist. My fingers shook violently, and bile rose in the back of my throat. I couldn't look at her face, couldn't see what was being done to her body.

"You have to run," she forced out, panting through her pain.

"I'm not leaving you."

I almost got the first cuff free when pain slammed into me. A hard jolt ripped through my body. All my muscles tensed, then went completely limp. I dropped, hitting the concrete hard.

"I was curious to see if you'd help her," Alex said from above me, sounding no more than mildly interested. "Elena has told me all about you. How she hates you. How you think you're better than her. How jealous she is of you. Elena doesn't have any secrets from me." He cocked his head at me. "I wonder what secrets you'll tell me."

"You can't do this," I hissed, forcing the words out through clenched teeth. "Not even the CIA."

He laughed, the deep sound rich with amusement. "Welcome to Division 9-C."

"What is Division 9-C?" I managed.

"Your new employer," he replied with the same bland smile. "You're going to be a loyal agent by the time we're finished with you. Your file is very promising."

I tried to shove myself up and launch myself at him. His thumb pressed down on a small black device he held in his hand, and the bolt of pain hit me again. I fell back onto the concrete, boneless.

"Your new implant seems to be working," he said with clinical satisfaction, lifting the black device so I could see it more clearly. "This will prevent you from fighting me. It controls a small device I've implanted in your shoulder. I'll know where you are at all times, and if you step out of line, you'll get a nasty shock. But I think you've worn yourself out enough for one day. You need rest before we can start the program." He pulled a syringe out of his pocket and swooped down over me.

I tried to move away, but my body refused to so much as twitch. The needle sank into my neck, and drugs oozed into my veins.

"Get some sleep," Alex advised, as though I had a choice. "You're going to need it before we can begin your reconditioning."

When I awoke, the torture started.

AFTER

Jason

Natalie's dark blue eyes were blank, devoid of any emotion. She stared out at nothing. Her bloody lips parted, accusatory words spilling from them.

"You let me die. You left me. You're weak. A failure. I never should have trusted you."

I reached for her in desperation, even as her words shredded my insides. My fingers brushed her too-pale cheek. It was ice cold.

"Please," I begged. "Come back to me."

She laughed, a hollow sound devoid of life. It echoed in my head, growing louder and boring into my brain. I pressed my hands against my ears, trying to block it out. But the cold, insane laughter was inside me, tearing at my soul.

Terror jolted me back to consciousness. I realized that the maddened sound issued from my own throat. It trailed off on a strangled groan.

I groped at the sheets beside me, searching.

Empty.

She's gone.

She's dead.

Frantically, I took a deep breath, holding onto the impossible hope that I could somehow catch her scent. I'd returned to *our* motel room in a desperate attempt to find something that belonged to her, something real I could hold onto. But the room had been cleaned, and even her delicate, floral scent had been eradicated, as though she'd never been here at all.

I reached beneath my pillow and grasped at the thin strip of leather I'd tucked there.

Her collar. It was all I had left of her: the symbol that she belonged to me, that she'd always be mine.

Always.

The horrible, hollow laughter sounded again. It ended on a rough shout, and I flung the collar away from me, unable to bear the feel of it in my fist, not when I knew I'd never see it around her delicate throat again.

The loss sent pain knifing through my gut as soon as the leather left my fingers.

I scrambled out of bed, searching. I found it across the room. I dropped to my knees to retrieve it and didn't bother to get back up. I didn't think my shaking legs would support me.

Obsessively, I rubbed my thumbs over the soft, supple leather, desperate to remember the elegant curved shape it took when it encircled her throat.

"I'm sorry," I murmured brokenly. "I'm so sorry."

I couldn't live without her. I couldn't.

Promise me you'll be okay. Promise me...

Damn her for those words. Why wouldn't she let me follow her into death?

Maybe I wouldn't have to end my own life. Maybe my ravaged heart would give out on its own. Or maybe it'd simply go insane. Would I be consumed by images of her death, or would I forget about her altogether if my mind broke?

I couldn't bear that. I couldn't forget her.

She was mine. Always mine.

Natalie

Cool air slid over my bare skin, making me shiver. How long had it been since the pretense of my hospital gown had been stripped away?

The jolt of pain had torn through my body, rendering me immobile. Alex had stripped me in seconds, his hands lingering on my exposed flesh before he gathered me up in his arms and carried me to this cell.

It was pitch black; my world had been devoid of light and sound for... How long?

It could have been hours. It could have been weeks. Time had no meaning in the dark.

I'd explored the space as best I could. I could pace six times in either direction before hitting rough concrete. It surrounded me: under my groping hands, beneath my bare feet. There was a smooth metal door, but it didn't have a handle. I'd searched for an opening until my fingernails broke and bled.

There was a musty cot for sleeping, and facilities for my more basic needs. The humiliation of using them had faded quickly. What did my embarrassment matter in the dark, where no one could witness my shame?

Food and water were brought to me intermittently, pushed through a small slot that opened at the bottom of the door. Light would flash into my prison briefly, blinding me as it winked in and out of existence in a matter of seconds.

I considered going on a hunger strike, possibly starving myself to death.

But I couldn't give up yet. I had to get back to Jason. He thought I was dead. It must be tearing him apart. I had to save myself, and then I'd save him, too.

Pain jolted through me, and I dropped. Light spilled into the room as the door swung open. Alex materialized as my vision cleared. He took a moment to study me where I lay helpless on the cold floor. Then he bent and picked me up. My skin crawled everywhere he touched me. He held me carefully, almost tenderly. It made my stomach turn.

"Where are you taking me?" I managed to make my thick tongue work as he carried me out into the hallway.

He gave me the soft, bland smile I'd quickly grown to hate. "It's time for our first session."

My stomach dropped. *Session?* What did that mean? Alex had mentioned *reconditioning*.

I had a horrible suspicion what that might entail. I'd seen what was being done to Elena when I'd tried to save her.

That won't happen to me. It can't.

My mind vehemently rejected the idea.

But I quickly came to learn that my denial was a useless, pathetic thing. That day, Alex began stripping me of my dignity, my will, my spirit. Thoughts of getting back to Jason were the only thing that got me through the torment. Without him, I'd shatter into a thousand pieces.

☙✦❧

Jason

I didn't allow myself to contemplate how long it had been since Natalie had been ripped away from me. I chose not to think about losing her at all. Except in my nightmares, when I couldn't force my mind to hide from the terrible memories of her bloody and broken body, her blank eyes.

In my waking hours, I threw myself into work. I settled into the Chicago field office and somehow managed to convince everyone around me that I was able to function without her. No one in Chicago knew that I'd been in love with a recruit. Parkinson and my father had kept it quiet, both too embarrassed of my weakness to let it get out.

That suited me just fine. I'd rip apart the first person to so much as whisper their condolences. That would make her death real. And I couldn't contemplate that.

I never mentioned her name aloud. I couldn't bear the pain of it on my tongue.

But I thought it often, playing it through my mind like a prayer.

My Natalie. My kitten.

I kept her alive in my head, choosing to remember her as she had been in my arms: sweet and submissive, but so much stronger than I could ever hope to be.

⊛

Natalie

Alex cradled my spent body against his hard chest as he carried me back to my cell. He always held me like this after our "sessions," as he called them. At first, it had disgusted me. He'd already violated me in so many ways. Why did he have to hold me tenderly in a perverse parody of comfort after he finished torturing me?

I wasn't sure how long I'd been here, or even how many sessions I'd endured. Time had no meaning in the darkness of my cell, and the only time I saw the light—the only time I saw anything at all—was when Alex came to retrieve me for torment. He was the only person in my world, my only tie to humanity.

Even if he was barely human. I'd never imagined

anyone could be so unfeeling, so utterly devoid of compassion. No matter how much I screamed or begged, he remained no more than blandly interested in my condition. It would almost have been easier if he'd been overtly cruel. He never touched me with a harsh hand. He didn't have to. The drugs hurt me for him.

I'd been horrified to realize that I'd started clinging to him when he held me as I cried. My body was always too weakened to even sob, but my tears soaked his crisp white coat.

Now, I couldn't bring myself to care that my face was tucked against his chest, my fingers curling into his coat as I clung to my only source of comfort.

He carried me back into my cell and sat down on my cot, still holding me.

This was different. He didn't usually linger once he brought me back to my prison. The fine hairs on the back of my neck lifted, and my tears stopped as my senses went on high alert.

His long fingers brushed my cheek, taking up a stray lock of hair and tucking it behind my ear.

"Tell me about Jason," he said gently.

I stopped breathing. I couldn't tell him about Jason. Jason was mine, my secret haven in my mind. He was my sanity.

"Now, Natalie," Alex chided. "You know you don't have any secrets from me. Did you think I would forget Agent Harper was the first person you asked for when you woke up?"

I licked my dry lips. "I was confused. Disoriented."

"Then why do you cry out his name during our sessions?"

My blood froze in my veins. I didn't realize I ever spoke his name aloud.

"I could arrange to bring him to you," Alex continued on calmly. "Is that what you want? For me to bring him here?"

"No!" I couldn't let my torturer get his hands on Jason. I had to protect the man I loved from the monster who tormented me.

That day, I stopped thinking about Jason to escape my reality. I gave up all hope of getting back to him. If I was ever near him again, Alex would find him. He'd hurt Jason to punish me. I couldn't allow that to happen. I'd die first.

Without my fantasies of Jason, my mind broke. It wasn't long after I gave him up that Alex molded me into what he wanted me to be. Without Jason, I wasn't strong enough to survive.

CHAPTER 16

Natalie

Five Years Later

Alex's hand rested on my shoulder in a familiar gesture. After years of having him watch my back in the field, the weight of his touch was comforting. There was no sensual undertone to the contact, simply a reassurance that my handler would be here for me, no matter what I faced.

"You did well in Colombia," he praised. "I'm sorry to drag you to the States on such short notice."

I waved him off. "If this is where I'm needed, this is where I'll be. What do you need me to do?"

He gave my shoulder one final squeeze before stepping away and taking a seat in the chair across the narrow table from me. We sat in the dated kitchen of some safe house he had set up in Chicago. Division 9-C had them all over the world, and they started to blend into one amorphous, run-down apartment after a while.

Although, I'd never been brought to the US on a mission. Alex had helped me unlock my potential of learning foreign language, so I was his go-to girl abroad. Particularly in South America, where I'd been on assignment combating drug trafficking and the war-like violence that surrounded the trade.

For months, I'd hunted my target: Cristian Moreno, a Colombian drug lord who'd primarily dealt in cocaine until recently. Last year, he'd partnered up with the Russian Bratva to start dealing a new date rape drug, Bliss.

"You're aware that the Bratva were crippled in New York recently," Alex said, refreshing me on the situation.

"Yes," I replied. "Leadership shattered and Moreno stepped in to take control of trafficking Bliss on the East Coast. So what am I doing in Chicago?"

"Moreno is trying to broker alliances with the Latin Kings here," Alex said. "The feds in New York are making things difficult for him, so he's expanding to new territory. The Kings are still widespread and powerful in Chicago, but divided into tribes. They're an ideal group to recruit and control if Moreno wants to distribute Bliss on a wider scale quickly."

My stomach turned. Bliss was a nasty drug, something between coke and rohypnol. Apparently, it made sex feel incredible and increased the user's sensual appetites. Whether they wanted it or not. A key component in its manufacture was Scopolamine, which originated in Colombia. It made the victim highly suggestible.

I'd been disgusted by the abuse I'd seen in my months tracking Moreno, and I knew he was setting up a lucrative human trafficking ring to go along with dealing Bliss. It kept the women compliant.

"What's my mission here?" I asked, eager to get one step closer to killing Cristian Moreno and putting a stop to his plans.

Alex slid a manila folder across the table. I picked it up and began to peruse its contents as he spoke.

"The feds are about to bust a club where the Kings have been meeting with Moreno's men. I want you to go to the club and facilitate contact. When the feds come in, you will help Moreno's men get out. The building schematics are in the file, along with potential routes for you to take. I'll have a van waiting for you outside.

"Save Moreno's men, make them indebted to you," he continued. "Earn their trust and infiltrate his organization. You haven't been able to get close to any of his key people yet. This is where you work your way in. When you get deeper, we'll bring in Nathaniel as your associate and put him in the organization as backup."

I nodded my agreement, pleased to have Nate at my back. Although he was quieter than he had been when I'd first met him, I preferred working with him over ice cold Elena or Trent, who was so detached he might as well be robotic.

"When and where do I go in?" I asked, glancing at the information in the file. "Tonight at Aqua Lounge," I read before he could answer. "A dance club?"

"Yes," he replied. "You'll arrive at ten fifteen. I've laid out an appropriate outfit for you in the bedroom. You'll be unarmed, but I know you can handle yourself."

"That won't be a problem," I confirmed. I was skilled enough in hand-to-hand combat that I could kill a man with my bare hands. Unless someone pulled a gun on me, I'd be able to take down anyone who threatened me. And while that was a possibility, I could easily disarm a man at close range. Besides, the threat of death didn't register any fear in my system. That instinct had been eliminated from my psyche a long time ago. I'd give my life for my division without a thought.

"I know you can do this," Alex said, his eyes bright with pride. "Moreno will be dead in a matter of weeks. Get close to him and take him out. When his organization is thrown into chaos, we'll step in and dismantle his operation."

I nodded again, determined to put a stop to the disgusting flesh trade Moreno had established.

"Check in with me once you're in tonight," Alex ordered. "Then, you'll go dark until the op is over or you need Nate to join you. I won't risk unnecessary communication if you're being monitored."

"Understood," I confirmed.

Alex pushed back from the table and got to his feet. "I'll talk to you in a few hours." He circled around the table and squeezed my shoulder again, staring down into my eyes. "Good luck, Natalie."

"Luck will have nothing to do with it," I replied.

He smiled. "I'm sure it won't. I'll see you soon."

Patting my shoulder in one last show of reassurance, he turned and left the shabby townhouse. I redirected my attention back to studying my case file, memorizing every word before I went into the field.

A LOW, SENSUAL BEAT THRUMMED THROUGH MY bones as I stepped into Aqua Lounge. Several male gazes turned toward me, taking in my skin-tight, leather-look leggings and low cut top that clung to my curves. Alex had selected a decidedly sexy outfit for me, but it was appropriate for my task; the flexible fit would allow me to fight without the challenge of a short skirt, and I'd attract the attention of the men I targeted.

I threaded my way through the gyrating bodies on the dance floor, heading for the bar. When I reached my destination, I leaned one elbow on the black bar top and surveyed the clientele, searching for my marks. Their pictures had been in my file, and I knew who to look for.

I caught sight of one of Moreno's men. Carlos Lopez was a heavily muscled, darkly tanned figure covered in tattoos. I allowed my eyes to fix on him until he felt my gaze. After a few seconds, he looked in my direction. I curved corners of my lips up in a seductive smile and thrust out my chest in physical invitation. He flashed a sharp, white grin and began making his way toward me.

"Hi," I purred when he reached me. "I'm Natalie." Instead of offering my hand to shake, I touched my fingertips to his arm, tracing the line of his muscles. His dark eyes flared.

"Carlos," he answered. "What are you drinking, Natalie?"

I cocked my head at him with a knowing smile. "Nothing you'd offer me," I said, my cool tone contrasting with my saucy expression. My fingers firmed on his arm. "I'd rather not be drugged and raped tonight."

His smile dropped to a scowl, and he took a step toward me, abruptly towering over me as he entered my personal space. "Who the fuck are you?" he demanded. "If you're a fucking cop—"

"I am," I lied easily, cutting him off. "But I want a piece of the action. So I came here with a peace offering. The feds are about to bust this club. They'll be here in approximately five minutes. I'll help you get out. I have a van waiting outside to take you and your friends to a safe place. In exchange, I want you to take me with you so I can meet your boss. I want in."

"And why the fuck would I trust a cop?" he snarled.

"Because you're going to find out I'm telling the truth in, well, four minutes now. I'm ready for a more lucrative career. Follow me, and I'll get you out before they arrive. But we have to move right now."

That moment, chaos exploded through the club as cops and agents poured in. Carlos' eyes widened with fear.

"Looks like they're early," I said calmly. "Do you want a ride out of here or not? My van's parked in the alley out back. We have less than a minute to get out."

He hesitated a few seconds, then grabbed my arm with a snarl. He began dragging me toward the emergency exit, shouting for his friends as we went. Two equally large men joined us as we hustled to the back. The cops were held back from us by a sea of panicked people.

"Who the fuck is she?" one of the new men demanded.

"Our ticket out," Carlos said. He glowered at me. "She'd better be." His tone was harsh with a clear threat.

I didn't deign to reply, instead hurrying along with them.

An alarm sounded when we burst out into the cool night air.

The way wasn't entirely clear. Two policemen and an agent in a suit were waiting to block our escape, guns drawn. My black van was at the mouth of the alley, idling and ready to go. The men at my side drew their own weapons.

"Don't shoot!" the agent and I shouted at the same time.

My heart stopped, and the world fell away around

me. Bright green eyes stared at me, wide with shock.

Then they narrowed, and Jason advanced on me.

"Who—?" he began, reaching for me with barely restrained violence.

I acted in blind panic. Dodging him with lighting speed, I slipped to the side and behind him, wrapping my arm around his throat. Gunshots rang out on either side of me, and the cops dropped.

My heart swelled, straining against my ribs as I applied pressure on Jason's carotid artery. My training overrode my shock and fear, making me act on instinct rather than emotion. Nothing could get in the way of my mission. And I couldn't even begin to face the horror of what I was doing, as my body acted of its own accord. I had to get away from Jason.

He dropped to his knees with a grunt, and I followed him down, not letting up the pressure.

"I'm sorry." The words left my lips as though issuing from someone else's mouth.

"Natalie," he groaned. I knew he was capable of fighting me, but he didn't. I wasn't sure if it was because shock had given me the upper hand, or if he wasn't willing to harm me.

Hot tears leaked from the corners of my eyes as he sagged in my arms, slipping into unconsciousness. I dropped him with a harsh cry.

Carlos grabbed my arm and began dragging me toward the van. "Let's go," he barked.

I followed him as numbness set in. I went on autopilot, my training taking over completely, blotting out all thought as my mind shut down. Somehow, I was in the driver's seat, and my foot slammed down on the gas as I rammed my way into traffic and sped off into the night.

CHAPTER 17

Jason

"Jason? Jason!" Small, delicate hands shook me awake.

My eyes snapped open, and my hands shot out to grip the woman who crouched over me, my fingers digging into her upper arms.

Sky blue eyes widened in shock.

Sky blue. Not soft navy.

"What the hell, Jason?" Sam demanded, jerking against my bruising grip. My new partner—Samantha Browning—was too green to fight me off. I didn't release her.

"Where is she?" I ground out, shooting to my feet and dragging Sam up along with me.

"Who?" Sam demanded. "Let me go. You're hurting me."

Forcing my fingers to unfurl, I shoved away from her. My eyes searched the alley frantically. The two officers who'd gone into the bust with me lay on the ground, groaning as paramedics hovered over them. They'd been wearing Kevlar, so they'd survived, but they'd be in pain after being shot at such close range.

A medic approached me, but I warned her away with a glare.

I growled my frustration when I didn't see the woman who'd surely been a ghost.

My neck ached. For an apparition, she'd been surprisingly solid.

"Natalie," I growled, jerking my fingers through my hair. She couldn't have been real. My eyes had deceived me.

I'm sorry. Her soft voice, rough with pain...

It'd been *her.* Her gentle, floral scent had surrounded me, clouding my senses and wrapping my chest in agony as I'd been thrust back into impossible memories.

How could she be alive? I'd watched her die. And if by some miracle she had survived, how could she have left me and allowed me to believe she was gone forever? My sweet kitten wouldn't have done that to me.

Rage burned through my veins, driving away disbelief.

"Natalie?" Sam said with shock. "You mean, *your* Natalie? But she's dead. I read all the files on it."

I glowered at her at the reminder of how the tech geek had hacked into my life, prying into my darkest, most painful secrets. She knew me better than anyone, and I hadn't given her permission to access that knowledge. It had only been recently that she'd accidentally confessed to breaking into my psychologist's notes on my trauma.

My rage burned impossibly hotter.

"If you read all the files, then tell me how the fuck you didn't know that she survived."

Sam's eyes widened, and her cheeks paled so her freckles stood out starkly on her delicate face.

"That's not possible," she said faintly. "I watched the feed from the body cams when she died."

"She's not dead!" I roared. "I just saw her! She fucking attacked me."

I pressed my hands to either side of my head, as though I could stop my pounding brain from cracking my skull apart.

How could she do this to me? How could she let me live without her?

How could she live without me?

I wouldn't have imagined it were possible. But

then again, I'd never imagined her survival to be possible.

And she was with Moreno's men.

What the fuck was going on?

Sam raised her hands in a gesture meant to calm me. "Let me get back to my computer. I'll look into it more. There has to be something buried in her files. Something I didn't think to look for. If it really was her you saw—"

"It was her!" I shouted, knowing it deep in my bones. I'd recognize her striking eyes and sweet scent anywhere, even after all these horrible, painful years.

"I want to know where the fuck she went, and why she was with Moreno's men," I continued, my mind racing. "There was a van at the mouth of the alley. I want traffic cam footage. I want to know where the fuck she is."

If my Natalie were alive, I wouldn't stop until I hunted her down. I wasn't sure if I wanted to take her in my arms and claim her body all over again, or if I wanted to punish her for the hell she'd put me through. Probably both.

I'd sate my needs and get the answers I craved. And then I'd never let her out of my sight again, no matter what it took. I'd bind her to me and never let her go.

After I made her regret ever leaving me.

✦

"THE TRAFFIC CAMS WERE DISABLED," SAM TOLD ME, watching me warily. "I can't track her."

"You're supposed to be the techie geek genius," I snapped, looming over her where she sat hunched at her desk. She shrank down under the weight of my maddened rage. "Recover the feed."

She ran a nervous hand through her fiery hair. "There's nothing to recover," she insisted, no longer able to meet my eye. "They didn't record anything."

"Then someone hacked them. Who did it?"

Her hands twisted in her lap. "I don't know. But I can look into it. I will look into it. I've got this. I mean, I can figure it out. I promise." She took up her frenetic pattern of speech that was her default when she was intimidated.

I couldn't rein in the rage that still rode me hard, mingling with agony that ripped at my insides. Over and over again, I watched Natalie die in my mind. Memories I'd buried deep spilled out from where they'd been locked in a dark corner of my brain. I hadn't suffered a panic attack in years, but I could feel my chest beginning to seize. I threw myself into my fury. It was my only protection from the horror and grief.

"What's going on? Why are you yelling at Sam?"

Agent Dexter Scott appeared behind my partner, his considerable bulk increasing as he drew himself up to his full height. His ice blue eyes glowered at me.

Sam flushed crimson and appeared to shrink into herself more. For months, she'd hardly been able to bear his presence, but he seemed oblivious to the fact that he'd broken her heart when he found his soul mate, Chloe. I suspected that heartbreak was a major factor in Sam's decision to transfer from analyst to field agent. She was trying to make a change in her life. Or maybe she was trying to prove something.

Whatever was going on with her, I couldn't bring myself to give a shit. All I could think about was getting to Natalie.

"Stay out of this, Scott," I warned Dex. "My partner and I are discussing a case."

He frowned. "Sam shouldn't be looking at traffic cam footage. She's not an analyst anymore." His lips twisted in disapproval as he said it, but otherwise he made no comment on his opinion regarding her choice to move into the field.

"She's the best tech analyst we have," I countered. "I'm not trusting anyone else with this. And that includes you. Go mind your own business, Scott."

"I don't think—" he began, but Sam cut him off softly.

"Just go, Dex. Please. I need to talk to Jason." She

was looking at her computer screen, reading something I couldn't understand.

"What did you find?" I asked quickly. I shot a glare at Dex when he didn't walk away immediately. "Leave," I snapped.

He blew out a heavy sigh and finally gave us some privacy. I turned my attention back to Sam.

"What is it?" I urged.

She looked up at me, her eyes cautious. "I did some research into Natalie's old files. There was a heavily redacted document. I never thought anything of it before." She had the grace to blush. "I just wanted background information on you. I didn't do any digging into her. Sorry about that. I didn't mean to pry. I was just curious. I mean, I—"

"Stop," I barked before she could start babbling out of nervousness. "I don't care about you spying on me. What about this redacted document?"

"Well, I just found the original," she said, still watching me as though I was a particularly unstable bomb that might detonate in her face if she breathed the wrong way. "The day Natalie died, after the shootout. The bodies weren't recovered. They were all missing, except Agent Thurman's body. There was a brief investigation, but when nothing was found, it seems the Bureau decided it was best to suppress the information."

"What?" I exploded.

Without waiting for her to respond, I tore off toward Director Parkinson's office. Parkinson had been transferred from Quantico to the Chicago field office three years ago when the previous Director, Franklin Dawes, had been killed. I suspected my father had sent her here to keep an eye on me. He'd always trusted Dawes to keep me in line, and Parkinson had proven to be a formidable replacement. She knew all my dark secrets, and I'd never dared to step a toe out of line under her watch.

But now, I knew one of *her* secrets. How could she have kept this from me for all these years? I would have torn apart anyone who stood between me and Natalie if I'd known there was even the slightest chance she'd survived.

And now, Parkinson fit into that category. She'd kept me from my kitten for five long years. Rage blinded me, and I kicked my way into her office, the door splintering on its hinges as I stormed in. She stood quickly, her dark eyes flaring in alarm.

"Harper!" she gasped. "What are you doing?"

"How could you not tell me?" I roared as I advanced on her.

She stood quickly, dropping into a defensive stance. All my muscles vibrated with barely suppressed violence as I restrained myself from physically extracting answers from her.

"What are you talking about?" she asked with surprising calm. The woman was ice cold, unfeeling.

"Natalie!" I raged. "There wasn't a body. You let me go to her fucking funeral, and she wasn't even there."

A horrible memory of that day assailed me: Natalie's family and friends weeping over her casket while I watched from a distance. Daffodils had been strewn on top of it, perversely cheery as they followed her into the dirt.

Parkinson's eyes narrowed. "Why are you asking about Simmons?"

I ground my teeth, unwilling to tell her I'd seen Natalie with Moreno's men. I didn't understand what was happening, but I couldn't betray Natalie to the Director. If she was going to be punished, it would be by my hand and no one else's.

"Why didn't you tell me?" I countered, not answering her question.

"Because you would have reacted just like this," she said coolly. "You were a loose cannon and a liability. You have no business being in the Bureau at all, and you'd have been fired that day if I'd had my way. I didn't need you tearing your way through our investigations in an attempt to find a dead body."

I tensed impossibly further, seething. I bit the inside of my cheek, the slight pain helping center me. I couldn't tell Parkinson that Natalie was alive, not until I had answers about what the fuck was going on. Where had she been for the last five years? And why the fuck was she with Moreno's people? They'd shot two cops, and she'd attacked me.

How could she do that? How could she do this to me? My life had been empty, hollow for years. I hadn't gone through with my suicide attempt, but I'd died inside the day I lost her. Everyone who knew me now had no inkling that the carefree persona I projected was nothing more than a mask, a way to hide from their concern. If no one knew I was a dead man walking, they couldn't remind me of my loss every day with their looks of pity.

But now, I was coming apart at the seams. And if I stayed close to Parkinson for one more minute, I wouldn't be able to contain the violence that simmered just beneath my skin.

"I won't forget this," I ground out. Gathering up my willpower, I jerked my limbs toward the door and stiffly strode out of her office.

"Neither will I," she warned as I retreated.

I hurried back over to Sam. She peeked up at me timidly.

"I have to find her," I said, my voice rough with

the effort of suppressing my emotions. "I need your help."

"Of course," Sam said, her face pale but determined. "I'll try to figure out who hacked those cams."

I nodded. "I'm going to set up surveillance on every one of Moreno's known associates in Chicago. I'll need you to work up a file on them."

"But I'm your partner," she countered. "I'll come out and run surveillance with you. One of the analysts can work up a file. You shouldn't be alone with this."

Her concern should have been touching, but I couldn't focus on anything but my task. "No," I refused. "I'm doing this on my own. I need you to sit behind your computer and do what you do best." She opened her mouth to protest, but I spoke before she could. "I need your help, Sam. Please."

She pressed her lips together, considering for a moment. "Okay," she finally said. "I'll be on desk duty. But you're going to wear a tracking device. I want to be able to find you if we lose contact. I don't like you being out there by yourself."

I won't be alone for long, I thought, dark anticipation racing through my veins. I'd find Natalie and get the answers I so desperately needed, by any means necessary.

CHAPTER 18

Natalie

I wandered lonely as a cloud
That floats on high o'er vales and hills,
When all at once I saw a crowd,
A host of golden daffodils;
Beside the lake, beneath the trees,
Fluttering and dancing in the breeze...
And then my heart with pleasure fills,
And dances with the daffodils.

The familiar poem flowed through my brain without conscious thought, calming and focusing me.

My encounter with Jason was utterly absent from my mind. All that existed was my task, my mission.

Carlos and the other two men I'd rescued spoke in hushed but angry tones as they huddled together in the entryway of the nondescript brick townhome. It wasn't the most reputable area, but it didn't strike me as a place where lower-level dealers distributed their product.

I shifted on my feet, uneasy being exposed on the sidewalk while they blocked the door, clearly debating whether or not to let me in. I knew Alex would have seen to the traffic cams around Aqua Lounge being disabled so my movements couldn't be tracked, but my instincts told me to get to cover as quickly as possible.

"Are we going in or what?" I asked in English. The men were speaking Spanish, but I wasn't ready to reveal that I could understand them. It would be so much easier to gather intel if they thought I didn't have a clue what they were saying.

As it was, they were speaking too softly at the moment for me to hear, but as we'd driven here, I'd caught their barked curses and heated argument over who the fuck I was and whether or not they could trust me. Carlos seemed to have convinced them that I was a dirty cop, but they still weren't letting me into the building.

Putting on my most confident persona, I hustled up to them and got right in their faces.

"We can't just sit out here all night," I said acidly. "Let's get inside."

Carlos gave me an oily smile I didn't trust for one second.

"Okay, *chiquita*. Let's get you inside."

I kept a carefully relaxed demeanor as I sauntered across the threshold, but my senses were on high alert. The men had come to a decision, and it wasn't in my favor. If they made a move against me, I'd be ready for them.

A low groan of tormented pleasure greeted me when I entered the townhouse. The sound made the fine hairs on the back of my neck stand on end, and unpleasant memories stirred.

Strapped down. Helpless. Forced pleasure. Pain.

And then my heart with pleasure fills,
And dances with the daffodils.

The memories instantly evaporated, and I forgot they'd even surfaced. I turned to Carlos.

"Where are we?" I asked, coolly composed.

"This is where we keep the whores," Carlos replied before he made a grab for me.

I dodged easily, but one of the other men's fists

tangled in my hair. I hissed when he yanked me toward him, my back hitting his heavily muscled chest. I hesitated, uncertain if I should demonstrate my lethal skills. I didn't want the men to see me as a threat, but I couldn't allow them to overpower me, either.

The decision was made for me when Carlos produced a syringe from his pocket.

Bliss.

If the drug entered my system, I'd be lost to mindless lust, powerless and suggestible. I'd probably be on my knees sucking their cocks in a matter of minutes. I'd seen it happen to women often enough while I was operating in Colombia, and I wasn't about to let that happen to me.

I jabbed my elbow back into the stomach of the man who held my hair. He released me with a grunt, and at the same time, my arm whipped out, knocking Carlos' wrist aside so it smashed against the wall. The threat of the syringe dropped from his hand. He snarled and reached behind him, drawing the gun that had been tucked in his waistband. I grabbed the weapon before he raised it, disarming him and taking it for myself. I swung it in an upward arc, clipping him hard beneath the chin. He dropped with a curse.

"Don't," I warned the other two, training the gun on one man, then the other as I took a step back out of their physical range. "Don't fuck with me ever again," I said coldly. "I came here to deal with your boss. I could be an asset in expanding his business in Chicago."

"You'd be a better asset as a whore," Carlos seethed.

I kicked him in the stomach, and he went back down, wheezing.

"Not interested," I replied, still ice cold. "Call your boss and set up a meeting. If he wants to take control of Chicago, he'll need help. I have a few friends on the force who would be interested in facilitating his business in exchange for a cut. I'm here to set it up." The lies were all established from the file Alex had given me. If Moreno's men chose to look into my story, there would be falsified documents in the CPD database to back me up. "Make the call," I commanded.

Carlos struggled to his feet, but this time, he kept a wary distance. He'd learned his lesson.

He glowered at me with undisguised loathing, and I firmed my grip on his gun, keeping it trained on him. He spat on the floor, but he retrieved his phone from his pocket and connected the call.

After a few seconds, he spoke into the receiver in rapid fire Spanish. I kept my face carefully blank, not betraying that I understood every word he was saying. It took a few minutes of argument, but finally Carlos came to an agreement with the person on the other end of the line.

He put his phone away, still scowling at me. "Come back tomorrow night. Six o'clock. Juan David wants to talk to you."

I nodded, even though Moreno was my target. I wasn't surprised that I would have to work my way up to gain access to him. After all, I was an unknown to these men. They'd want to check my story and vet me with their immediate boss before allowing me to meet with Cristian Moreno himself. I'd bide my time and establish trust. When the time was right, I'd bring in Nate under the pretense that he was another dirty cop. Then we'd move on Moreno.

"I'll be back tomorrow, then," I agreed. I didn't give Carlos his gun. "But I'm keeping this," I informed him. No way was I going to leave this place unarmed. They'd probably shoot me out of spite as soon as I was vulnerable.

I didn't turn my back on them as I eased toward the front door and slipped out into the night. I quickly made my way back to the black van and hopped into the driver's seat before speeding away from the danger they posed. If I lingered, they might decide to take out their rage on me. Men like that didn't take it well when a woman kicked their ass.

I allowed three minutes to pass before I retrieved my phone from the console and called Alex.

"Natalie," he answered after it rang once. "Update me."

"I'm in," I replied. "I meet with Juan David tomorrow evening. It'll take a little while, but I'll work my way up to Moreno. This is the first step."

"Good. Take me through the events of tonight. You established contact with Moreno's men at the club?"

"Yes," I confirmed. "I got in with Carlos Lopez right before the feds arrived."

The feds.

The agent waiting for us in the alley.

My arm around his neck as I took him down.

Jason.

"Natalie? What's wrong?" Alex's voice penetrated my mounting panic and horror. How could I have forgotten about attacking Jason? How could I forget *him*?

"Natalie, talk to me."

I couldn't tell him about Jason. I couldn't think...

I wandered lonely as a cloud
That floats on high o'er vales and hills,
When all at once I saw a crowd,
A host of golden daffodils;

Beside the lake, beneath the trees,
Fluttering and dancing in the breeze...
And then my heart with pleasure fills,
And dances with the daffodils.

"I'm here," I said to Alex, all thoughts of Jason melting away. Calm settled over me, and I flowed back into conversation with my handler. "Moreno's men followed me into the van. They gave me directions to a brothel. They tried to dose me with Bliss, but I convinced them to call their boss and arrange a meeting instead. They think I'm a dirty cop, and I told them I have friends on the force who want in. The way is clear for me to bring Nate in once I gain their trust."

There was a pause. "Something upset you," Alex said calmly. "What happened?"

Bright green eyes, wide with shock.
His voice rough with disbelief as he uttered my name.
Jason, going limp in my hold.

And then my heart with pleasure fills...

My mind cleared. "I hate the Bliss trafficking," I said to Alex. "What they're doing to those women is awful. It's upsetting."

"You'll help take out Moreno," he reassured me.

"Yes," I agreed.

"Go dark for now," he ordered. "Check in when you're ready for Nathaniel to join you."

"Understood." I ended the call, obeying my handler.

Idly, I wiped at my cheeks. I didn't understand why they were wet.

It didn't matter. All that mattered was my mission.

CHAPTER 19

Jason

I wiped the blood from my knuckles and stormed back to where my black sedan was parked at the curb outside the run-down apartment complex. I'd spent the last three hours tearing my way through the neighborhood, interrogating every one of the dealers I came across. They were easy prey here: mostly addicts who dealt for the Latin Kings to support their habit. It was the best place I had to investigate until Sam got back to me with more intel. If Moreno's men were networking with the Kings to establish themselves in Chicago, then this was where I'd start. I'd destroy anyone who stood in my path to Natalie. As it was, I'd already resorted to *unsanctioned* interrogation methods to get the answers I wanted. The blood on my hands wasn't my own. No one had died, but I'd certainly left the men I'd questioned in bloodier condition than I'd found them.

Unfortunately, I didn't have any solid leads yet. The men I'd encountered so far dealt in cocaine, not Bliss. They had ties to the Kings, but they weren't able to give me more than first names of their connections, and they were unable to provide locations where I might find their bosses.

As I slammed my car door behind me, my phone buzzed in my pocket. I answered immediately when I saw the caller ID.

"Sam," I said in clipped tones. "What do you have for me?"

"You've been busy," she replied drily. "I've been tracking your movements. I thought you were running surveillance, not infiltrating locations with a pattern of drug dealing."

Fuck. I'd forgotten about the damn tracking device she'd insisted I wear in the inner lining of my jacket.

"Did you call to scold me or because you have new intel?" I growled.

"I'm not scolding you. I'm worried about you." She sighed. "But yes, I do have something for you. I checked the CCTV cameras around Aqua Lounge. They were still live fifteen minutes before the bust. I have footage of three of Moreno's suspected associates entering the club. So then I backtracked, following their movements through traffic cams to see where they were before they came to the club. They all left a townhouse at eight fifty-three PM before heading to Aqua Lounge."

"What's the address?" I demanded, throwing my car into gear and preparing to track the men down.

"You can go there if you want, but Natalie's not there anymore," Sam replied.

"*Anymore?* You mean she was there earlier?"

"So after I found the location, I checked traffic cams in the timeframe after we busted Aqua Lounge. A black van arrived at ten forty-six. Natalie and the men got out and went into the townhouse. She left seventeen minutes later."

"Where did she go?" I ground out, eager to have a direction so I could start closing the distance between us.

"I followed the van to another townhouse several blocks away. She went in at eleven eighteen and hasn't come back out."

I glanced at the clock on the dashboard: three forty-one AM. Natalie would be sleeping. That would make my task easier. She wouldn't get the upper hand if I caught her by surprise. She wouldn't escape me again.

"Give me the address," I ordered.

Sam complied, and I slammed down on the gas as I sped in that direction.

"What are you going to do?" Sam asked. "Should I tell Parkinson you're bringing Natalie into the field office?"

"No," I snarled at the idea of Parkinson knowing Natalie was alive and within my reach. "I won't have anyone at the Bureau coming near her. They left her for dead five years ago. And I have no idea what she's been doing all this time. I need answers."

"You're not..." Sam began hesitantly. "You're not going to hurt her, are you?"

"Why would you even ask me that?" I demanded, my fury rising. Of course I'd never harm Natalie. I had plans for interrogating her if she proved reticent, but none of them involved her in pain.

"You seem... I don't know. Kind of crazy. And definitely angry."

"Of course I'm angry!" I burst out.

I took a deep breath, struggling to calm myself. If

Sam decided I couldn't handle this, she'd turn every-thing over to Parkinson. It was a small miracle that she hadn't done so already. I wasn't sure exactly why she was helping me behind the Director's back, but I didn't have time to puzzle over it. All I could think about was getting to Natalie. Now, I was only minutes away from her.

"Parkinson let me think Natalie was dead all this time," I said, more calmly. "I can't trust her to know anything about this. I won't have the Bureau getting their hands on her, especially when I don't know why she was with the Colombians. If the Bureau suspects she's involved with Moreno, she won't be treated gently. Once I have more information, I can decide how to move forward."

"All right," Sam said after a moment of hesitation. "I get it. I do. I know what losing her did to you."

I grimaced. I'd briefly forgotten that the curious little geek had hacked into my psychologist's files and read up on all of my darkest secrets. Maybe it was a sense of guilt over that violation of trust that was causing her to help me now. Or maybe she really did care about reuniting me with Natalie, knowing how her supposed death had destroyed me. After losing Dex to another woman, Sam knew the pain of heart-break. Even if the man she loved was still alive, he was out of her reach. That pain bound Sam and me in a way I'd never have thought possible. Now, I was grateful for it. I would need a friend in the Bureau in the coming days, and Sam was one of the most intelligent agents I'd ever known.

"But you have to promise you'll keep me updated on what's going on," Sam continued in an uncharacteristically stern tone. "If you're not bringing Natalie to the field office, where are you going to take her?"

"My apartment," I replied. "The place where she's staying might be compromised if Moreno's people know where to find her. I don't want any nasty surprises."

"And how will you convince her to come with you? She attacked you before. She might again."

"You let me worry about that," I said grimly. I had a plan in place. Natalie wouldn't escape me again. "I want you to cut the feeds on the CCTV around where she's staying, and I want you to erase any footage you've found of her in the city."

"What? Why?"

"Because I don't want Parkinson to have anything on her."

And because I don't want a record of what I'm going to do.

"Okay," she agreed. "But swear to me that you'll call me tomorrow with an update."

"I will," I promised. I had no choice but to trust Sam. I needed her to stay on my side, or she might betray me to Parkinson. "In the meantime, I want you to keep looking into Natalie's ties to Moreno. I want to know what she was doing with his men and where the fuck she's been for the last five years."

"I'm on it," she confirmed. "I'll update you when you check in with me." It was a subtle threat; she was implying that she'd withhold any information she found if I didn't keep contact with her. The shy little mouse was bolder than I'd thought.

"Fine," I agreed and ended the call. I was nearly at my destination, and I didn't want to waste any time finishing off a conversation with Sam when I could be getting to Natalie.

I pulled up onto the curb directly in front of the address Sam had given me. I needed to be able to move from the townhouse back to my sedan as fast as possible. I planned to subdue Natalie, and I didn't want to be seen. Although considering the time, it was unlikely anyone would be around to see me.

As I crossed the sidewalk to the front stoop, I rested my hand on the gun holstered at my side. I'd made sure to gather a few provisions from the Bureau before I'd started my hunt. Natalie wasn't going to slip through my fingers again.

There was no point knocking. Natalie was well

trained enough that she wouldn't open the door for anyone at this hour. And picking the lock would only give her time to plan a counterattack when I managed to get in; she'd recognize the scrape of a pick in the lock, even if she was sleeping.

I took a deep breath and then launched into action. I kicked the door open, the wood splintering as it gave way. Natalie barely made a sound as she scrambled out of bed to meet the threat I posed, but I caught her gasp before she fell silent.

I didn't allow her time to gather her wits. Or a weapon.

I headed straight in the direction of the soft sound she'd made, speeding down the short corridor before shoving my way into a darkened bedroom. Natalie's silhouette raced toward me, framed by the streetlight that glowed through the drawn blinds.

I fired the gun.

She didn't slow. Her body collided with mine, forcing me back a step as her weight barreled into me.

I didn't meet her with aggression. I simply wrapped my arms around her and waited for the tranquilizer to take effect. She jerked and writhed, struggling in the cage of my arms.

"Jason," she slurred my name as she softened against me. I wished it was because she didn't want to fight me, but I knew it was the drugs settling into her system.

"I've got you," I murmured as she sagged in my arms. I wasn't sure if it was a statement of reassurance or dark triumph.

PART III
REUNION

CHAPTER 20

Natalie

Fear surfaced along with consciousness. Awareness that I was bound hit me like a blow to the chest. I could feel the supple leather around my wrists and ankles, trapping me in place for torment.

Bound. Helpless. Tortured.

Pleasure. Pain.

Fear.

A low, horrified moan left my lips, but I didn't fight the restraints. I'd given up fighting a long time ago. I was powerless to break free. The acceptance was almost as terrifying as the sensation of being trapped.

A large, warm hand cupped my cheek in a soothing gesture.

Alex.

I choked on a sob and began to tremble. I both craved and dreaded that touch. It meant the torment was over, but my secret desire for the comforting contact made my stomach turn.

"Look at me," he commanded. "Open your eyes, Natalie."

I didn't dare disobey a direct order. I opened my eyes and sucked in a sharp breath. Bright green eyes stared down at me.

Green eyes. Not gold.

"Jason?" His name shook as it left my lips.

His fingers sank into my hair, running through the silken strands in an achingly familiar motion.

"I'm here," he murmured. "I've got you."

I've got you. Those words were the last thing I remembered before the drugs pulled me under and I passed out in his arms.

I started to tremble again as panic spiked through my system.

I had to get away from Jason. He wasn't safe with me.

I looked around wildly, searching for a way out. I was in a utilitarian bedroom, a place devoid of decoration or personality. There was a single chest of drawers and a nightstand beside the massive iron four-poster bed. I lay on the mattress, my body spread out. Leather cuffs encircled my wrists and ankles, anchored to the bedposts by thick chains.

My breath came in short, shallow gasps.

I was trapped. I couldn't fight my way out. I couldn't put distance between me and Jason.

"Easy," he urged gently, still stroking my hair. "You're safe with me."

But you're not safe with me.

I kept the words locked behind my lips. I didn't fully understand it, but I couldn't deny the blind panic that gripped me at Jason's nearness.

"Let me go," I begged.

His jaw firmed. "No. We're going to have a talk. And I'm never letting you go again."

His eyes took on a feverish light as he said the last. He appeared maddened, almost feral.

I struggled to find calm, even though I couldn't stop shaking. There had to be some way I could reason with him.

"You can't keep me here against my will," I asserted, trying to make him see how insane the prospect was. I ignored the dark part of myself that yearned for him to follow through on his promise and continued to defy him. "You can't do this."

His nostrils flared. "I can and I will." I recognized

the steely determination in his tone. "I'm going to keep you tied to my bed until you tell me where the hell you've been and who you're working with. If I'm satisfied with your answers, I'll figure out a way to protect you from the Bureau. If not..." He trailed off, leaving the threat hanging in the air.

I swallowed hard. Division 9-C would disavow me if I were caught by the FBI. I'd go to prison for drug trafficking. Possibly even human trafficking, now that I'd become involved with Moreno's people on US soil. Or my division might just assassinate me before I was even taken to the Bureau. They wouldn't risk me spilling their secrets; they'd rather see me dead.

But worse than that was the danger I posed to Jason every second I remained with him.

"You have to let me go," I pleaded, tugging against the cuffs. "I know you don't want to hurt me. You're a good man."

He barked out a bitter laugh that sounded nothing like the Jason I remembered. "Anything that was good in me died with you. You've let me believe you were dead all this time. You owe me answers. Hell, you owe me five years." He leaned in close, his warm breath teasing across my lips. "No, I'm not going to hurt you. But I am going to punish you. If you won't answer me willingly, I have other methods of interrogation."

Dark arousal stirred in response to his nearness and his deviant threats. Memories of how he'd once disciplined me in his office, bending me over his desk for my first spanking, stirred in my mind, surfacing for the first time in years. How could I have forgotten?

Something inside me softened as an ache pulsed deep in my chest. His familiar, masculine scent surrounded me, intoxicating me, tempting me. I'd never forgotten Jason, but he'd become an abstract in my mind. I'd locked away all of the bittersweet memories of the time we'd shared together because I couldn't bear them. Not when getting back to him was impossible. I wouldn't risk his safety by returning to him.

Confusion threaded through my mind. I didn't understand how I was a threat to Jason, but I knew it deep in my bones.

I have to keep him away from Alex.

I wasn't sure why I couldn't allow Jason near Alex, but the prospect made fear grip my heart.

"I can't tell you anything," I whispered.

If I told Jason about Alex, he'd go after my handler. I had to keep them apart, no matter what. And I had to get away from Jason, or Alex would eventually come looking for me and find him.

Jason's face settled into a forbidding mask. His

eyes were harder than they'd once been, and the fine lines around them were deeper than I remembered. But he was unmistakably the same man I'd fallen in love with, and something tugged at my soul, even under the weight of his fury.

Mine.

Something white-hot filled my chest, pressing against my lungs with burning heat as it expanded within me.

Love.

I'd forgotten what it felt like. This painful, beautiful, all-consuming emotion that made my heart soar and ache at the same time.

I loved Jason. I had to save him.

"Please let me go," I begged. "You have to let me go."

His eyes flashed. "You're not going anywhere. You're going to answer my questions. And then, I'll decide what to do with you. But understand this: even after I extract the answers I want, I'm not letting you get away from me. I lived without you for five years, and I'm not going to do it anymore. I don't care what I have to do to keep you with me. You're mine, Natalie. By the time I'm finished with you, you'll remember that. You'll never forget it again."

A thread of fear twined through the yearning that filled my chest. "You can't do this to me."

"What about what you did to me?" he roared, his tenuous control snapping. "You ruined me! But you just went on with your life! And now, you're working with the Colombians? They shot two cops, and you fucking attacked me and ran. Why did you run from me?" His shout broke on the final question, and his eyes tightened with pain.

"I'm sorry," I whispered through my own agony. "I'm sorry I couldn't come back to you. And I'm sorry I can't tell you anything about where I've been or what I've been doing. You have to trust me and—"

"Trust you?" he seethed. "That ship has sailed." He leaned in close again. "I'm going to get the truth out of you, the only way I know how."

"What are you going to do to me?" I asked, my voice small. Fear still nipped at me, but my core began to throb with excitement I hadn't felt in years.

"I'm going to remind you of who I am. I'm your Master. I always have been. I always will be. And you don't get to keep secrets from your Master." His fingers curled beneath my chin, angling my face so my lips were offered up to him. "You belong to me, Natalie. You'll never forget it again after today."

His mouth slanted over mine, gentle for only a moment. At the first contact, forgotten lust slammed into me, igniting my system with bliss. Tears formed at the corners of my closed eyes as the pure joy of his touch soared through me.

He must have felt it too, because he snarled against my mouth, and his teeth sank into my lower lip. I parted for him on a gasp, and his tongue surged inside to tangle with mine. He kissed me in a frenzy, nothing refined or controlled in the way he claimed my mouth with raw intensity. His big hand cupped my jaw, tipping my head back farther so he could plunder more deeply.

I moaned into him, and chains rattled as I struggled to hold him. My moan turned to a whimper when I couldn't return his touch, but the fear of my restraints was absent. Memories of how he used to bind me, fuck me, love me, filled my mind, and my body heated for his domineering brand of lovemaking. I remembered everything, the recollections spilling out of a forgotten corner of my brain.

Tears flowed, trailing over my temples and falling into my hair. He finally released my lips, only to brush feather-light kisses over my wet lashes. I shivered as emotion and carnal need overwhelmed me. His tenderness tore at my soul, the knowledge that I'd lost years with him causing me physical pain.

But that pain wasn't enough to blot out the desire that coursed through me.

"Jason." His name left my lips on a tormented whisper.

"I'm right here," he promised, pressing a reassuring kiss against my forehead. "I'm not going anywhere."

He drew back slightly, his hands bracketing my face so I couldn't look away.

"Where have you been?" he asked softly. "Why did you leave me?"

"I can't..." I choked on the refusal, but I forced it out. "I can't tell you. I'm sorry." I had to keep him safe. "You have to let me go. Please."

His eyes darkened with pain, but his lips firmed with determination. "That's not happening. You're not leaving this bed until you give up your secrets. I'm not going to let anything keep us apart any longer, not even you. You're mine. You know that, don't you?"

"Jason, please..."

His fingers curved around my throat, asserting his dominance with the slightest pressure. "Tell me," he demanded. "Tell me what we both know. Say you belong to me."

My vision blurred as the tears fell faster. He gently wiped them away with his thumbs.

"I can't," I whispered. If I gave in, I'd never be

able to leave him again. And I had to leave him. To keep him safe.

He regarded me intently, his jaw set. "You can and you will. I won't let you hide from me. Not one second longer."

His hands fisted in my thin camisole, and the fabric tore with one jerk of his powerful arms. He'd come to me in the night, when I only wore the flimsy top and my white cotton underwear. Now, I was nearly naked, exposed in the one second it took him to strip me of so much more than my clothing. As his eyes devoured me, flaring with hunger and lust, he looked deeper than my flesh. There was nowhere for me to run, nowhere to hide. He stared at my soul, his gaze penetrating me as though he could discover all my secrets without a word passing through my lips.

My nipples pebbled to hard buds, throbbing for attention as cool air washed over them. I arched my back in mindless invitation, tugging against my bonds as I instinctively sought to draw him closer.

He didn't touch me in the way I craved. Instead, he reached into the nightstand drawer and removed a pair of scissors. Fear coiled in my belly as they glinted silver in the light that filtered through the closed curtains.

He rested his free hand on my stomach, the firm pressure reassuring me even as he pinned me in place.

"Don't move," he ordered. "I'm not going to hurt you."

The cold metal whispered across my hipbone as he slid the blade beneath the band at the top of my panties. With a soft *snick,* the fabric parted. He quickly severed the other side before setting the scissors aside. Then, he gently pulled the ruined panties away from my body, exposing every inch of me to his ravenous gaze.

I blew out a shaky breath. Adrenaline rushed through my veins in the wake of the hit of fear, making me lightheaded. My entire world centered on him: his touch, his will. I was completely helpless, laid out before him like a sacrifice.

The prospect should terrify me, but all I felt was hunger. Yearning. I ached for him, a physical pain between my legs and in my heart.

"Please," I begged tremulously. "Touch me."

His eyes locked on mine, and the pressure of his hand on my abdomen increased slightly, a reminder of his possession of my body and soul.

"Who am I?" he demanded.

Master. My Master.

I bit the inside of my cheek to hold the words in.

After watching me for a few tense seconds, his fingers trailed down to tease at the upper edge of my

JULIA SYKES

soft curls. His other hand came up to cup my jaw, his thumb tracing the line of my cheekbone.

"I know my sweet kitten's in there somewhere," he said with calm certainty.

I'm right here, I wanted to say. *I'm yours.*

He rubbed his thumb across my lips. "If you're a good girl for me, you get to come. But you have to submit first." His fingers teased through my curls to rest above my throbbing clit. "Surrender," he urged. "Tell me you belong to me."

"Please..."

A low, tormented sound eased up his throat. "I forgot how fucking sweet you are when you beg. But I can't give you what we both want. Call me *Master*, and you get to come."

Two fingers teased around my clit in an excruciatingly slow circular motion. My core fluttered around nothing, craving for him to fill me and fuck me. I groaned my frustration and rotated my hips up toward him, seeking more stimulation.

His hand left my sex, and a sharp sting flared on my inner thighs as he spanked them in rapid succession. I cried out as my skin began to burn, but the restraints around my ankles kept me open and at his mercy.

"Naughty kitten," he chastised. "You know better than that. I control your pleasure."

The burn turned to a delicious warmth that seeped into my flesh, moving up my thighs to heat my core. My labia became swollen and slick with my arousal.

He stopped spanking me and trailed his fingertips across my enflamed skin, petting me where he'd disciplined me.

A strangled sob left my chest. Everything about my predicament made my body and my soul ache.

"Shhh," he soothed me. "You're okay. I'm going to take care of you. All you have to do is say you're mine."

I whined in wordless protest. There was a reason I couldn't give in. I couldn't...

Two fingers traced the line of my slick folds, gathering up the wetness there. He eased farther back, until his touch brushed across my asshole.

"No," I whimpered. I couldn't handle it if he penetrated me there. I'd always been sensitive, but something about being touched in that forbidden way always made me melt for him.

"I'm sorry, kitten," he said roughly. "That's not going to stop me. There's only one way this ends. And that's with you screaming out my name."

His fingers circled the puckered bud, teasing. At the same time, his thumb applied light pressure on my clit. I gasped, and my back arched as pleasure shot through me. His free hand left my face to toy with my breasts, pinching and tugging at my nipples in slow, glorious torture.

"Your body remembers its Master," he said, his voice dropping to that impossibly sexy, deep register that he found in his dominant headspace. I shuddered at the sound of it as my body responded with a flood of lust.

"Tell me you're mine," he prompted, his voice floating to me as I fell into his intoxicating power. All thoughts of resistance were wiped away. There was no thought at all; only the sensations he was inflicting upon me and his will washing over me.

His fingers pressed against my asshole, slipping inside me. The sensation of being filled by him tore what was left of my conscious mind to shreds.

"Master!" I cried out as I clenched around the intrusion, my body uncertain if it wanted to push him out or invite him in. He continued to press in, pene-trating me in a slow slide, my slick juices on his fingers easing the way.

"Good girl." His voice was thick with more than lust. "Come for me. Come for your Master."

His thumb pressed down hard on my clit, rubbing in an expert rhythm to wring ecstasy from my body. He continued to pinch and roll my abused nipples, lighting up my system with pleasure and pain.

"Jason!" I exploded on a scream. White lights popped across my vision, and my eyes slid closed as ecstasy wracked my body. My inner muscles contracted around him, reminding me of the taboo way he filled me. He owned every inch of me, and I was powerless to resist the pleasure coursing through my system.

Powerless.

I began to twist against my bonds, my body writhing helplessly as the pleasure claimed me.

Trapped.

My blissful scream morphed into a horrified shriek as I fell into dark memories that I'd carefully locked away.

A fresh jolt ripped through my body, the implant in my shoulder disabling my attempts to fight. Alex was coolly composed as he arranged my body on the padded table, cuffing my wrists at my sides and lifting my feet into the stir-rups so I was spread open. I was in the horrific room where I'd found Elena being tortured. And my body was strapped down and vulnerable, just as hers had been.

I tried taking deep breaths through clenched teeth, staving off the panic that threatened to bubble up and consume me.

Cool air rolled over my skin, sending a chill through my flesh. It penetrated deep, seeping into my bones. My teeth began to chatter as Alex positioned my limp body where he wanted it.

"This is going to be a difficult process," he informed me calmly. "But I'll be with you every step of the way."

"Fuck you," I spat.

He smiled, the sharp glint in his golden eyes belying the benign curve of his full lips. "Unfortunately, that's not one of the perks of my job. We will have a purely professional relationship, Natalie."

"I don't want this," I forced out, struggling to make my thick tongue shape the words. "You said I had a choice to work with you or not. I don't choose this."

His smile remained fixed in place. "You were allowed to choose to cooperate willingly. You chose wrong. You're going to be a loyal, obedient agent. How long the process takes is up to you."

"What process? What are you going to do to me?" I couldn't stop my voice from shaking. All my instincts told me to fight, but I'd been effectively and efficiently rendered completely powerless. I was naked and at Alex's mercy. He could do anything to me, and there was nothing I could do to resist him.

He picked up a syringe from a metal table set beside me. I tried to shrink away, but he easily sank the needle into the crook of my arm.

"You're going to start feeling it soon," he told me. "Your

heartbeat will pick up. Your pupils will dilate. Today, I'll monitor your physical responses and get a baseline."

He began sticking wires at strategic points on my body: above my heart, on my temples. They were attached to machinery I didn't understand, but Alex watched whatever readings he was getting with keen interest.

My heart hammered against my ribs, and my blood pumped hot in my veins. My entire body flushed, and my skin pebbled.

Alex moved between my legs, staring at my sex. After a few horrible, tense minutes, he reached out his gloved hand and touched my labia. Horror seized my soul when his fingers came away wet with the undeniable sign of my arousal.

"Pleasure is a powerful tool," he remarked. "As is humiliation. You won't have any secrets from me by the time we're finished."

He picked up a long, silvery probe and pressed it against my slick entrance.

"Don't," I pleaded, shame and terror expanding in my chest.

"This won't hurt," he said, as though that was supposed to reassure me. "We'll get to that part later."

I screamed as the violation began. I lost count of how many times he wrung an orgasm from my drugged system before he injected me with a different cocktail. Then the pain came, and my mind shattered.

CHAPTER 21

Jason

Natalie's screams ripped through my chest, clawing at my heart. One second, she's been crying out my name in ecstasy, and then next, she was shrieking in unmistakable agony. Her eyes were open wide, but she wasn't looking at me. They were glazed over, staring at some horror I couldn't imagine.

I quickly freed her from the restraints, leaving the cuffs locked in place but unhooking the chains that connected them to the bedposts. I didn't want to waste time fiddling with the small padlocks that kept the leather wrapped around her wrists and ankles, but I had to get her free so I could cradle her in my arms.

She thrashed and writhed, moaning in horror. I clutched her tightly against my chest, pinning her arms at her sides as I held her close.

"You're okay," I tried to reassure her, but my voice broke.

Had I done this to her? All I'd wanted was to give her pleasure and coax out her submission, to remind her of our connection. I wanted her to put her trust in me and tell me her secrets, but I'd managed to push her into a waking nightmare instead.

Was this what I'd been like when I used to have PTSD episodes? Trapped within the horrors in my own head?

My blood ran cold. If Natalie was having an episode, something terrible had happened to her. What had she suffered in the last five years that she would react this way when I pushed her to let go? Was this why she'd resisted me? Because she feared that if she gave up control, she'd be lost to darkness?

"I'm sorry, kitten," I murmured against her hair. My eyes burned, and regret twisted my gut. "I'm so sorry. Come back to me. Please."

Slowly, her thrashing calmed, leaving her shaking in my arms. She closed her eyes and began whispering something I didn't understand.

"And then my heart with pleasure fills. And then

my heart with pleasure fills." Over and over again, she recited the words.

"Natalie?" I prompted, struggling for a calm, even tone. "Natalie. Look at me."

She blinked, and her gorgeous sapphire eyes focused on me at last. I heaved a sigh of relief and pressed a kiss against her forehead.

"I'm sorry," I said again. "I had no idea..." I trailed off, unable to put the magnitude of my sin into words.

Her brows drew together, and she touched my cheek with her soft fingertips. "What are you sorry for?"

"I didn't mean to push you so hard," I said. "I never wanted to hurt you."

One corner of her lips ticked up in a wry smile. "You didn't hurt me."

My arms tightened around her. Something was wrong. Although her cheeks were still wet with tears, her eyes were clear. There was no hint of fear or distress in her countenance. She appeared eerily serene.

"I didn't mean to upset you," I said carefully. "You were screaming."

She stared up at me. "I don't know what you're talking about."

Was it possible that she didn't recall her episode

because it was too traumatic for her conscious mind to face? I wasn't sure if that was how this worked. She was the psychologist, not me. My own experience with PTSD hadn't prepared me for what I'd just witnessed. I'd suffer through the panic and fear that used to grip me a thousand times over if it meant I never had to hear Natalie scream like that ever again.

I cuddled her closer, unable to put a millimeter of space between our bodies.

"What were you saying?" I pressed gently. "When you started to calm down. 'And then my heart with pleasure fills.' What does that mean?"

She stiffened. "I don't know." Suddenly, she shook her head as though to clear it. When her eyes found mine again, they were beseeching. "You have to let me go, Jason."

Fury threatened to rise again, driving me back toward madness.

"Not happening," I refused her. "I'm sorry I pushed you to..." I couldn't put the horrible episode into words. "I'm sorry. But you're staying here with me. I'm going to take care of you."

I still needed answers about where she'd been and what she was doing with Moreno's people, but that could wait. It was imperative that I convince her that she was safe with me, and I feared that I might push her into her trauma again if I pressed too hard. We had to establish trust again.

I'd start by proving to her that I could care for her, just as I'd promised. Keeping her cradled in my arms, I retrieved a small coil of rope from the night-stand drawer. She kept her face tucked against my chest, and I was grateful she didn't seem to notice it. I didn't like the idea of restraining her again after her distress, but I'd do what was necessary to keep her with me until I could figure out what the hell was going on with her and where she'd been for the last five years.

I continued to hold her as I stood and began to walk out of my bedroom.

"Where are you taking me?" she asked, and the tremor in her voice nearly broke me. I never wanted her to be afraid of me.

"I'm going to get you something to eat." I moved us into the open plan living room/kitchen and settled her down in a chair at my small dining table. I stayed in her personal space for a few seconds longer, debating. She studied me with equal intensity, and I could practically see her mind working to devise a way to escape me. I didn't understand why she so desperately wanted to get away from me. It pained me like a knife to my heart, but I was beginning to understand that there might be good reasons why my kitten was skittish now.

"Do I need to tie you to this chair while I feed you?" I asked, barely managing to keep my shame from coloring my tone. I'd meant it when I told her I wasn't letting her go, no matter what I had to do to bind her to me. I didn't want to traumatize her further, but I wouldn't risk her escape. I'd lived without her for far too long. Now that she was back in my life, I'd die before I let her leave me again.

When she didn't answer, I settled into grim determination. I uncoiled the rope that was wrapped around my wrist. She eyed it with unease, noticing it for the first time. I captured her jaw in my free hand, gently lifting her face so she had to look into my eyes.

"I'm not going to hurt you," I promised. "But I can't trust you right now. I want to take care of you. I wish you'd let me." I finished on a strained whisper. "Why do you keep trying to run from me?"

She bit her lip and cut her eyes away. I firmed my grip on her jaw, redirecting her gaze to mine.

"I don't want you to get hurt," she finally said, her eyes tight with desperation.

A low, humorless laugh left my chest. "You already ripped my heart out when you died. You can't hurt me worse than that. And now that I know you're alive, I won't allow you to leave me again. I won't give you the opportunity to try to fight your way free." I began to loop the rope through the D-rings attached to the cuffs around her wrists, binding her arms together behind the back of the chair. "You're going to accept my protection and tell me your secrets. Whatever you're scared of, I'll keep you safe. You used to trust me. You still can. The only way for you to hurt me now is to leave me."

"Not me," she said quietly. "I'd never hurt you. That's why you have to let me go. You're not safe with me."

I finished tying her in place and crouched beside her so I could look into her eyes, wishing I could look straight through them into her soul and learn her secrets.

"What do you mean?" I asked. "If you're in danger and you're worried it'll affect me, I don't give a shit. I'll arrange protection for you. Whatever you were doing with Moreno's men, I can keep you safe from them."

She shook her head. "I'm not working with them. I'm black ops, Jason. You can't get involved in my world."

I sucked in a breath. Natalie was black ops? That would explain what she was doing getting involved with scum like Moreno.

But it still didn't explain why she'd chosen to leave

me all those years ago and start a new life as an operative. My heart twisted. I'd known Natalie was ambitious, but I'd never thought that ambition would drive us apart. I would have done anything for her. I would have died for her. But she'd left me for a job.

I stood and turned away from her so she couldn't see the pain in my eyes.

"Jason?" she asked tentatively. "Do you understand now? You have to let me go."

I didn't look at her. Instead, I moved into the kitchen and set about preparing food for her.

"You need to eat something," I said. "We can talk after."

She sighed, but didn't offer any further protest. I selected a mac and cheese micro-meal out of my freezer—the only food I had in stock. I wished I had something better to offer her, but I'd never bothered to learn to cook properly. My apartment was a place to eat and sleep. I lived for my job. It was the only time I could fool myself into thinking I was a good man. If I did good things, maybe I wasn't the shell of a man who'd allowed the woman he loved to get killed while he helplessly watched.

It had always been a fleeting fantasy, but it helped me stay sane. It helped keep me from using again.

I wasn't entirely without the aid of prescription drugs, though. The one I allowed myself was sleeping pills. It was the only way to get through the night without nightmares of watching Natalie die.

I glanced over at her. I'd tied her so she was facing away from the kitchen. She wouldn't see what I was doing.

While the microwave emitted a soft buzzing sound, I slid three pills from the bottle and crushed them against the counter with the back of a spoon.

I was uneasy about the idea of drugging her again, but I needed to talk to Sam without being overheard. I had to know what she'd found on Natalie. If my kitten were part of a black ops division, Sam would be skilled enough to hack into any database and uncover the truth. I needed to make the call to check in, but I didn't dare take my eyes off Natalie for one second while she was awake and alert. She'd been formidable as a recruit. I could only imagine how skilled she was after training as an operative for years.

I wouldn't risk her getting away while my back was turned.

When the microwave dinged, I removed the hot plastic container and placed it on a plate. Then I spooned the crushed pill powder into the dish and mixed it in. I hoped the salty flavor would mask any bitterness.

I carried the steaming food over to the table and pulled up a chair beside hers. Her brows rose.

"You cook like a bachelor," she remarked.

"Of course I'm a bachelor," I said more harshly than I intended. "There's never been anyone but you." Jealous rage clawed at my insides. "Has there been anyone for you?" I demanded.

Her eyes softened, and she jerked against her restraints, as though she wanted to reach for me. "Of course not. I still... I've always—"

"You should eat." I cut her off before she could say what I feared she might. If she told me she still loved me, I wasn't at all sure I'd be able to maintain my tenuous control over myself. It was difficult enough holding myself back when I thought she'd chosen to leave me and didn't want to be with me anymore. All I wanted to do was take her in my arms and make her mine again. I wanted to bury myself inside her and never let her leave my bed.

But I couldn't do that until she came clean, until there were no more secrets between us and I could trust her. If I claimed her again only to have her leave me at the first opportunity, what was left of my soul would wither and die.

Her eyes dropped from mine, and her perfect lips twisted in sorrow. She appeared utterly defeated. I hated the sight of it, even though I knew I couldn't risk freeing her from her bonds.

If I couldn't free her as she desired, I'd just have

to prove to her that she could trust me. And that trust would be established as I took care of her.

A dark part of me liked the idea of having her completely dependent on me, and a deviant surge of lust pulsed through my veins when I lifted a spoonful of pasta to her lips. The Dominant in me wanted her bound and helpless, relying on me to see to her every need. Even the simple act of feeding her brought me pleasure. After the long years of loneliness, I wanted to bind her to me in every way possible. She was still naked from when I'd stripped her in my bedroom, and the sight of her exposed, beautiful body tied in place while I was fully clothed in my suit affected me more than was healthy.

I blew on the food to cool it so it wouldn't burn her mouth. "Open up, kitten," I urged, a gentle command, but a command nonetheless.

She didn't look at me, but her lips parted. I fed her in silence, not pressing her to talk. I simply enjoyed the act of nurturing her. Even in our messed up circumstances, she allowed me to look after her needs. If she was hungry, I'd feed her. If she needed a shower, I'd wash her. And if she needed pleasure, I could certainly see to that.

As I fed her, I fell into my Dominant headspace, getting high off the power dynamic. There was nothing sexual about our interaction, but I felt greater pleasure than I had in all the years since I'd lost her. I took to it like a starving man to a feast, gorging myself on the perfection of her submission to me.

When she finally finished the meal, I reluctantly set the dish aside, hesitant for the moment to end. She yawned.

Fuck. I'd forgotten about the sleeping pills. I wasn't ready for her to slip back into unconsciousness. Even though we weren't talking, I craved her company.

She blinked slowly, her lids growing heavy as she slumped forward. I caught her so her wrists didn't strain against her restraints, wrapping my arm around her shoulders and curling my fingers beneath her chin so she looked up at me.

When her eyes found mine, they were accusatory. "You drugged me," she said thickly.

"I did," I responded calmly. "You can sleep, kitten. I'll be right here with you the whole time."

"Why?" she asked faintly, her eyes sliding closed.

I stroked her hair and waited a few more seconds, until her breathing turned deep and even as she fell into sleep.

"Because I love you," I admitted on a whisper.

She didn't respond in any way. That was for the best. I still wasn't ready to hear her say the words.

JULIA SYKES

Not until the truth was revealed and I could trust her again.

Resigned, I untied her and carried her limp form back into the bedroom. I laid her on the bed and unlocked the cuffs around her wrists. After a minute's deliberation, I left one ankle cuffed and attached it to the chain on the bedpost. I was going to make my call in the next room, and I couldn't risk Natalie stirring somehow when I wasn't watching her.

I took a few moments longer to drink in the sight of her perfect, naked body before covering her with blankets. I didn't want her to get cold, even if I'd rather strip down and keep her warm with my own body heat.

Not yet, I reminded myself. Honesty had to come first. Then I'd mark her with my cum and make her mine again.

Tearing my gaze from her, I strode out of the bedroom, cracking the door behind me so the sound of my conversation with Sam would be muffled. I doubted Natalie would awaken anytime soon, but I didn't want to take any chances. If she wouldn't tell me the full truth about who she worked for and where she'd been, then I'd have to rely on Sam's skills to get me the information I needed.

I pulled my phone out of my pocket and connected the call. She answered immediately.

"Jason. What's going on? Is Natalie with you? I mean, your tracker says you're at your apartment. And I, um, watched the CCTV feed when you went to her townhouse. So, yeah. I know she's with you. But don't worry. I erased the feed, like you asked."

She was talking a mile a minute, almost like a stream of consciousness rather than conversation.

"What's wrong?" I demanded. Sam wouldn't be babbling unless she was nervous. "What did you find?"

"Well, um, I looked into where Natalie's been recently. It wasn't easy. She has at least three aliases I uncovered, and that's just in the last year. It looks like she's been running drugs in South America."

"She hasn't," I countered. "She told me she's black ops. She's been undercover." I'd known my sweet kitten couldn't be involved in Bliss trafficking. Nothing had made sense until she admitted she was an operative.

"No, she hasn't," Sam said. "I thought of that. I've been digging through every FBI and CIA database there is. There's no record of Natalie or any of her aliases. As far as the US government is concerned, she's been dead for five years."

"That's not possible. You didn't dig deep enough."

"You know I'm too good to miss something that important," Sam replied. "I dug as deep as I could go.

If Natalie's black ops, she's not working for us. I can keep tracking where she's been. I've only gotten back thirteen months so far, and she's good at covering her tracks. Like, really good. She must have help."

"Yeah, from the CIA," I asserted.

"Stop it, Jason," Sam said with uncharacteristic steel. "She's not CIA. Pretending she is will get you nowhere. You want answers? I'm working on getting them for you. But you should probably ask her some questions yourself."

"You think I haven't tried that?" I demanded. "What do expect me to do? Torture her?"

"Of course not. Jesus, Jason. Get a grip. If you can't handle this, I'll go to Parkinson. I should have done that already, but I understand what... I didn't want to... Well, I just didn't want to," she finished after stumbling over her words. Again, I wondered exactly why Sam was helping me behind the Director's back, but I didn't bother to press her about it. She was being decent enough not to question what I was doing with Natalie, so I wouldn't pry into her painful secrets about her own heartbreak.

"Thank you," I said, genuinely grateful. "I can't let Parkinson know Natalie's alive. Not until we figure this out. If she really isn't working for the US government, she'll be arrested. I have to know I can protect her from whatever's coming before we make our next move."

"I agree. I'll keep looking into her activities."

"I'll check in again tomorrow," I promised and ended the call.

As soon as I hung up, I hurried back to Natalie. She still slept, her dark hair spilling over my pillow. She looked so fucking perfect there, in my bed.

My mind spun. If she wasn't working for us, she would face worse than arrest and prison time. She could be shipped off and thrown into a dark hole where I'd never find her.

I knew deep in my bones that it didn't matter what she'd done, or who she might be working for. I'd never let her go. I'd protect her, no matter what.

CHAPTER 22

Natalie

Alex carried me back into my cell and sat down on my cot, holding me close to his chest. His long fingers brushed my cheek, taking up a stray lock of hair and tucking it behind my ear.

"Tell me about Jason," he said gently.

I stopped breathing.

He rubbed his big hand up and down my back in a soothing motion. "Now, Natalie," he chided. "You know you don't have any secrets from me. Did you think I would forget Agent Harper was the first person you asked for when you woke up?"

I licked my dry lips. "I was confused. Disoriented."

"Then why do you cry out his name during our sessions?"

My blood froze in my veins. I thought of Jason often as a way of coping with what was happening to me. The fantasy of being with him was my way to escape the horror. But I didn't realize I ever spoke his name aloud.

"I could arrange to bring him to you," Alex continued on calmly. "Is that what you want? For me to bring him here?"

"No!" I gasped out. I didn't want Jason anywhere near my torturer.

"We usually only take on new recruits," he continued, as though I hadn't spoken. "But I've looked at Agent Harper's file. He would be a promising asset."

"Leave him alone!" I shouted, my voice ragged from hours of screaming.

"You seem so desperate to have him with you," he said, as falsely benign as ever. "I can make it happen."

"No." I choked on a sob. "Please."

Alex studied me for a long moment, his golden eyes searching my soul. "If you don't want him here, then you're going to have to let go of these fantasies. I know you're thinking of him when I bring you to orgasm. If you want him to be with you, I can always arrange for him to come and watch."

The idea of Jason witnessing my destruction, my humiliation, was too horrible to bear. I wanted him to remember me as I had been with him. He thought I was dead. It was better that way. If Alex got his hands on Jason, he'd do so much worse than make him watch as I was tortured. I *couldn't allow Alex to hurt Jason the way he was hurting me.*

"I'll do anything," I gasped out. "Just leave him alone."

"All right, Natalie. Agent Harper won't be touched. If you promise me you'll stop escaping into these fantasies during our sessions. I need you present with me for the process to work. Do you understand?"

I nodded as tears flooded down my cheeks. In that moment, I locked my memories of Jason away, never to be accessed again. His life depended on it. I had to keep Alex away from him, at any cost. Even the cost of my sanity, my soul.

"Natalie!" a deep, masculine voice called out my name. I curled into myself, fearing Alex's return.

His hands closed around my shoulders, shaking me.

"Open your eyes, kitten. Look at me. Please."

Kitten.

I'm with Jason.

I gasped, and I my eyes snapped open. Fear thundered through my system.

"Run," I begged on a ragged whisper. "You can't be here."

He pulled me into his arms. "You're okay, kitten. You're safe with me."

I twisted beneath him, trying to get free. My leg

jerked against a leather cuff, and I realized I was chained down. My tears came faster, blinding me.

"No," I moaned. "He'll hurt you. I can't let him…" My throat closed up, unable to put what Alex would do to him into words.

"We're in my apartment, Natalie," he told me calmly. "No one else is here. No one will hurt me. Or you."

I squeezed my eyes shut, unable to cope with the terror that was ripping my brain to shreds. I couldn't think, couldn't fight.

"And then my heart with pleasure fills," I whispered the familiar words like a prayer. "And then my heart with pleasure fills."

"Why are you saying that?" I was distantly aware of Jason's frustrated question, but it didn't stick in my mind.

I repeated the mantra, until the full stanzas of the poem flowed through my mind, filling it with the cheery image of a field of bright yellow daffodils. Nothing could hurt me here. Nothing bad existed in this peaceful place. All concerns, all my dark memories and fears, melted away into nothing.

I blinked up at Jason. His eyes were tight with worry. I reached out trailed my fingertips along the creases in his brow, as though I could smooth them away.

"What's wrong?" I asked.

"Where did you go just now?" he pressed. "You were crying in your sleep. You were scared when you woke up. You thought I was in danger. And now... You said that line—'And then my heart with pleasure fills'—and it's like nothing happened. What does it mean? Why did you think I was in danger? Did someone..." His voice roughened to a barely intelligible growl. "Did someone hurt you?"

I shook my head. "I don't know what you're talking about. The last thing I remember is falling asleep at the table. After you drugged me," I added with reproach.

"You're cold," he noted instead of commenting on my accusation. He rubbed at the goose bumps on my arms.

Now that he mentioned it, I did feel chilled down to my bones. I shivered and burrowed into his warmth. I realized that I could feel his bare skin against mine for the first time in years. The sensation was so sweet, it brought tears to my eyes. Confusion briefly flashed through my mind when I noted that my cheeks were already wet. I hastily wiped at them and put it out of my mind, instead focusing on the joy of being in Jason's arms.

I traced the lines of his muscles, re-learning the shape of his hard chest and abs. They rippled beneath my touch, flexing under my fingers. I explored lower, feeling the sexy V at his hips that led down to...

His hand closed around my wrist, stopping me. "No," he ground out. "I promised myself I wouldn't. Not until you come clean with me."

"I already told you I'm black ops. I can't say more than that. I'm sorry. And you really do have to let me go. I can't stay with you."

"Because you think someone will hurt me if you do?" His green eyes were incisive, flashing in the dim evening light that filtered through the curtains.

I flinched. I couldn't think about that. I knew I had to get away from Jason, to keep him separated from Alex.

But I couldn't allow myself to contemplate why that was. It was a base knowledge, burned deep into my psyche.

"My life is dangerous," I said to reason with myself as much as with him. "You can't be part of it."

"That's not good enough," he told me. "You'll have to be more honest than that. I can't protect you if you don't tell me the truth."

"I am telling the truth," I insisted. "I've just told you all the truth I can. I won't pull you into my world."

He studied me carefully, and when he finally

spoke, his tone was cautious. "You're not CIA. They don't have any record of you working for them."

"Of course they don't," I replied levelly. "Not officially, anyway."

"No, Natalie. They don't have any record of you at all. Everyone thinks you're dead."

I shook my head. "You don't understand. They'll disavow me if they even suspect someone at the FBI is aware that I exist. No one will come to save me from justice. They'll let me go to jail for drug and human trafficking. If they don't kill me first."

"That's not how we work," he told me. "The US government wouldn't assassinate one of their own. Who are you really working for, Natalie?"

I shrugged. "You're lucky enough to live in a world where you think that's true. Well, it's not. My job is dangerous."

"Then why do you do it?" he asked, his voice strained. "Why did you leave me for a job where your employers would rather see you dead than be exposed?"

My heart twisted. "I couldn't come back to you. I'm sorry."

"Why?" he pressed, his eyes shining. "I would have died for you. I wanted to die *with* you. How could you leave me like that?"

Dark memories stirred.

I don't want this, I'd begged. *You said I had a choice to work with you or not. I don't choose this.*

Alex's bland smile flashed through my mind. *You were allowed to choose to cooperate willingly. You chose wrong.*

"Stop saying that," Jason's voice ripped me out of the past.

I blinked at him. "Saying what?"

"That line. 'And then my heart with pleasure fills.' Every time you say it, I lose you. What does it mean?"

I shrugged. "I don't know."

His big hands bracketed my face, his eyes piercing into me as though he could look into my mind. "What happened to you? Where have you been?"

"I can't—"

He cut me off with a warning growl. "Don't say you can't tell me. I won't accept that as an answer."

I pressed my lips together. If he wouldn't accept the only answer I could give him, then I wouldn't reply at all.

"I'm sorry," he said abruptly, his face firming into hard lines of determination.

"For what?"

The question barely left my lips before he flipped me onto my front. He was on me in an instant, straddling my lower back so I was pinned down beneath him. My fingers scrabbled at the sheets, but there was nowhere for me to go.

"What are you doing?" I asked, panic and lust twining inside me in a confusing cocktail. I wanted to be trapped by Jason. A selfish, dark part of me didn't want him to release me. But I also instinctively knew that I couldn't allow him to trap me. I couldn't indulge in the feel of his strong body dominating my own.

He didn't answer me. He reached over to the nightstand and grabbed the length of rope he'd used to bind me to the kitchen chair. I twisted beneath him, but he easily caught my wrists and looped the rope over them. The feel of the slightly rough fibers running over my soft skin made me shiver involuntarily. I shouldn't be enjoying this. I couldn't.

He quickly subdued me, securing the rope around my wrists in a grip that was tight enough to ensure I couldn't slip out, but it wouldn't cut off my circulation. Jason would never harm me. But he would bind me so I couldn't try to escape him. He tied the rope to one of the metal slats at the head of the bed, which seemed to have been crafted with the precise purpose of trapping me exactly where he wanted me.

A soft whimper eased up my throat. I wasn't sure if it was a sound of desire or fear. A little voice deep inside my mind shouted at me to struggle, but it was growing fainter by the second. Being overwhelmed by Jason felt so *good*. If he wouldn't allow me to fight or flee, I no longer had the option to defy him. I didn't have to worry about making the hard choice to leave him, because he was taking it from me. In binding me, he freed me. I shuddered and relaxed beneath him, giving in to the power he'd always wielded over me.

"There's my sweet kitten," he said with painfully tender approval. He stroked my cheek, catching the tear that had spilled over. "You can cry. It's okay. You're safe with me," he promised, giving me permission to finally release the roiling emotions that had been bottled up inside me for years.

Another tear fell, and he kissed it away.

His weight finally eased from my back, and he shifted to free my cuffed ankle from the chain that had kept me bound to the bed in my sleep.

"On your knees," he ordered, his voice gently coaxing, even though it was an unmistakable command. His unique ability to be so careful with me while still controlling my entire being made me melt.

I shifted my knees so they were tucked beneath me. With my arms tied in front of me, my torso remained pressed against the mattress, forcing my back to arch. My ass was offered up to him for his use. The position made my core contract in anticipation of his cock, and wetness gathered between my legs as my body prepared to take him.

His fingers stroked my slick folds, grazing over my clit as he petted my pussy. I whined and wriggled my hips, craving more even as I reveled in the reverent touch. He lightly slapped my sex, a gentle reprimand that made me moan.

"Stay still," he commanded. "I don't want any hits to land where I don't want them to."

"What…" I asked faintly, trying to get my lust-drunk brain to work.

"Shhh," he hushed me, still petting me to keep me calm. "I don't want you to talk unless I ask you a question. Do you understand?"

"Yes," I said meekly.

He slapped my pussy again, hard enough to make me cry out in shock.

"Who am I?" he prompted.

"Master," I released his title on a moan, loving the feel of it on my tongue. "Yes, Master."

"Good girl. I'm going to discipline you now. You need it badly. You need the release. And I need your obedience."

Before I could formulate a response, he briefly left me to retrieve something from his chest of drawers. He took a few seconds to rummage through the top drawer before he returned to me. He held the black leather paddle up so I could see it clearly, slapping it against his hand.

"Do you remember what this feels like, kitten?"

I bit my lip and nodded, my cheeks suffusing with heat. He'd paddled me before, the night he'd taken me to the BDSM club to celebrate my impending graduation from the FBI academy. So long ago. Before I'd died, and everything changed.

"I've kept it," he told me, his voice hitching slightly. "I've kept this, too."

He lifted the other item I hadn't seen wrapped around the handle of the paddle: a thin strip of black leather with a silver ring set into the center.

A lump formed in my throat, and my lower lip quivered as more tears spilled over.

My collar.

The symbol that marked me as his.

He gathered up my hair and brushed it to one side. His gorgeous eyes were shining as the leather encircled my throat. He took his time buckling it closed, savoring the moment. When he finished, he traced the line of the collar with worshipful fingers.

"I never thought..." His voice broke. He continued to touch the collar, as though he couldn't help himself. "I never thought I'd see you like this again. All mine. Always mine."

"I love you," I whispered, the words issuing from deep within my soul.

A single tear slipped down his cheek, and he drew in a shuddering breath. "I love you, too." His fingers sank into my hair, his fist closing in a possessive grip. "Fuck, Natalie. I love you so much." His features twisted with something between regret and resolve. "That's why I have to do this."

"Do what?" I asked with little more than idle interest. His statement should have made me nervous, but I was too consumed by love to muster up concern about anything.

He traced the line of my spine with the cool leather paddle, making my nerve endings flare to life and sending pleasure racing straight to my head, intoxicating me.

"You let me worry about that," he said. "I just need you to relax and trust me. Can you do that for me?"

"Yes, Master," I sighed, surrendering.

"Good little kitten," he praised, and I basked in the glow of his approval. "Take a deep breath and relax into the pain."

I did as he instructed, drawing oxygen into my lungs and easing all the tension that lingered in my muscles.

The first hit was sharp, shocking. It drew a cry

from my chest, which amplified to a wail when he rained down several more blows in quick succession. Stinging heat flared, spreading across my skin like wildfire. I choked on a sob, and the hits stopped. The smooth leather skimmed over the areas it had enflamed, achingly cool against my flaming skin. I whimpered and wriggled, uncertain if I was wordlessly asking for more or begging for reprieve.

"Relax," he urged. The smooth edge of the paddle traced the seam of my wet pussy, sliding through the slick arousal that coated my labia. I shivered as pleasure washed through my system at the light touch, and a low whine eased up my throat.

"Are you ready for more, kitten?" he asked, lightly slapping my burning ass. Only, the burn wasn't uncomfortable anymore. It pulsed erotic heat deep into my core, making me ache for him to fill me.

"Yes, Master," I whispered, completely losing myself in him.

"Good girl." He struck me again, taking up a harsh, punishing rhythm. I moaned and cried out, but I wasn't sure if I made sounds of protest or pleasure. All I knew was his utter possession of my body, my mind, my soul. Master marked me as his with the collar and the heat of the paddle, ensuring that I wore signs of his ownership.

The knowledge that I was his calmed me, and

my mind went utterly quiet as I settled into peace. My breathing turned deep and even, and my eyes slid closed as I floated in bliss. My pussy still ached for him to fill me, but a languorous content- ment had taken hold of my soul, and I fully surrendered to his will. He would fuck me when he chose to do so; my pleasure was his to give. The knowledge of his complete ownership kept me in a joyous state, even though my body still craved him. My Master would always take care of me. I trusted him and loved him with every fiber of my being.

I was dimly aware of the rope around my wrists sliding free, and he gathered me in his arms. I was curled up in his lap, my face tucked into his chest as I breathed him in.

"I need you to be honest with me, kitten," he said, his voice in the deep register that let me know he was just as drunk on me as I was on him. "I need you to trust me."

"I do," I murmured, snuggling into him. "I love you."

He kissed the top of my head. "I love you, too. But I need you to tell me where you've been. Who are you working for?"

Golden eyes flashed through my mind, studying me like a butterfly pinned to a board. I shuddered and curled further into myself in a fruitless effort to protect my more sensitive areas.

"And then my heart with pleasure—" I began desperately.

A strong hand clamped over my mouth.

"No," he said sternly. "Stop saying that. Stay here with me."

I squeezed my eyes shut tighter. I couldn't say the words, but I could think them. I had to think them. I couldn't bear it...

> *And then my heart with pleasure fills,*
> *And dances with the daffodils.*

But it wasn't my own voice I heard echoing in my head.

Alex held my exhausted and aching body cradled against his chest. I cried silent tears, my fingers curling into his white coat in a desperate attempt to cling onto the only kindness in my world. The disgust I'd once felt for him was utterly absent. I needed him too desperately.

"You did very well today, Natalie," he told me.

I shivered at the praise, basking in the kind words.

"I think that you're ready to resume your training," he announced. "Our sessions could be over. Would you like that?"

I nodded vigorously, my voice too raw from screaming to manage to speak.

"Good. I'm very pleased with you, Natalie."

A warm glow pulsed in the center of my chest.

"If we're going to be working together, we should put all this negativity behind us and move forward. Don't you think?"

I nodded again, ready to agree to anything if it meant the torture would stop for good.

"I'm going to give you a tool to help you feel better. Daffodils are your favorite flower, aren't they?"

I blinked, surprise threading through my desperation. "How do you know that?" I croaked.

"They were on your casket at your funeral."

I shivered and clutched at him more tightly. He rubbed his hand up and down my back, comforting me.

"I'm going to give you some homework. There's something I want you to memorize. Do you know the poem I Wandered Lonely as a Cloud?*"*

"I... I think I've heard of it," I said tentatively, not understanding this new line of questioning. It seemed almost conversational, but Alex always had an agenda.

"I'm going to recite a few lines. I want you to close your eyes and listen. Visualize the words."

I closed my eyes, obeying immediately.

He began to recite.

> *I wandered lonely as a cloud*
> *That floats on high o'er vales and hills,*

When all at once I saw a crowd,
A host of golden daffodils;
Beside the lake, beneath the trees,
Fluttering and dancing in the breeze...
And then my heart with pleasure fills,
And dances with the daffodils.

"Can you see it?" he prompted.

I let out a shaky sigh. "Yes." The cheery yellow flowers filled my mind, their delicate scent wafting around me. It was so much nicer here than in my dark reality. I never wanted to leave.

"Good," he said softly. "I want you to keep visualizing it. Say the lines out loud. Repeat them. Don't stop until I come back."

He laid me down on my cot, but I kept my eyes closed, murmuring the words as I remained firmly in my fantasy. I wasn't even aware of the hated sound of my cell door clanging shut. My world was bright, the sunlight kissing my skin for the first time in longer than I could remember.

Someone pinched and rolled my nipples, calling me out of my reverie with a bite of pain. I shuddered and sobbed.

"No," I protested on a horrified groan. "You said it was over. You said I didn't have to anymore. Please, Alex."

"Who the fuck is Alex?" The question was a

barely intelligible snarl, and the arms holding me tightened around my body.

I froze, trying to make sense of what was real and what was memory.

"Jason?"

CHAPTER 23

Jason

Natalie trembled in my arms, tears streaming down her face.

"Who is Alex?" I demanded again, struggling for a calmer tone. Whoever he was, it was becoming clear that he was the man behind her nightmares.

"My... my handler," she whispered brokenly.

"He hurt you," I growled, unable to keep my voice gentle when rage was ripping through my system.

She flinched. "Yes." The admission was barely audible.

"Why do you work for a man who hurt you?"

"I didn't have a choice. I couldn't..." Her voice hitched. "I couldn't get back to you. He was going to..." She shuddered. "I couldn't let him get to you."

"Is that why you've been trying to run from me? Because you think Alex is a threat to me if he knows we're together?"

"I *know* he's a threat," she said desperately. "You don't know what he's capable of. I can't let him do that to you."

My arms tightened around her. "Tell me." I didn't want to hear it, but I had to know. "Tell me what he did to you to make you leave me."

She turned her face into my chest, hiding from me. "I can't."

"He's not CIA," I said. "You know that, don't you? The CIA wouldn't... wouldn't hurt you," I finished, not able to say the word I knew was true: *torture.* My sweet kitten had been tortured. They'd hurt her and kept her from me.

I had to know more. I had to know who Alex was and where I could find him.

He was a dead man.

"Who do you work for?" I pressed.

"Division 9-C," she said, still not looking at me. "Oh god." Her fingers threaded through her hair, tugging at the silken strands. "They're not CIA. I knew, I had to know. But I... I convinced myself I was doing good." She finally met my gaze, her dark blue eyes tormented. "What have I done? They're not... They're not good, are they?"

"No, kitten. They're not. But we'll find them. I have a contact at the Bureau, and she—"

"No!" she cried out, her fingers curling into my shoulders as she clutched at me. "You can't go anywhere near Alex."

"Don't think for a second that I'm going to allow you to go back to him," I growled. "You think you're protecting me. You've been trying to protect me for five years by staying away. I won't let you go again. It's time I started protecting you. I'm sorry. I'm so sorry I didn't keep you safe. I should have ripped apart anyone who tried to keep you from me."

She touched my cheek. Impossibly, she had the strength to comfort *me*. After everything she'd been through. After I'd failed her.

"You thought I was dead," she said softly. "Everyone thought I was dead. There's no way you could have found me."

"I'm going to find *him*," I swore. "I'm not going to let him hurt you ever again. Come to the Bureau with me. Sam can find anyone. Now that we have the name of your division, I'm sure she'll be able to track his location."

"Please," she begged. "You don't understand. I can't let him get to you."

"I'm not letting you go," I said fiercely.

She trembled. "I don't want you to. I don't want to go back to him. I'll stay with you. But you can't go looking for him. We have to arrange protection for you. Call your contact and launch an investigation if you want, but please don't try to find him yourself. If Alex finds out I'm with you, he'll hurt you to punish me. He'll... He'll break you."

"No one's going to break me," I promised.

"That's what I used to think," she whispered, her eyes haunted. "But he can. It doesn't matter what you do. Even your mind isn't a safe place to hide. I thought I could escape what was happening if I thought about you. But he took that from me, too. He told me he'd bring you to me if I didn't give you up. I couldn't let him get to you. I couldn't. That's when I... I didn't last long after that."

Her skin was cold against mine, and she started shaking violently, her teeth chattering. I held her closer to me, trying to warm her with my body heat. It didn't seem to have any effect.

I pressed a kiss against her chilled forehead. "It's okay, kitten," I said roughly, willing my rage to subside so I could take care of her. My retribution could come later. No matter what she said, there was no way I wasn't going to kill the fucker who'd hurt her. I'd tear him apart with my bare hands.

For now, I kept my hands gentle, rubbing away the chill that clung to her skin. Focusing solely on her, I forced back the violence that brewed inside me. I could unleash it on the man who'd hurt her later, once I'd taken care of my kitten. As much as I needed to punish her tormentor, Natalie's wellbeing was the most important thing in my world.

As I petted her, the tight lines of fear around her eyes began to ease, and she blew out a long, shuddering sigh. Her skin warmed beneath my tender touch, and her nipples drew to hard, needy peaks. She'd flinched and whimpered when I'd pinched and plucked at them before, but that was when she was lost to her memories. I didn't know what secrets were locked inside her head, what she'd endured that had kept her from me for all these years.

But whatever had happened to her, I could never allow her to fear my touch.

Carefully, slowly, I traced the soft swells of her perfect breasts with my fingertips. Her breath hitched, but her gaze remained locked on me. She arched her back slightly, silently inviting me to increase our sensual contact. I cupped her breast in my hand, savoring the weight and feel of her tight nipple against my palm. She let out a soft sound of contentment, and I continued to lavish attention on her breasts, keeping my other arm braced around her back so she was cuddled close to my chest.

Her head tipped back, offering her lips up to me. I moved with care as I slowly closed the distance between us, giving her time to flinch away if she wasn't ready.

She didn't flinch. But she was far too still as my mouth came down on hers. I shaped my lips around hers, gently coaxing until she opened for me on a soft sigh. My tongue dipped inside, testing. She returned a tentative stroke, and I explored more deeply, sliding my tongue along hers in a slow but firm rhythm. My cock stiffened, craving to claim her pussy the way I was claiming her mouth.

I continued the careful kiss as I moved my hand from her breasts, sliding it down her abdomen to tease at the upper edge of her curls. She'd panicked the last time I'd brought her to orgasm.

The way she tensed in my arms let me know she remembered it, too.

I pulled back just far enough so I could reassure her, my lips teasing across hers as I spoke. "I'm not going to hurt you."

"I know," she whispered. "I trust you. I love you."

"Good girl." I brushed a tender kiss across her lips and dipped my fingers lower, playing through her wet folds. "Stay here with me," I issued a gentle command.

Her eyes flickered for a moment, but she drew in a deep breath and calmed, remaining focused on me.

"I'm okay," she promised. She reached out and boldly directed my hand deeper, guiding my fingers to penetrate her slick entrance. "I want you, Jason. I want you, my Master."

A soft, pained groan left my chest. I'd never thought I'd hear those words ever again. She arched toward me and boldly captured my lips with hers. There was nothing tentative about the kiss this time. She greedily drank me in, and I answered her intensity on a low growl, nipping at her lower lip before taming her tongue with mine. She shuddered and softened in my arms, but her hips rocked against my hand, welcoming me to stroke her with greater intensity.

I couldn't bear it any longer. I gripped her hips and rolled, shifting our bodies so she was pinned beneath me. She spread her legs, wrapping them around my waist and drawing me toward her. My cock lined up with her pussy, and I entered her in one desperate thrust. She cried out, the sound tinged with pain.

I gritted my teeth and stilled. Fuck, she was even tighter than I remembered.

"I'll be gentle," I promised, running my fingers through her hair to reassure her.

Her fingernails curved into my shoulders, and her heels dug into my ass, driving me deeper.

"Jason," she moaned my name. "Fuck me. Please."

"I don't want to hurt you," I said, my balls aching as I held myself back.

"You won't," she promised. "I need to feel you inside me. I need you to fuck me, mark me. Like you used to do. I want you to make me yours again."

"You've always been mine. You always will be. My sweet kitten, my Natalie."

"Then fuck me, Master."

I couldn't hold back, not when she begged me so sweetly. Not when I needed to mark her as desperately as she needed to be marked. I shifted back slightly so I could grasp her legs, guiding them up so they rested against my shoulders. The position let me go impossibly deeper, and we both moaned as we were connected in every way possible. I captured her lips with mine again, and my fingers caught her wrists, pinning them against the mattress on either side of her head. She arched against me, rubbing her tight nipples against my chest as she mewled into my mouth.

I began to take her in harsh thrusts, withdrawing slowly before driving back in hard enough to make sure she felt an ache deep inside. She would feel me between her legs for hours after we finished. And when the sensation faded, I'd brand her with my heat all over again. I'd never let her forget who she belonged to ever again.

She panted into my mouth, drawing in sharp gasps when I gave her enough space to breathe. My head spun as I became drunk on her, my whole world centering on the woman in my arms. My Natalie. My kitten. She was alive and real and hot beneath my hands.

Mine.

The word rang through my mind as she screamed against me, her inner walls contracting around me as she came undone. My ragged shout vibrated into her mouth, my release triggered by hers. Pleasure rushed through my system in a tidal wave, ripping its way through my body. I thrust into her one last time, driving deep as my cum shot into her pussy, binding us together.

Both of our cheeks were wet, and I kissed at the salt on her skin, savoring its vital flavor.

"I love you," she said, her voice slightly ragged from crying out.

"I love you," I murmured, unable to stop myself from kissing her cheeks, her eyelashes, her lips. I had my sweet kitten back in my arms, and I was never letting her go.

CHAPTER 24

Natalie

I sighed in perfect contentment as Jason ran the brush through my hair, gently working out any knots he encountered. The stiff bristles massaged my scalp, and the slight tug with every long, slow pull made my eyes slide closed as I settled into bliss. After we'd made love, he'd taken me into the shower and bathed me, his hands worshipping my body as he cared for me. Now, he was brushing out my damp hair as he cradled my body against his on the bed.

I'd forgotten what this felt like: to let go and allow Jason to take care of me. I'd locked away the memories for so long, and even though they'd flooded back now, a memory couldn't compare to the real thing.

Jason was solid and whole and *real*. Finally, after all these years, he was more than an abstract in my mind. I remembered him. I remembered our love. And I thought I'd burst with it. If I had any more tears left in my system, I would have wept from the joy that filled my entire being. As it was, I rested my head against his shoulder, rubbing my cheek against his bare skin as I breathed him in.

"Sweet kitten," he rumbled. "Do you know how fucking perfect you are?"

I smiled and twined my arms around his neck. "Do you know how perfect *you* are?"

He grimaced. "Don't say that. I'm not. I didn't protect you. I failed you."

I touched my fingertips to his granite jaw. "You didn't know," I said softly. "You couldn't have known. I don't blame you for anything. And I won't let you blame yourself. We've been apart too long for this self-loathing to drive a wedge between us. I don't want to waste any of our time together with grief. I want to be with you, Jason. Don't you remember what I told you all those years ago? You're not a failure. You're not weak."

"But he hurt you." He couldn't seem to say the

words without snarling. "I didn't stop him. He'll die for what he did to you. I swear he will."

I cupped his face in my hands. "Please. You can't go after him yourself. Promise me you'll stay with me. I've lived without you too long. I can't lose you now."

"But he—"

"I know what he did," I said, more harshly than I intended. Now that the mental protection of my poem was broken, the memories of my torture were all too clear. "And I'm going to have to learn how to live with it," I continued more softly. "I need you for that. Please, Jason. I can't do this without you."

Now that I was safely back in his arms, I'd rather curl up and die than lose him again.

"Okay, kitten," he forced out after a tense moment. "I won't leave you. But we're going to the Bureau. Sam will help us dig up intel on Division 9-C, and that will lead us to Alex. He won't be a free man for much longer. He'll pay for what he did to you."

I didn't fully trust the steely glint in his eyes, but I'd have to deal with that later. I knew there would come a time when Jason would want to confront Alex. I just had to ensure that it never happened. Even in chains, I didn't believe Alex would ever be powerless. He always had something nasty up his sleeve, and I couldn't allow him anywhere near the man I loved.

"All right," I agreed. "Let's go in to the field office, then. We shouldn't stay here for too much longer, anyway. We're exposed without backup. I thought I could slip away from you and smooth things over, but now we're going to have to get to cover before Alex gets to us. I've missed the meeting I was supposed to have with Moreno's associate last night. Alex wasn't expecting a call-in, but that doesn't mean he won't check my tracker eventually if I don't make contact."

"Tracker? Where?"

"It's in my shoulder." I cringed when he scowled, but I carried on. "The Bureau can help me take it out. But we should be fine. Alex isn't expecting a call from me for a few more days. I told him I'd cut off any unnecessary communication until I was ready to bring in backup."

"What were you supposed to be doing with Moreno's associates?"

"I was supposed to work my way up and assassinate Moreno," I said. "I thought I was taking down his organization. But now that I know Division 9-C isn't CIA, I don't know what their agenda was in eliminating Moreno." I shivered at the prospect that I'd been molded into a mindless assassin for a clandestine organization.

I hugged Jason more tightly and pushed the worry aside. If I started thinking about all the terrible things I might have done, I'd break all over again. Possibly beyond repair this time.

"I need you," I said, clinging to him. "Please don't leave me, no matter what."

"I won't," he swore. "Never again."

He held me for a while longer, petting and soothing me.

"We should get dressed," he finally said. "If Alex is expecting a call in the next few days, we need to arrange a protective detail before then. Let's get you to the field office so Sam can get started tracking down the bastard."

"Okay," I agreed. I didn't want to leave the haven of his apartment, but I knew he spoke sense. "But I don't have any clothes."

He had the grace to appear chagrined. "I suppose I did destroy your nightshirt and panties. You'll have to wear something of mine."

I eyed him dubiously, but within minutes, he'd helped me into one of his huge t-shirts and a pair of sweatpants. He drew the drawstring tight around my waist and rolled up the pant legs so I could walk without tripping. He touched his fingers to the buckle at the back of my collar.

"No," I refused softly. "I want to wear it."

He nodded his approval and planted a swift kiss on my forehead before quickly dressing himself. He was glorious naked, but there was something about Jason in a suit that exuded power and confidence. It made my core pulse and my cheeks heat.

"Don't look at me like that, or we'll never leave," he warned, but a small smile played around his mouth.

He wrapped his arm around my waist and guided me out of the bedroom. We made it to the kitchen when pain shot through my body. All my muscles tensed, then turned to water.

"Natalie!" Jason caught me as I dropped, falling to his knees so he could hold my boneless body.

"Run," I tried to say, fear for him twisting my insides. The word strangled in my throat as the door burst open, wood splintering as it gave way.

I turned horrified eyes on the ruined doorway. Nate came in first, gun drawn. And trained directly on my heart.

"Don't move, or she's dead." My blood froze in my veins at the sound of Alex's voice. He stepped in beside Nate, resting a hand on my friend's shoulder, as one might idly touch a favorite pet. His golden eyes fixed on me. "You didn't really think you could come to Agent Harper's apartment without me knowing, did you?" he asked, his benign smile firmly in place. "It took me several hours to fly in the team, but it seems we've arrived in time."

Elena and Trent stepped in behind Alex, both holding guns trained at Jason's head.

"Don't hurt him," I begged, barely managing to form the words on my limp tongue.

"What have you done to her?" Jason snarled, pulling me closer to his chest.

Alex waved dismissively, but his keen eyes remained incisive. "Didn't she tell you about how her implant works?" He withdrew the hated black device from his pocket. "I touch this, and she gets a nasty shock."

"Nate," I pleaded with my friend, my mouth starting to function again even though my limbs were still useless. "You have to remember what he did. Stop him. He tortured you. How can you not remember?"

The hard planes of Nate's face remained impassive, as though he hadn't heard me at all.

Alex patted his shoulder. "Nathaniel and I are good friends. He'd never turn on me."

To my shock, Trent's hand began to shake on his gun. I captured his hazel eyes in mine. I saw emotion there for the first time in years. Something flickered: fear, pain, hate.

"Trent," I gasped out. "Help me. You know what he did. You know he hurt you. Stop him."

Trent's arm swung, his shaking gun shifting to point at Alex's head.

"What are you doing?" Elena asked, alarmed. "Trent, stop it!"

"Such a shame," Alex said, looking at Trent with no more than mild interest. "You were always a disappointing subject, but you've proven a valuable asset. Nathaniel," he said calmly. "Take care of the traitor."

"No!" I screamed as Nate briefly changed his aim from my heart to Trent's head. Blood and brain splattered from the back of his skull when the bullet exited, and he dropped. Nate's gun returned to my heart in the space of a second, resuming his target as though nothing had happened.

Elena glanced down at Trent's body. She blinked once. Then her ice blue eyes returned to me. Her gun never wavered from its aim on Jason.

"I'll come with you," I said brokenly. "Just leave Jason alone. I won't fight you."

"I know you won't," Alex said with an indulgent smile. He activated my implant, and pain jolted through me, rendering me helpless.

Jason snarled and clutched me more tightly. I could feel his body coiling for attack.

"Don't move, or I'll have Nathaniel dispatch her, too," Alex warned him. "She's always been my favorite, but I can't have my agents going rogue. But I won't cause her undue distress. Hand her over, and we'll leave you in peace, Agent Harper. She's always been so invested in your wellbeing."

"No," he refused, his arms iron bands around me. "She's not going anywhere without me."

Alex's brows rose. "Are you offering to join her?"

"I'm never leaving her again. I'll come with you."

"No," I moaned, horror washing over me. I couldn't let Alex touch Jason. "Please, Alex."

He touched the black device, and speech became impossible as all my muscles went limp.

"I'm talking to Agent Harper," he chided.

"Do that to her again, and I'll snap your fucking neck," Jason growled.

Alex cocked his head at him, completely unconcerned by the threat. "This is an interesting proposition. She must have told you about the process. You'd be willing to give up your dignity, your identity, for her?"

"I'd die for her," Jason swore.

Alex's lips twisted up at the corners. "That's not what I asked." He continued to study Jason. "You love her," he observed. "What if I told you I can make her love me, not you? Would you still want to come?"

"I never loved you," I forced out, the words garbled on my thick tongue.

He glanced at me, still smiling. "I have some ideas on how to fix that little problem." He looked back to Jason. "What if I told you I can make *you* love me? Would you still voluntarily come with me?"

"I'm not letting you have her," Jason ground out.

Alex laughed, a soft sound of amusement. "That's not up to you to decide." He reached into his pocket and pulled out a syringe. "The only choice you get to make is if you're coming with her."

Jason's eyes narrowed, his jaw fixing in a stubborn line. "I'm coming with her."

"No," I begged. "Jason, don't." I looked back to Alex, frantic. "He doesn't know what he's saying. Please leave him alone. I'll be good. I'll do whatever you want."

Alex took a step toward us, shaking his head at me. "You tried to run away from me, Natalie. I can't allow that behavior to go unpunished. You'll need to go through the process again before I can send you back into the field."

Terror solidified in my gut, and my blood turned to ice in my veins. I couldn't go through that again. I couldn't survive it.

"If I come with you, you have to swear never to hurt her again," Jason demanded.

"I'm afraid you don't get to make demands," Alex

replied. "Now be a good boy and stay still, or Nathaniel will shoot her."

Jason's corded muscles rippled around me, but he didn't flinch as the needle slid into his neck. A low growl left his lips, and he pulled me tighter to him one last time before his arms began to ease as the drugs took effect.

Alex caught my limp body before Jason dropped me. He fell to the floor beside me. I tried to reach for him, but my arms wouldn't work.

"Nathaniel, bring Agent Harper," Alex ordered. "Elena, make sure the hall is clear before we move them."

He produced a second syringe. I tried to shrink away, but I couldn't move.

"Don't," I begged. "Please, leave him."

"Oh, no," Alex replied with a small smile. "This is far too interesting. He's managed to undo all of my hard work with you. I'll have to come up with more creative ways of keeping you in line."

The needle sank into my neck, a horribly familiar sensation. The world around me disappeared, until I was left in stark fear and darkness.

Then, even that faded away, and I slipped into nothingness.

I KNEW WHERE I WAS BEFORE I CAME BACK TO FULL consciousness. The cuffs around my ankles and wrists; the exposing angle of my spread thighs; the sterile, clinical smell.

My eyes snapped open on a gasp.

No. No no no...

I squeezed them closed again, willing the horrible scene to change. I couldn't be back here. I'd been with Jason. We were going to get help. Until...

Alex. Alex has Jason.

"Where is he?" I demanded, my eyes focusing on Alex's white-clad figure where he sat on the stool beside me.

He finished applying the wires to my naked body before answering.

"Agent Harper?" he asked, as though little more than mildly curious. "I'm sure he's making himself at home in his new cell. Why? Did you want him to come and watch?"

"Let him go." I didn't care that I was groveling. "I'll do whatever you want. Just let him go."

"Oh, no. I don't think so. I've never worked with an older agent before. I've only ever been given new recruits. And considering your history with him, this gives me the opportunity to experiment. I want to see how he reacts when you come to love me, not him."

"You're insane," I flung out, finding my anger. It was so much less terrifying than facing the knowledge of my helplessness. "I'll never love you. I didn't before, and I won't now."

He stood so he could lean over me. "That's because I wasn't allowed before. Our relationship had to remain professional. However, in light of your *lapse,* I've been granted more freedom in your conditioning."

A block of ice solidified in my gut. "What are you talking about?"

He stroked his crotch, pushing his long white coat aside so I could see his erection straining against his slacks. "Did you really never notice? Or did you just not want to notice? All that time, I got to touch you, but you didn't touch me. You received pleasure over and over again, and I was denied."

Bile rose in the back of my throat. "Stay away from me," I warned shakily.

He leaned in close, so his hot breath washed over my face. "You're going to love me, Natalie. You used to love when I held you after our sessions. This will be even better. You're going to—"

Whatever vile thing he was going to say was cut off when my head snapped forward. Pain sliced through my forehead as his nose cracked beneath the impact. He jerked back with a muffled curse, blood running through his fingers as he clutched at his face.

Grim satisfaction settled over me at the sight of him, bloodied and hurting. For once, his perfectly placid façade was torn away.

A hysterical laugh bubbled up my throat. He snarled, then cursed when the vibrations hurt his ruined nose.

Glowering at me, he unzipped his slacks and fisted his flaccid penis. He pumped up and down. It didn't get hard.

I laughed again, the insane sound seizing my lungs and making my insides ache as tears dripped from the corners of my eyes.

He released himself and reached for a syringe on the metal table beside him.

"Very well," he said, his voice rough with anger. "I can see you're not ready for pleasure. You want to start the session with pain. That's easy enough."

I was still cackling when the needle slid into the crook of my arm and the drugs raced into my veins with stinging heat. This pain was familiar, but that didn't make it easier to bear. It started out slow, like someone punching their way through the inside of my body. Soon, it would feel like they were trying to claw their way out, ripping me to shreds.

At first, it was manageable. I gritted my teeth and

sucked in deep breaths, willing my mind to deal with the pain. I knew that no harm was coming to my physical body. I could endure this.

Alex touched his bloody fingers to the collar that still encircled my throat. I snapped at him, a feral act of defense.

He smiled a red smile. "Is this Jason's?" he asked.

"Don't touch it," I hissed.

Ignoring me, he dodged my snapping teeth and managed to unbuckle the collar, pulling it away from my throat. I cried out at the loss.

"It's mine now, Natalie," he told me, darkly triumphant. "You have nothing of his. Nothing of your own. You belong to me. Both of you."

Pain ripped into me, my anguish layering over the agony inflicted by the drugs. My back arched with the force of my scream, and the sound of my despair echoed throughout the room.

CHAPTER 25

Jason

I opened my eyes. Blinked.

Nothing.

Darkness surrounded me in a silent shroud. I lay on something lumpy that smelled vaguely of mildew.

I reached out my hand, holding it in front of my face. I couldn't even see the silhouette of my fingers against the faintest light.

Where am I?

Instinctively, I knew I wasn't blind. I was somewhere light couldn't reach.

I cast my mind back.

I'd been with Natalie. We were going to the Bureau. Then...

"Natalie!" I shouted out her name, sitting bolt upright. I became aware of cool air on my skin.

I was naked.

Natalie didn't answer me.

Silence.

I was alone in the dark.

"Natalie!" I called out again, as though I could summon her if I just yelled loud enough.

That fucker Alex had her. He'd said he would punish her for running to me. I understood now why she'd tried to escape me from the beginning. He'd hurt her, was probably hurting her right now.

And I was naked and blind, powerless to help her.

I swung my legs over the edge of whatever I'd been lying on. My feet touched cool concrete. I groped the air around me, searching. My right hand hit a rough wall, scraping my palm. I pressed against the surface, using it to steady me as I stood in the inky darkness. I took a cautious step, my toes searching for obstructions before I inched forward. My hand touched a corner. I paused and felt in front of me. The rough wall smoothed into cold metal. I banged on it.

"Natalie!" I shouted. My fingers frantically searched for a door handle, but they only met smooth metal. "Natalie!" I pounded harder, making as much noise as possible. They had to take me to her. I couldn't bear the thought of Alex hurting her. I'd seen the way he looked at her. There was more than just clinical interest in his eyes, although that had been chilling enough. If he touched her...

I roared out my rage and slammed my body against the metal, bruising my flesh as I mindlessly tried to break the door down.

A small beep sounded, and a mechanical lock clicked back. My body coiled, prepared to destroy whoever stood between me and Natalie.

Light seared my eyes, but I didn't allow that to slow my attack. I launched myself forward. A small, slight body gave way, falling to the floor beneath me. On instinct, my forearm went to their throat, ready to crush their windpipe.

"Jesus, Jason. It's me. It's Sam." If she hadn't been using her rapid-fire pattern of speech, I might have killed her before I realized who she was. "Get off me. Oh my god, you're *naked*. That's your penis. That's your penis on my chest. Holy fuck, that's big. Okay. Okay. We're good. That's fine. But you're kind of crushing me. Can you get off, please?" Her freckled cheeks turned red as my vision returned. "I mean, not like *get off*. You know? Just... Jesus, that's big."

"Where's Natalie?" I ground out.

"I don't know," she said, her pale blue eyes wide and a little frightened. "Dex is right behind me. I called in for backup when I found this place. You didn't call me to check in, and the tracking device in your jacket moved here. Only, when I got here, I found the jacket. Not you. Obviously, you weren't wearing it. Because you're... Well, yeah. I heard you beating down that door and came running."

"Tell me the schematics," I ordered, still not easing up. "Where are we? How many guards are here? How do I get Natalie out once I find her?"

"We're underneath the warehouse district. This is a subfloor level that's not on any of the blueprints I found of this place. And there don't seem to be many guards. I saw two people—a short blonde and a huge black guy—but I hit them with tranq darts and they dropped. I haven't seen anyone else. I didn't even hear anyone else until you started trying to break the door down." She held up her phone. "Lucky for you, I have an app for everything. Even unlocking super-secret electronic locks." She glanced down at her chest again. "Now, could you please get your dick off my boobs? It's making me feel really weird. And not in a good way."

A distant scream ripped through my consciousness. It was faint, but I knew it immediately.

Natalie.

I shoved off Sam and started sprinting toward the sound.

"Wait!" I was vaguely aware of her calling after me. "You don't even have a gun. Jason!"

A second scream tore through me, closer this time. I reached the end of the long corridor and flung my body against the metal door that separated me from her. This one wasn't locked, and it swung open easily, banging against the wall as I burst into the room.

I paused for one moment of absolute horror. My sweet kitten was naked, strapped down, her legs spread wide. And Alex was beside her, his hand pumping his limp dick as blood ran down his face.

An inhuman, feral sound ripped up my throat, and I launched myself at the fucker who had hurt Natalie. He turned just before I collided with him, his eyes widening in shock as I took him down. I didn't give him a second to recover. There were so many more efficient, less messy ways to kill a man.

Alex didn't deserve any of them.

I pulled my fist back and smashed it into his jaw, enjoying the feeling of the bones crunching as ruby droplets sprayed from his lips. I took another shot from the opposite side, ensuring he'd never open his mouth again.

He coughed and spluttered, his hands groping at me in blind pain.

I wasn't nearly satisfied. I reached between us and grabbed his balls. I dug my fingers in, pulled, ripped. Dark pleasure flooded me when I felt something rupture. He screamed.

Natalie's ragged cry tore my attention from him. I stood immediately, going to her.

I was vaguely aware of the sound of a man choking on his own blood beneath me, but I only had eyes for Natalie. Her beautiful face was contorted in pain, her body slick with sweat.

"I'm okay," she said before her back arched on a ragged cry.

I cupped her cheeks with bloody hands. "What's happening? How do I make it stop?" I ripped away the wires that were stuck to her skin, but still she shuddered and groaned.

"It'll pass," she said through clenched teeth. "I'll be okay." Her eyes strayed past me, looking at something behind me. I turned in the direction of her gaze. Her collar lay on a metal table beside where she was restrained.

I reached for it, my fingers fisting around it. "What can I do?" I asked, helplessness settling over me as she writhed and shuddered. "Backup is on the way. There will be a medic. Just hold on for me."

Her fingers splayed out as her wrist jerked against the cuff that held her immobile. "I want it," she choked out.

I lifted her collar. "You want this?"

"Yes," she said, her voice strained with pain. "Please. Just stay with me."

"How do I make the pain stop?" I urged, desperate to end her agony.

"It will. Eventually. Please..." Her fingers reached toward the collar again.

"Okay, kitten. Okay." Wet heat poured down my cheeks as I buckled the slim strip of leather around her neck. I traced the line of it, my thumbs grazing her throat.

She groaned, a tortured sound that tore at my soul. "Thank you."

A long sigh left her chest, and her eyes slid closed. Her body began to convulse.

"Help!" I cried out brokenly. "I need help in here!"

People poured into the room, the space suddenly cacophonous. But none of the babble could override the sound of her screams. Medics closed in, pushing me away. I stepped back so they could tend to her, knowing I was powerless to do anything.

Her tormented cries echoed inside me, tearing at my soul as I sank to the cold floor in despair.

CHAPTER 26

Natalie

Fear flooded my system as consciousness returned. Not fear for myself, but for him.

"Jason!" I cried out, jolting awake.

A strong hand settled on my shoulder, pinning me down. I shrieked and tried to twist away from Alex.

His fingers tangled in my hair at either side of my head, a tender but firm touch that grounded me.

"Easy, kitten. I'm right here."

My blind panic melted away, and I focused on Jason's perfect face. His expression was drawn with worry, but he didn't appear to be in pain.

I looked around wildly, trying to get my bearings. I lay on a hospital bed in a real hospital. I could hear the bustle of people around us, and the ceilings were white, without any exposed piping.

"You're safe," Jason promised. "He's dead. I've got you."

"Alex?" I asked, casting my mind back. "He's dead?"

The needle sliding into my arm; Alex's bloody hand pumping his cock; pain consuming me.

Jason...

Jason had burst into the room like a naked god of vengeance, ripping my tormentor apart with his bare hands.

"You killed him," I said. It wasn't a question.

Jason nodded, his lips twisting with disgust as his eyes clouded over. "They tried to save him, but he didn't make it. He'll never hurt you again."

I touched his tight jaw. "What's wrong?"

He blinked and focused on me again. "Alex was our only lead on Division 9-C, the people who took you from me. Nathaniel and Elena are getting psychiatric care, but they're in no condition to be answering any questions. They're still loyal to Alex." The fine lines around his eyes deepened. "But I had to kill him. I couldn't let him live. Not after he..." He swallowed hard. "Not after what he did to you."

I shuddered. "I didn't want you to see that," I said quietly. "I didn't want you to know." Something awful occurred to me, and I clutched at his shoulders. "He didn't hurt you, did he? Before I woke up, did he..." My eyes burned, and I was unable to put into words the horrors that were running through my mind.

Jason's fingers stroked through my hair in a reassuring motion, but his muscles remained tense. "He didn't touch me. But I would have taken the pain a thousand times over if he would have spared you."

"He was never going to let me go," I said. "He would have used me against you. He would have broken you, too."

"You're not broken," he countered fiercely. "You're mine, and you're perfect."

I was far from perfect. I was damaged, scarred. But with Jason, I felt whole for the first time in years. I could face anything, as long as he kept me firmly in his protective arms.

"I'm glad you killed him," I said softly. "Thank you."

He grimaced. "He should have suffered more."

I cupped his cheek in my hand, smoothing away the harsh lines around his mouth with my thumb. "He's gone. That's all that matters."

"But now we can't find the people he answered to. He couldn't have been operating on his own, with only you, Nathaniel, Elena, and Trent. There has to be a larger organization behind this. How did they know where to find you when you went out on your test mission? Alex couldn't have orchestrated all that by himself."

"I'm sorry," I replied, wishing I had answers. I needed them, but not as desperately as Jason seemed to crave them. He wasn't content with his vengeance on Alex. He wanted to punish everyone who had ripped us away from each other. "I'm sorry I don't know more," I continued. "I only ever answered to Alex. He made me think I was working for the greater good. The things I did..." I trailed off. I'd killed people in cold blood, a robotic assassin. How many of them had truly deserved it? And what would Division 9-C have gained from my actions?

"You didn't do anything wrong," Jason promised me. "Nothing that's happened is your fault."

"I know," I whispered. I wasn't sure how I'd cope with the knowledge that I might have been doing evil things for years, but as long as Jason supported me, I could make it through anything.

That moment, a doctor entered my room. I shrank back at the sight of the white coat, dark memories stirring. I didn't like being in the sterile environment, barely clothed in my hospital gown.

"Miss Simmons," the doctor said with a warm smile. It reached his rich brown eyes, but that did little to quell my unease.

Jason's fingers closed around mine, squeezing reassuringly. And his other hand continued to pet my hair, tethering me to him in a silent promise that he would take care of me.

"I'm glad you're awake," the doctor continued. "I think you're ready to move to the psychiatric ward. Considering your trauma, you've been recommended for—"

"No," Jason growled, his hand tightening on mine. "She's coming home with me."

I clung to him. "Yes," I agreed. I didn't want to be locked away again, especially not in a hospital. My skin was beginning to itch with the need to escape into the fresh air, my instincts driving me to seek freedom.

The doctor hesitated. "I don't know if that's best. Miss Simmons is—"

"Coming home with me," Jason finished for him, his eyes flashing in warning.

"Are you family?"

Jason glowered. "I'm her..." He couldn't seem to find the right word to describe what we meant to one another. At least, not one the doctor would understand.

"I'm his," I said firmly. "I'm going home with Jason. I'll see a psychologist for private sessions," I added quickly. "I know I need to work through...

everything."

The doctor sighed, capitulating. "If it will cause you distress, I won't force you to stay. I'll refer you to an excellent psychologist. She can make an appointment for you immediately. I'll get you her contact details."

"Thank you," I said.

He nodded and left the room to see to the arrangements.

Jason seemed to forget about him immediately, his bright green eyes fixing on me in wonder. He traced the line of my jaw, my cheekbone.

"Mine," he said softly, as though he wasn't aware he spoke the reverent word aloud.

I turned my face into his touch, basking in his warm strength. "Yours," I agreed, kissing his palm.

He closed the distance between us and captured my lips with his. I opened for him, welcoming him home. Together, we could face anything, overcome all the terrible things that had separated us for all those painful years. Jason belonged with me, and I belonged to him.

EPILOGUE

Jason

One Week Later

"**O**h darlin', are you sure you won't come back home to North Carolina with us?" Natalie's mom pleaded, lingering at the threshold to my apartment. She seemed reluctant to leave her daughter, as did Natalie's father, who was still hugging her after a full minute.

The Simmons had been in Chicago for a week, having flown in as soon as they found out their daughter was alive. They appeared to have aged much more than five years since I'd last seen them at Natalie's funeral. There had been tears of joy when they reunited, and they couldn't seem to stop holding their only child, who they'd thought was gone forever.

Natalie had appeared bewildered by their affection, but by the end of the week, she returned their embraces with equal ferocity. I remembered what she'd told me about her parents being withholding, but that seemed to have changed now that they miraculously had her back in their lives.

"I'm staying here, Mama," Natalie said, sounding apologetic but not regretful. "Jason will take care of me."

She extricated herself from her father's embrace and returned to my side. I wrapped my arm around her waist, pulling her close. Mrs. Simmons studied us for a moment, then nodded her approval.

"Yes, I think he will," she said. "But promise you'll come visit soon. And call us every day. Please, honey. I need to hear your voice."

"Of course I'll call," Natalie promised. "I love y'all."

Her mother approached to plant one final kiss on her daughter's cheek.

"We love you too, sweetie," her father said, his voice thick with emotion. "We'll talk to you as soon as we get back to Raleigh."

"Yes, please call to let me know you got home safe." Natalie's accent was more pronounced around her family. It was adorable. And more than a little sexy.

When her parents finally left, I pulled her against me, holding her tight as I smiled down at her. "Such a sweet Southern belle," I said. "Why don't you talk to me like that?"

She grinned. "I tend to lose most of my accent when I'm not in the South. Why? Do you like it?"

"I love everything about you," I said earnestly, tucking a stray lock of hair behind her ear.

My phone buzzed in my pocket, interrupting us. "I need to get this," I said, releasing her reluctantly.

I glanced at the caller ID, surprised when Dexter Scott's contact details came up, not Sam's.

"What do you want, Scott?" I asked in clipped tones. "Sam was supposed to call with an update hours ago." I was careful not to mention the name of Natalie's division aloud. She was aware that Sam was helping me track down the people who had hurt her, but I preferred for her to focus on her therapy, not the investigation. I could handle that for both of us.

"Sam's missing," Dex growled.

"What?"

"Are you fucking deaf?" he demanded with uncharacteristic anger. "One of my best friends is missing, and it's your fault. She was doing off-the-books research for you, and now she's gone. She hasn't answered her phone in days."

"I talked to her yesterday," I said, but worry nipped at me. "Maybe she just doesn't want to talk to you."

"I just got to her apartment. She's not here. Her phone is going straight to voicemail, and she's not at the office."

"Maybe she's somewhere else," I countered.

"You know how she is," Dex snapped. "She never leaves her apartment unless she's coming in to work. She's not the type to socialize."

That was true. The little geek preferred to lose herself in online games when she wasn't working. It wasn't like her to go out on her own. She was painfully shy around new people. Hell, she was still skittish around me, and I'd known her for years.

"I'll try calling her," I said and hung up on Dex.

As I found her contact details, I hoped that she was just finally sick of Dex's painful company and had decided to kick him out of her life. Maybe she was out on a date.

My gut twisted when the call went straight to voicemail, just as Dex had said. I disconnected and slid my phone back into my pocket.

"What's happening?" Natalie asked, her tender touch on my cheek grounding me.

I kissed her forehead, reassuring her. "Nothing you need to worry about. Sam's taking a day off, and Dexter can't deal." I wished I could be certain of that, but doubt chewed at my insides.

"Oh," Natalie sighed in relief. "Okay. She deserves a day off after everything she's done for me."

I nodded, locking my worry away for a moment. I couldn't leave Natalie to go into the office and check to see if Sam had hidden herself away in the archives or somewhere else obscure. It wasn't unheard of for her to get so caught up in work that she zoned everything else out. I'd try to call her again in an hour.

For now, I wasn't leaving Natalie's side for anything. Alex might be dead, but she still woke up screaming in the night. She needed me to stay close, to hold her and tell her everything was going to be okay. I'd taken an extended leave of absence from work so I could care for her. I'd have quit altogether, but I needed my contacts at the Bureau if I was going to find the people who had kept my kitten from me for five years. Once we had a lead, I'd go back into the field. Until then, I wasn't letting Natalie out of my sight.

I sank my fingers into her hair, reveling in the silken feel of it against my skin. I couldn't bring myself to stop touching her, to stop reassuring myself that she was alive and whole. I had her in my arms, and I'd never allow her to leave them again.

And she didn't seem to want to. She leaned into my touch, purring as I massaged her scalp.

"Sweet kitten," I murmured. "It's getting late. You should eat something." Her wellbeing was my top priority, and she seemed to relish when I took care of her as much as I reveled in nurturing her. She needed me, just as I needed her.

"I'm not hungry," she said.

"Kitten," I said sternly. "You know it's my job to look after your needs. And you need to eat."

Her arms twined around the back of my neck. "That's not what I need right now. That's not what I want. I want you, Master."

A low groan left my chest. I couldn't resist her when she molded her soft body against mine and stared up at me with lust in her lovely eyes. The sound of my title on her tongue was painfully sweet. My cock instantly stiffened, aching to get inside her and claim her hard.

She arched up into me, and I met her halfway, crushing my mouth to hers in a fierce kiss. I'd never get enough of her: her scent, her flavor, her touch. Her love.

"I love you so much," I said against her lips, my

breath coming fast and my heart racing as though I'd sprinted a mile.

She smiled against my mouth. "I love you too. Can I have my collar back now?"

She'd taken it off while her parents visited, and neither of us had liked it. I needed to see it around her throat as badly as she needed to feel it there.

I reached into my pocket and retrieved the thin strip of leather. With careful, worshipful hands, I buckled it closed at her nape. My forefinger hooked through the silver ring at the front, and I tugged her toward me, capturing her lips again.

Natalie was all mine, always.

The End

The Impossible Series

Impossible

Savior (An Impossible Novel)

Rogue (An Impossible Novel)

Knight (An Impossible Novel)

Mentor (An Impossible Novella)

Master (An Impossible Novel)

King (An Impossible Novel)

A Decadent Christmas (An Impossible Series Christmas Special)

Czar (An Impossible Novella)

Crusader (An Impossible Novel)

Prey (An Impossible Series Short Story)

Highlander (An Impossible Novel)

Decadent Knights (An Impossible Series Short Story)

Centurion (An Impossible Novel)

Dex (An Impossible Novella)

Hero (An Impossible Novel)

Wedding Knight (An Impossible Series Short Story)

Happily Ever After (An Impossible Series Christmas Special)

Valentines at Dusk (An Impossible Series Short Story)

The Subversive Series

Dark Lessons

Sweet Captivity (Coming Soon!)

The RENEGADE Series

TARGET

SPY

SUBJECT

ASSASSIN

AGENT

Made in the USA
Monee, IL
22 May 2021